A
Sadness
WITHIN

A
Sadness
WITHIN

Sara Fiorenzo

MAD HATTER PRESS

Editing services provided by TJS Literary Editing
Book Cover by Book Fabulous Designs
Photography by Life In Motion Photography
Formatting Services provided by Mad Hatter Press, LLC

ISBN Number 978-0-9906852-0-3

Second Edition, 2015

To My Girls

Chicago
1910

I FIRST REGISTERED THE PAIN. White and hot, coursing through my body, and so intense, I could not tell which part of me had been hurt. There had been laughter before. And love. Always love with my family. Then I remembered the accident — a derailment. I had been looking into the laughing eyes of my wife, Elizabeth. They sparkled when she looked at me, and I felt the connection we had shared for the past 30 years. She clasped my hand and smiled, but then a shift in the railcar had thrown us apart. Men were all around us, and the screams of the other passengers filled my ears. Were we being robbed? Were they taking advantage of the disaster? Or maybe they had planned it. One minute we had been sitting there, talking about our plans for the next day, and then ...suddenly, I felt very alone.

Will! Celia! Elizabeth! My dear, sweet Elizabeth. I tried to sit up, to find them. Had they survived? Then I saw them. Will and Celia were on one side of me, both lying in hospital beds, their bodies seemed to be writhing in pain. Elizabeth was on my other side, her beautiful face grimaced with pain, and I instantly felt her turmoil rolling through me. Her pain was different than my own. I could feel it, our connection bonding us. She stirred and turned toward me. Our eyes met briefly, the once bright, blue irises, now dark and sad. Her skin was pale and droplets of dried blood surrounded her once soft lips.

I tried to speak, but could barely get a sound out, my voice nothing more than a harsh whisper. All she seemed to be able to do was cough, blood trickling out with each burst of air. Consumption. It had to be. Perhaps we had all been exposed while on the train. But there had been an accident. I couldn't quite put my mind around these circumstances. Something wasn't making sense.

I don't know how long we lay there, fading in and out of consciousness. I began to have a hard time deciphering reality from dream. At one point, men were standing at the foot of my bed talking.

"These three will make it. Their bodies have already begun accepting the change," I heard a voice say.

"This one will not," added another. "I fear the Consumption will take her instead of save her."

And then they were gone.

This was the reason my own pain was so intense. I could feel hers as well. Something was happening to us. Something within us was changing, and the stronger I began to feel, the further away Elizabeth felt. Whatever was happening to me was not happening to her. I was healing and she was dying.

Will, Celia, and I seemed to be growing stronger, our bodies mending. Finally, I was strong enough to move. I swung my legs over the bed and practically leapt at the bed next to me. By now, Elizabeth's body was weak, withering away. She coughed frequently, droplets of blood covering the sleeve of her gown as she tried to cover it. I encased her in my arms, holding her, giving her strength, feeling the connection between us fading and wishing I could make her stay.

I knew the moment she slipped away because the physical pain was gone, and the ache moved into my heart. For many years afterward, I longed for the pain to return, because it would mean that she had come back to me. I longed to fill the empty void that having someone like her in my life meant.

My son, daughter, and I had all survived the train accident, only to be attacked with this immortal disease. We were cursed in this new life. Nothing would ever bring Elizabeth back, so instead, I focused on what I had... helping my children know the kind of love that I had shared with their mother.

Chapter 1
Will

NUMB. THAT'S HOW I WOULD describe myself. Not meaning that I couldn't feel, but that I didn't care if I did or not. I was desensitized to the world around me. My head was a mess, and I was unable to make sense of it all, an unexplained weight always pulling me down. As I raced down the highway, storm clouds were building over the lake and would soon overtake the sun that had been beating down and warming my skin. I felt nothing. Neither the wind I was racing against, nor the warmth of the sun; not even the pain I wanted to get away from. Today wasn't any different, though. I hadn't felt anything real in a long time. I wish I could say it was because of my actions over the past several years, or even the last few days. No remorse, no regret, and certainly no sadness. I suppose one could argue that I felt *something* as I was heading back to the only place I had ever considered home. Or maybe there was simply no difference between ignorance and apathy.

Eventually the grey asphalt beneath me speckled with the

cool autumn rain that was beginning to fall. Within minutes, the rain beat down in a steady pulse, assaulted my face and eyes, and slid off of my jacket. I pressed the pedal down even further, urging the motorcycle for more speed. I glanced behind me, still expecting someone to be following me. It wouldn't take long for them to realize I was gone, and I was certain they would follow. This journey felt like forever.

The events of the night before had been coming to me in pieces. The bodies. The booming bass of a horrid song. The copper tang of blood. A scream. Fear. Shame? Remorse? Did I feel remorse? Was I sorry that things kept on ending like last night with bodies and blood? I suppose it could be argued that *that* is exactly why I was running away. Or maybe it was her voice. '*Please, Will. Please come back home,*' the message on my phone had said. A simple plea from my sister miles away is what I thought had suddenly sent me heading back on the road to this place. I hadn't been there for a long time. My father and I argued too often. Our lives, our believed purpose, too different. A way of life that I never asked for but was given. All of us were.

I suppose we were considered immortal, the three of us, my father, sister, and me. Ravaged by an incurable disease decades ago that left our bodies frozen. Lifeless. Empty shells. Not really living, but not dying. We needed blood to survive, to run through our veins and feed our organs, to keep our heart beating ever so slightly. Of course, the opinion on how to get the blood is part of what differed between the three of us. It's what made me move to Chicago in the first place. I was angry when the change happened, and didn't want to hide. I didn't want to pretend to be something I wasn't. I didn't want to play at being a human.

The rain finally began to subside as I pulled off the highway and onto my exit. It would only take a few minutes until I pulled into the driveway. Still, I wasn't quite ready to walk through the doors of the old house, announcing my presence. Instead, I found myself meandering down a familiar shaded drive and into the cemetery; there was a stop I needed to make first.

A cool north wind swirled through the leaves as I parked my bike. The rain had fully stopped, leaving everything with a wet sheen; the wood around me smelled vaguely like cinnamon. Closing my eyes, I breathed in deeply and absentmindedly grabbed my chest, feeling the heavy numbness sink back down into me. The large iron gate creaked as I pushed it open. Walking forward, my eyes scanned the manicured lawn in search of my objective. I followed the winding path deep into the sunken meadow. Protected on three sides by the trees on the sand dunes, it was still there and hard to miss. The maple tree, with leaves turned a brilliant red hue that clashed with its smooth grey trunk. The gigantic tree wasn't the only thing I sought out. At its base sat four granite stones. Gravestones. The leaves stirred in the breeze, waving to me, beckoning me to come closer, while some fell around me like thin sheets of paper.

I stood at the foot of the tree and filled my lifeless lungs, deeply drawing the smell of the damp and decaying leaves and enjoying the burn. I leaned against the tree and glanced down, letting my eyes wander to the old, moss-covered granite stones that lay below. A shudder went through my body as I stared. I hadn't come to this place in a while but somehow needed it now, to remind me of what I was; to remind myself that coming back here should be temporary. They would come for me eventually, even if it wasn't today.

Again, thoughts of last night invaded my mind. I had left Chris at some party, but as I was leaving, I heard a whimpering sound from the corner. It came from a girl who was crouching down, her arms fiercely hugging her knees. She shook as she looked around the room at the bodies. Her lips had parted and a small noise escaped, while around us, the stereo was blaring some stupid classic rock song. An unwarranted anthem for a party such as this. It would have been easy to end it for her. To continue the life I had been living for many years. But then I hesitated, realizing that I was at a crossroad and didn't know which way to turn. I hadn't ended a life but instead, had walked away from it. From Chris. I was tired of the darkness that seemed to settle over me. It was time. Something had to change, although I knew it was only a matter of time before he would come looking for me, and right now, I wasn't sure that I didn't want to let him find me. Just because I had left, didn't mean that I knew what I needed to do. Maybe I would go back and maybe I wouldn't. Either way, I needed some time away.

"Just leave. No one will hurt you," I had whispered, letting the girl go. I then found myself aimlessly wandering the streets of the city for the rest of the night, unsure of what was happening. Over and over, I listened to the pleading message from my sister, trying to find the answers I was seeking.

Perhaps that's why I came here first, back to this cemetery. To find something. It took only a few moments to realize that the stones at my feet held no more answers than my sister's voicemail.

DRIVING BACK TOWARD THE HOUSE, thoughts about last night and the carnage I had left behind continued to cloud my mind. At the time, leaving Chicago and coming back here had seemed like the right decision, but now that I was on my way, I hated myself for letting my father and sister influence me. Once I got there, I knew what would happen. They would try to convince me to stay, to live like they did, pretending we were like everyone else; as if we were human. I would stick around for a few days, as always, then tell him what I thought of that life and find somewhere else to go. That thought made me smile and press the accelerator down even further. Yes, this is what I needed. Just a few days away from Chicago so I could let things clear. Then everything would go back to normal... whatever that was.

I slowed a little as I neared the familiar surroundings of my ancestral home. Following the hidden driveway to the sprawling house that I knew was just barely visible beyond the trees, I slid to a stop on the front walk, spewing gravel every which way. Taking my helmet off, I looked up at the house that most people would consider an old Victorian. It was three stories, with ornate detailing around the windows and a tower with bay windows and stained glass. Hydrangeas surrounded the front of the wraparound porch. To the right of the house was an English garden, complete with a trellis of wisteria. My mother's rose garden was just past that. Pathways wound their way through the landscape to a koi pond just beyond the gardens as well. The front of the house was obscured from the main road by trees, but the back opened up and sloped gently downward, offering a view of Lake Michigan off in the distance. It was exquisite. Anyone who knew it was back here thought it was a perfect restoration when in reality, it was the same house that we had lived in for 100 or so years, meticulously preserved.

In its former glory, the house had been part of a 50-acre fox farm. My family had made its money at the turn of the century selling fox pelts. Then the accident and infection happened, and we were forced to remain out of sight, to hide our immortality. Eventually, my father, disguised as a relative, sold off several parcels of land. Now, all that was left of this farm was the ten acres surrounding the house and a few outbuildings scattered around the neighborhood that had built up in the fields. The neighborhood had been here for 30 years, but it was still hard for me to see what happened to our old farm.

Standing on the porch, I looked around the yard at the gardens, breathed in the lake air of my hometown, and prepared to make my arrival known to my family. I stood quietly by the front door for a moment, readying myself for the scene that would surely follow once I walked in. I raised my hand to knock, and then dropped it back to my side, reminding myself that this was as much my home as his. Only guests knocked.

I shoved the door open and called out.

"Father, your favorite son has returned," I announced sarcastically. The house was quiet, except for the ticking of the grandfather clock in the hall. Not the homecoming I had expected. Hadn't they been calling me for days, begging me to come back?

"William, glad you decided to grace us with your presence." My father emerged from his study with a furrowed brow. He had been about 50 when he was infected and just like me, still looked the same, his age frozen in time. He was tall — over six feet, with wavy salt and pepper hair. His eyes were a deep brown, framed by a pair of round glasses. Once a literature professor at the local university, he found that he couldn't gain enough knowledge, a condition that was made worse by being granted so much time after the infection. He was the perfectly preserved specimen of the father that I had known for over a century.

"Glad to see you too." I hesitated, and we stared at each other, neither one wanting to back down. "Celia called me and I had a few free days, so what do you want from me?" I asked boldly, although I was sure I already knew.

"I read about the recent antics of your Chicago crowd, and there was more on the news this morning." He stood straighter, as if to look down on me, which was difficult when I was equally as tall.

Of course, he knew about it. He was constantly keeping tabs on me, which was why he continued to call. I felt a flash of something rush though me. Disgust? Guilt, perhaps? I shook it off quickly and clenched my teeth.

"How I live my life is none of your business." It didn't take long for me to become defensive and ready for a fight.

"Oh, yes it is! I am still the head of this family, and I will not have a member of my family running about undisciplined!" He turned away quickly, but not before I saw his face soften. "You just don't seem to understand. I don't know what would happen if I lost you."

And therein lay the cause of my sudden guilt and perhaps the reason I came back here at all. I could feel the sadness coming from him, but I wouldn't let it get to me. I knew what he was trying to do and it wasn't going to work. It didn't work the first time, and it certainly wouldn't work this time. I refused to let it.

"I have no idea what you're talking about," I said in denial, as I slid into the soft leather of the arm chair, propping my feet up on the worn ottoman. "And I am not the one who killed anyone." I crossed my arms in front of me, making a show of standing my ground. I would not let him intimidate me.

"Oh, so now you are killing? Never mind, it doesn't matter! You are associated with those *people* and are therefore responsible for what they do. Do you really have to be so reckless? Being immortal only guarantees you long life. It doesn't make you any less vulnerable to dying." He was angry again. "I just wish that you would stay here and leave that life behind you." He faced me, his eyes pleading.

I stared at him for a minute, contemplating what he was really asking. Despite the fact that he was right about Chicago, my answer would not be what he wanted to hear.

"No. This is not the life I chose."

Disappointment etched across his face before he pulled the hard mask back in place. I realized this had been a mistake. I may need a change, but I don't think this is it. Guilt or not, I could read into what he was really asking, and I didn't want to stay. This was the life he had chosen for my sister and himself. I didn't want to pretend that I was human. I didn't want to pretend that I was something I was not. We were different, and the sooner he accepted that, the better off all of us would be. I glared back at him, daring him to continue this argument.

"If you won't stay for me, stay for your sister. She misses you. You don't have to stay forever, just stay for a while. Stay for her." His voice was soft, all the ire from a moment before was gone.

And just like that, my resolve wavered. My father knew my sister was my weakness, and using her would make me consider it. I have never thought that this sedentary life was for me. I liked to live on the edge. Then there was my sister. As much as I had loved living it up with the others in Chicago, I knew that I didn't really want to hurt her. There was an unexplainable bond that still pulled me toward her... toward them. It really was her phone call that brought me back and at the very least, I should give her a few days of my time. The time away would clear my head.

"Fine," I answered calmly, "but only for a few days. Then I'm going back *home*." I emphasized the last word, as if to point out that this was not my home anymore.

A soft thank you was his only reply before he turned back the way he came and left me sitting there all alone.

Sighing loudly, I stood up and walked up the staircase to find my bedroom. It was actually more than a room, it was a small apartment. The space consisted of three rooms, a sleeping area, a sitting area, and a bathroom. A four-poster bed stood against the wall at the far corner, with a small bedside table to the left of it. The sitting area included a chaise lounge, a desk and a chair. Even though this had been my room off and on for over 100 years, there was nothing personal in it; nothing that would necessarily link me to this house. If I were planning on spending any length of time here, I would have to send for my things. Fortunately, I didn't plan on staying more than a few days.

The springs of the old mattress croaked under my weight as I sat cautiously on the bed. Oddly, there wasn't a speck of dust on any of the surfaces, even though it had been a long time since I had stayed here. The evening sun was streaming through the window and I could feel it heat my cool skin. I closed my eyes and thought back through the last week. My father was right. There was something going on in Chicago, but he was wrong about my involvement. It wasn't that bad. I knew what I was doing. Or did I?

I lived with a rogue group of immortals in a Chicago brownstone. It was like a fraternity, I guess. We went out a lot, drank frequently, and yes, sometimes things did get out of control like last night, or worse. Three weeks ago, there was an incident in Millennium Park. Chris, the so-called leader, got a little carried away. Two people were attacked and killed in the open, while others stood by. The group took care of most of them, either killing them or convincing them that they didn't see anything. I didn't want to kill innocent people, but sometimes it was necessary in order to protect our identity. It was a matter of self-preservation. If I was going to live unexposed, I wanted to continue to live a free life; to do what I wanted and not what someone else told me I should do. Wasn't that what being an immortal was all about? I had escaped death once, and now I might as well enjoy it. The Chicago incident was all over the news and there was a lot of speculation as to what actually killed those people. Since then, there were whisperings of a serial killer on the loose. Then again, Chicago was a big city and was not immune to random killings. I guess in hindsight, it had been reckless, being out in the open like that. While I didn't necessarily participate, I did nothing to stop it, either. Now that I was here, back in my former bedroom on the old fox farm in this boring town, I couldn't wait to get back to the excitement of the city. I felt the ache in my chest again. The one that never seemed to go away. In fact, when I thought about the events of the last few days, the ache increased. Or maybe it was just because I was back here with all the memories.

I glanced around my room at the few artifacts that remained. My bed stood against the wall, providing a view of the lake from the window. A Tiffany lamp sat on the bedside table. The quilt was homemade, a gift from my grandmother many years before. Its tattered ends the only indication of how old it really was. Either my father or my sister had placed two pictures on the oversized bureau; one of my mother sitting in the garden looking out over the lake at the setting sun and one of my sister smiling broadly as she played on the beach. I walked over and gathered them up, throwing them in the top drawer. I hated looking at the reminders, which is precisely why I had left the weathered photos here. I was not that same person anymore.

I threw myself on the bed and folded my arms under my head, turning to get a view of the waves crashing on the shore in the distance. I wondered what my next step should be... how many days should I stay and where should I go next?

I felt a pang in my stomach and knew I needed blood. Finding fresh blood in this small town would be a risk, so I walked back downstairs to the very large kitchen. It hadn't been used in years, but I could almost smell my mother's cooking. It was one thing about being human that I missed. While I could still eat, it did nothing for me. It wasn't the nutrition found in food that the disease needed. My father walked by at that moment, breaking up my thoughts.

"There is human blood in the refrigerator," he eyed me cautiously from the doorway. "I have a connection at the blood bank and can get an unlimited supply." I knew this of course; this is what allowed my father and my sister to exist in this human world. They remained civilized and continued to lead a semi-normal human life but still needed human blood to survive. I knew that they would have to find fresh blood from somewhere.

"And how is Cee getting along here?" I leaned on the

countertop and casually asked, just to be polite. My sister, Celia, was seven years younger than I was theoretically. Considering we were both immortal, she was actually much older than sixteen, as she appeared.

"Actually, quite well. She has enrolled in high school. She doesn't really have any friends, but she is enjoying the time she spends there."

"High school! How could she ever enjoy high school? I mean, hasn't she had enough already after all of these years?" I poured myself a glass of blood just to appease my father but made a show of turning my nose up at it.

"She's never finished and she felt that it was high time. We have only been in the open in this town for three years. It has made it much more enjoyable." My father and sister had moved around a lot to keep suspicions at bay. People would notice if they never aged or if my sister never got married. They had come back here, often for weeks at a time, but had never lived in the open until now.

"Well, alright then. If that's what makes her happy... maybe I could visit as her guest." My eyes flashed mischievously for a moment, but my father already knew what was on my mind.

"William, don't you dare. She is truly happy here for the first time in her new life! You cannot ruin this for her," his voice yelled icily. He eyed the glass of blood in front of me, knowing that it wouldn't satisfy my need. My physical need, yes, but it was my mental need that he was concerned about. "I have warned you before. Do not cause trouble here. We don't want to expose ourselves. You chose your lifestyle when you let the disease decide your life, but you must respect that we have not, and have chosen differently for ourselves."

"Hey, you asked me to come here, don't forget," I reminded him, raising my hands up in mock defeat. "Don't worry, though. I won't blow your cover of the loving father and daughter. Besides, I was only joking," I spat back. "I promise not to do anything while I'm here. Contrary to popular belief, I can control myself." And I could, though it wasn't always easy. I would be able to do it for a few days, and a few days was all I needed right now. "Just keep plenty of blood in the refrigerator, and I'll stay out of sight. I have to feed this disease somehow, don't I? And if you are so worried, why did you even want me back here anyway?" It was always like this. The back and forth about whose life was better. He wanted me to stay but threatened to kick me out for being me.

My father shrugged and turned to go but stopped abruptly next to me.

"I do wish that you would at least give this," he gestured around, "a try, for more than just a few days." His voice was sincere, the previous anger gone as he put his hand on my shoulder.

"You know that I don't think I would be able to last here for long. I can't change what I am now. Chicago is a better place for me," I answered soberly. This was half true. It just seemed that no matter where I was, I still felt hollow inside. Sometimes I wished that it would work for me, but I knew better. Still, the guilt returned... and with it came the confusion. I turned my back to him and gazed out the window at the lake. My body tensed. He didn't know the nerve he had hit.

"You think I don't understand, but I do. It's not the blood; it's the loss of control." He knew me better than I thought. My father was always intuitive. "Just please stay out of trouble while you're here. Celia is a senior in high school and she very much wants to finish."

"Don't I always?" I rolled my eyes at him, even though I knew he was right. It would be a struggle. I would find ways around it. A hollow spot deep inside burned at the thought.

My thoughts were interrupted by my sister running at me. She jumped before I realized what she was doing and knocked me down.

"Will! I knew you would come. Oh, please tell me that you will stay a while. It feels like forever since I have seen you!"

"Considering our immortality, forever is possible," I joked back. "I'll be here for at least a few days." I sprang to my feet and planted a kiss on top of her head. I was a good six inches taller than she was. Other than a slight similarity, she was my opposite. Her blond hair hung in curls past her shoulders, a stark contrast to my own dark waves. Her features were perfect; wide blue-grey eyes, defined cheekbones, and full, red lips. Despite her pale skin, she was stunning. She may not agree, but being immortal agreed with her. The change had made her hauntingly beautiful.

My sister was one of the only things I truly missed about my life before I was infected. We had been close before the accident, and while we had remained in contact, we had hardly spoken in recent years, most of our conversations taking place through email or text messages. The longer I stayed away from here, the more I found myself pulling away for good. But now that I was with her again, it was easier to let my guard down a little.

"So, tell me about your latest stint in high school. Are you finally getting good grades?" I nudged her a little, and it was enough to get her to talk. Apparently, she was really enjoying being in high school. She was adjusting to life in the open. Her eyes sparkled as she talked about it. She looked radiant, and I could tell that she was happy. I was surprised at how happy it made me, that she had found some peace after all these years. I thought about my own inner turmoil and shuddered. Maybe being at home was better than I thought.

She dragged me back out to the living room and plopped down on the sofa, dragging me with her. I sighed, and looked around as she continued talking. The house never changed. My mother's touches were everywhere, and it was clear my father was still feeling her loss as well, even after all of these years. Then again, the house was just like us; it never aged. It would always be here. A timeless refuge.

After a while, my father came to join us, and we sat around the fire, talking late into the evening. I had to admit, it felt good for a while. When we weren't trying to best each other, conversation with my father was easy. Celia told me more about her latest exploits in high school, her attempts to fit in, and the occasional human who would actually talk to her. She was a favorite among the teachers, but apparently, most of the students were terrified of her. I shifted in my chair, and then shifted again, my eyes darting to the clock. Clearly, I was reaching my fill of family time. The sun had set and the moon had risen, giving way to the evening. I stood up to stretch, my muscles aching from the inactivity.

"I think I need to go out for a walk and get a breath of fresh air."

My father raised an eyebrow at me cautiously. Yes, I was restless. Being back here had awakened something in me. A need perhaps, or something else... I just didn't know what. I was aware of my father's rules. I would stay in the shadows and out of trouble. I truly just needed some fresh air and time to think.

"Don't worry, I gave you my promise. I'm just not used to being stuck in a building at night. I need some fresh air," I reminded him. "Don't wait up." There was no immediate response and I didn't wait for one as I slipped from the house before he could argue or try to get Celia to join me.

Immortals do still need sleep. Perhaps not as long as humans, but there was still a basic need to close our eyes and rest. Sometimes, though, I slept out of boredom. When you had forever, sleeping a day away meant absolutely nothing. In fact, in Chicago, I was known to sleep through the daytime hours and go out only at night. This immortality is a disease. We aren't vampires, although with the need for blood and sleeping habits such as ours, this may be where some of the myths had begun.

Outside, the moon was full and light cascaded down the

otherwise unlit road. I loved the night. I could see quite clearly through the dark curtain before me, once my eyes adjusted. I walked quickly at first, feeling the cool breeze on my sensitive skin, tasting and smelling the air around me to get my bearings in this neighborhood. All the while, my mind was busy sorting out the memories that were emerging with every step I took, in the places that used to be my family farm.

It was a small neighborhood, shaped in an L and consisting of about fifteen houses. Our house stood back from the road where it looked down at a cul-de-sac. When my father sold the property off, he sold some of the existing outbuildings as well. I could see that many of them were still standing. What once housed the foxes, now stored garden hoses and wheelbarrows or the occasional car. They looked out of place next to the newer houses. I crept around the old barns, taking in their scent and trying to remember how things used to be. The neighborhood was quiet, with only the sound of crickets accompanying me on my self-guided tour.

The air only slightly calmed my nerves. I couldn't seem to shake my restlessness no matter how much I walked. I was about ready to give up and head back home, when I caught the scent of something unusual. The metallic scent of blood filled the air around me and it made me wonder if I wasn't alone. Sadness and despair seemed to drape around me in a thick blanket. The disease loved all blood, but seemed to be most attracted to the blood of those who felt sad and desperate. I guess it didn't make me as heartless as everyone thought. I chose to fill my need from those who were void of hope, perhaps a reflection of who I was.

The fragrance was unusually strong, and again I wondered if someone was lurking about. A quick glance around revealed nothing and I felt assured that I was alone. I passed by the old slaughter house, which now served as an outdoor shed and I wondered if I wasn't picking up on the old blood that at one time had soaked through the floor and into the surrounding soil. But that blood was old, and after passing the slaughter house, the scent was still there. My promise to my father lingered in my mind, but suddenly I needed to know where the scent was coming from. I continued to the end of the cul-de-sac anyway, telling myself the whole time that if it were someone, I wasn't going to do anything. I simply wanted to see what was drawing me in. Could I really stop myself?

It was dark, other than a solitary light coming from the front window of a house to my left. The light spilled out into the blackness of the front lawn. Puzzled, I crept closer to the window, wondering if this was the source of my intrigue. I had to see what or who it was, unsure of what I would do next. I was sure of one thing; I had never experienced a need this strong before. Slowly, I peered in the window and that's when I saw her. A girl was sitting on a bench, her auburn hair cascading over her shoulders in beautiful waves, accentuating an oval face. She squinted closely at something, which wrinkled her brow. My eyes followed her slender hand, as she raised it up to grab the chewed-up pencil from her mouth. She wrote something quickly and placed the pencil back between her full lips, cocking her head slightly. I had never seen anything or anyone I wanted more. The sadness I had sensed disappeared, and instead, I was filled with pure happiness. It was like the scent of fresh grass after a rainstorm, or an open field of lavender, or fresh cut roses. It was clearly coming from the girl, who seemed to be everything all in one.

That's when the most fascinating sounds came from her fingertips. I had been so distracted that I didn't even notice that she was sitting at a piano. Long-fingered hands flew over the keys in perfect arches. They pressed down delicately on the ivory, her thin wrists arching gracefully. And then the melody. The music vibrated through my skin, through my bones, and deep into the emptiness that was once my soul. In my hundred plus years, I had never seen or heard anything this perfect. It was as if she was playing just for me. I felt the notes radiating into the hollow spot in my chest, and there was no longer any trace of the despair that had drawn me to her. The need I had felt all these years was gone, and my body was filled with something new.

I staggered from the window, my back slamming against a nearby tree, confused by this turn of events. How could I have been so drawn to this one person? I had felt the darkness moments earlier, but then when the music started, there was passion unlike anything I had ever experienced. She fascinated me. I knew that I would not hurt her. *Could not hurt her.* How could I harm someone so captivating?

My confusion was strong and I forgot who or where I was for a moment. I got clumsy and stepped on a twig outside her window. She looked up, peering out into the darkness just as I melted into the shadows, hoping that she hadn't seen me. She walked close to the window, peering out into the night. Only then could I see her eyes. They were a bright jade green, edged with a rich caramel and they were peering into my soul. I was startled by what I saw. There was turmoil and sadness hidden deep, but there was also something different. I didn't have time to figure it out before she turned from the window, turned off the light, and disappeared in the dark house.

Staring at the empty window for a moment, I registered the encounter in my mind, realizing this girl had left me shaken. I could still hear the melody long after she had stopped playing and the air was still redolent. It was at that moment I felt that maybe there was another need that existed within me. A need for more than just blood. I knew I needed *her*. Somehow, it was as if my empty soul depended on it. I turned and glared out into the night, more restless than before. With confusion mounting, I did the only thing I knew to do. I ran.

"WHERE HAVE YOU BEEN ALL night?" my father asked accusingly, as I was quietly closing the door. So much for sneaking back in. "Did you go into town? Did anything happen? I knew I should have made your sister go with you."

His tone implied that he didn't think that I was actually keeping my promise. No, I had not done anything that stupid, although it had been almost dawn when I returned. My mind had been shaken, and I had stayed out all night walking, just trying to make sense of it all. After I left the girl's house, the pain and the need for blood returned, as did the confusion which fought with the new aching sensation I felt, frustrating me even more. How quickly I had gone from the numbness I felt in Chicago to the turbulence that engulfed me here.

"No," I sneered, irritated. I was quick to anger when my father accused me in this way. "I was just out." My temper felt shorter than usual, and it bothered me that my father seemed unaware that my mind was a blur right now.

"I am not just thinking of me," he bellowed back, unaffected by my snarling. "Do you think this life is easy for your sister? I am trying to give her as much normalcy and I can. Can't you think of someone other than yourself for once, Will?"

The force of his words hit me hard, and I blinked, stumbling back stunned. It was selfish, wasn't it? Wanting something more. I thought of the girl standing at the window and did indeed want more.

"I know, I am sorry," I stammered, my anger leaving as quickly as it came. "Nothing happened, no one saw me. I just walked." I looked up into his concerned eyes and nearly choked on my own pain, causing me to pause. "I think I just need some time alone. I will be upstairs for a while," I said, as I scrambled up toward my room. What was happening to me?

I suppose my father deserved to know about my encounter, but I was still too shaken. I felt strange, like I wasn't myself. For many years, all I had thought about was blood and hurt and for the first time, it wasn't the only thing on my mind. I certainly had some thinking to do. Seeing the girl, hearing her play stirred things in me that I hadn't felt in a very long time. I couldn't make sense of this new longing. I didn't know what it was and for once in my life, I was not sure what to do. I lay on the bed and stared at the ceiling. I sighed loudly and squeezed my eyelids closed. I could still see her and hear the sweet melody playing in my mind. Eventually, I drifted off to sleep, still ruminating about the mystery girl and her song.

Chapter 2
Celia

I LISTENED FOR MY BROTHER to come back but fell asleep sometime in the quiet hours of night. Thank god tomorrow was Saturday and I wouldn't have to get up early. Or so I thought. I woke to the sound of feuding voices downstairs. The light of dawn was slowly trickling through the windows, and it was clear that my father was arguing with Will about something. Quietly, I crept to the top of the stairs to try to hear better.

"I think I just need some time alone..." my brother's voice finished, and I heard him heading in my direction. I scrambled back down the hallway and within a second, I was back behind my own closed door, hopefully undetected by either one.

It wasn't unusual for my father and brother to fight. They often fought when Will was home, although rarely in front of me. They tended to be slightly overprotective and treat me as if I were still six. When I was around, they'd pretend things were fine. Neither one of them would try to understand the other's point of view. I wished they would. I wanted my brother home again.

As much as I wanted to go to Will and see what was going on, I knew that it would only annoy him at this point. He clearly needed his space and I would grant him that. Instead, I just messed around in my room, listening to music, finishing my homework, and reading a little. After a while, I couldn't stand it anymore and decided to find out what was going on. I knew where every floor board creaked and carefully avoided the worst. My hand was poised over the door to knock when I hesitated. Breathing in the familiar smell of oak, I sighed deeply and rapped the door slightly.

"What." His voice sounded muffled as if he was smothering it.

"Can I come in?" I called out softly.

"I guess." A slightly inviting response, I suppose. "Can't a guy get some sleep around here?" he mumbled.

I entered Will's room tentatively and walked over to sit on the edge of his bed where he was still lounging. He sat up and smiled, pretending everything was fine and trying to hide the fact that he looked awful. His skin was pale and the purple crescents under his eyes only drew attention to the wild look deep in them. He looked like a startled animal. Unease was not something I was used to seeing from him.

"What's up? How's school?" He asked, leaning over to muss my hair as if I was still ten. I ducked out of the way, but not before his fingers caught in my curls.

"School's great. We talked about that yesterday,

remember?" I answered, rolling my eyes. Small talk was not why I had come in here, so I hastily changed the subject. "Hey, you look like hell. You really should drink or something. What's up with you?"

"Cee, I'm sure that people will warm up to you eventually," he said ignoring my insult and leaning back against the headboard, with his hands behind his head.

"Gee, thanks. That's very comforting. And you still haven't answered my question." He wasn't going to escape my questions that easily.

"Seriously, what's going on? You were fine, and then you went out all night and I heard you fighting with father this morning. Not to mention the fact that you've been holed up in here for hours. Is everything okay? I mean, I know that you don't love being here, but usually you're at least a *little* social with me." I stared intently at him, trying to show him how serious I was. I could sense a darkness rolling off him in waves, but it was happening so quickly that I couldn't decipher anything. Reading people is something that I've always been good at, especially when it came to my brother. He could never hide a thing from me. "You just aren't yourself. I mean, you just seem... I don't know, murky. What happened?" I prodded again.

"Nothing, it's just..." His words faded off as he lay back down and rolled over, turning his back to me before continuing. "Celia, you have been acting like a human far longer than I have."

I smiled. It was going to be *that* kind of conversation. Well, at least he was talking.

"I don't act like a human, Will. We live in a human world and I don't like to think of myself as being so different. Besides, technically, we *are* still humans. Just humans with an incurable disease that requires ingesting blood to survive and grants us an unnaturally long life." I tried the joking approach, but Will didn't even crack a smile.

"Come on Cee, that's not what I mean. I'm talking about really being human. Do you remember what it was like to have human feelings?"

I continued to scan his face, but his features were still unreadable and I couldn't tell where this was going.

"Yes. I mean, I still get angry and happy. I miss you when you're gone too long. I don't think I feel them as intensely, but I do feel them," It was a cruel part of immortality. Our senses may be heightened, but our ability to truly feel has almost disappeared.

I wondered where he was going with this. I was no stranger to odd conversations with my brother, but he had never talked this candidly with me about our affliction, and I couldn't help but wonder what it meant.

"When I was out last night I saw a girl," he finally said, looking at his hands, and I immediately thought the worst. I could feel my eyes widen at the thought of him killing someone innocent. He sensed where my mind was going.

"I didn't kill her. What is it with you two! I didn't even touch her. I only saw her from a distance," he quickly assured me. "Actually, that's not entirely true. I went out for some air, to get away from the whole *happy family* vibe, when I was hit with the most intoxicating scent. It was full of so much pain, sadness, and despair. I followed it, curious, and it led me to a nearby house. This girl was sitting at a piano. I could feel the disease aching for the taste of her blood. It wanted it so bad. *I* wanted it so bad. I wanted it worse than anything I have ever wanted before. Then the strangest thing happened. She started playing a melody and everything I had thought I wanted before disappeared, and in its place, something new. Something strange. She was no longer full of gloom and loss, but of hope and longing. I stayed and listened to her play, and when she was done, I just couldn't get that feeling out of my mind. I have never changed my mind this quickly about anything. One minute I wanted to appease the disease and the next minute, I was filled with something different. I just can't explain it." He turned to look out the window and my eyes followed to the lake. I could see the waves in the distance lazily crashing on the shore.

I turned and studied his profile carefully, trying to read him for the truth. He stared innocently as if in deep concentration. A frown played at his lips, but his eyes, which were wild before, were bright and calm. The confusion on his face explained the barrage of energy I was getting from him.

"So you didn't... hurt her?" My voice was hesitant. I wanted to believe him. I wanted to trust him.

"No, I couldn't. I didn't want to. The craving was gone and was replaced with something new. My chest hurt, but not like the need for blood where your muscles feel fatigued. It was like a heaviness constricted me and I couldn't breathe. Even now, I can still feel it," he said sadly and for the first time, I could really see how conflicted he really was.

"Do you think you are actually *feeling* something? I mean, is that why you were asking me about human emotions?" I asked tentatively, already forming a hypothesis in my head.

"I don't know. Maybe. I guess I don't know what to think anymore." He shrugged off my question nonchalantly.

"Will, you aren't as awful as you think, you know." He always had such low opinion of himself, refusing to believe that he could ever be good. "I mean, you do still come back here once in a while, and there are times I still see the old you. You shouldn't be so hard on yourself. It isn't impossible for you to be feeling." I stopped to see if there was a reaction before I continued. "I think you've been away from human life for such a long time that you don't recognize it. Whatever this girl did, she stirred up something in you. Perhaps, what you're feeling is loneliness."

He gave me a look of disbelief, but I could also register relief rolling off of him.

"Lonely?" he quipped and our brother/sister moment was gone. "But I live with a bunch of guys. Plus I have you," he answered sarcastically. There he was again, the Will that he had become. The one that only cared about himself. The one I didn't quite trust. The one that let the disease take over. Still, something inside of me wanted to keep hoping, especially considering the sliver of innocence he just revealed. I would never give up on him, which is why I kept pushing.

"Well yes, but even humans can feel lonely despite the fact that they have families. It's different. I don't know how to explain it, as it's something I scarcely remember myself. Maybe even immortals can want more." I paused before continuing hoping my words would sink in and finally reach him. "Perhaps this life isn't supposed to be all about blood and disease. I think maybe you want more."

He began laughing and I looked down at my hands, suddenly annoyed with his reaction.

"I think you've been hanging around humans for too long," he suggested, while he rolled out of bed and began pulling clothes out of a giant duffle bag.

"I don't think that's very funny, Will," I said quietly, working hard to control the annoyance that was welling inside me. "I was only trying to help." Sometimes he can be so frustrating. If it weren't for the fact that he was my big brother, I would have just left him there on his own. Screw trying to help. But, of course, he was my brother, and I felt someone needed to help him.

Will looked back at me, and the laughter on his face instantly disappeared.

"I'm sorry, Cee. I really would like your help. Maybe you could help me figure out who this mystery girl is and then I can go from there," he continued.

I stood for a moment, contemplating. If only I could say no. No matter how many times I tried to convince myself to walk away just like he had done to me many times before, I never seemed able to do it. He was looking at me intently, the softness returning to his face, and it was evident that he really wanted this, and there was no way I could turn my back.

"Fine," I sighed, giving in, "but you need to fill me in on everything. And quit trying to be so damn tough."

He explained again in detail, the events that had happened again, and included a description of the girl and the house this time. I knew that house, and I knew that girl. Her name was Julia Cavallo, and she was my English teacher. I didn't know very much about her because she was new and young enough to frequently be mistaken for a student. It was common knowledge that she lived alone in the house down the road and that there had been some horrible tragedy in her past. I didn't concern myself with gossip, so I never bothered to learn what it was. She kept to herself and didn't seem to be a bother to anyone.

"What are you thinking about, Will. You won't hurt her, will you?" This new Will was something that would take a bit of getting used to. While my brother hid things around me, I wasn't an idiot and knew that he wasn't always the best at self-control.

"No, no, of course not! I gave my word. And to tell you the truth, maybe I am a little tired of that," he said, although I wondered how truthful his words really were; I was still a fledgling in my attempt at trusting him. "I just want to know more about her so that I can figure this thing out."

"Okay, good. Because she really is nice, though she is a little sad."

Will pulled on a clean t-shirt and a pair of pants over his

boxers as I looked away.

"Do you think that I could get a job in the school or something?" His expression was quizzical yet held a hint of trouble, and I suddenly realized that he didn't mean any of this. I had been right to hesitate. Was this all just a game to him? Did he really want to be there to be closer to her or would he just cause trouble. He said that he would behave, but I still wasn't positive that he could be trusted around so many humans. It had all just been a lie!

"What?" I yelled out. "You want to work at my high school? You really are unbelievable. Here I thought that things were going to be different, and you wouldn't try to ruin things again. You tell me all about this girl, and I thought that just maybe, you were coming back to me. To think you almost had me convinced to help you." I stood up and stormed toward the door, but before I could get there, he was in front of me with an iron grip on my shoulders, silver-grey eyes peering into mine.

"No, I didn't come here to ruin things. You both asked me to come home and I didn't object because . . . well, because the truth is that I have to lay low for a while. It's just that ...please, Celia. You have to trust me. You're the only one left who can." He loosened his grip and let me walk away. There was a pleading in his eyes and a longing as I had never seen. There was nothing to do but believe.

"Will, I'm still not totally sure what you need from us, but I have to ask... what is it that you want? I mean *really* want." I turned to ask before I reached the doorway.

His back was to me as he stared out of the window. Running a hand through his dark hair, he sighed.

"I don't know anymore, Celia. I just don't know," he whispered.

"Well, perhaps that's something you need to figure out first."

The angst was evident in his posture and I no longer knew what else to say. This was something for him to figure out on his own, at least for now. I slipped out of the room and left him to his thoughts.

AN HOUR LATER, WILL CAME into the living room where my father and I were both reading. He stood silently, his posture defeated, and both of us looked up expectantly.

"Will," our father greeted him curtly, a touch of annoyance still there.

"Father," Will started, "I was thinking. Maybe I should stay here for a while." His face was expressionless. "Perhaps I could get a job at the school or something." He let out the breath he had been holding after he rushed out the last part of his statement.

Our father breathed in deeply and closed his book, using a slender finger to mark his page.

"Will, we have talked about this before. I would love for you to stay for a while, but your sister and I enjoy our life here and can't afford to have you ruin it. You are welcome to stay, but it's too soon for you to think about being out in the open."

"I know that I've made mistakes before," he stammered, "but I would like to try."

Visible shock registered across our father's face. Will had stayed or rather, been forced to stay out of obligation before, but he had never actually come right out and said that he wanted to try. My father stood and approached Will, still standing in the doorway. The sides of the sofa engulfed me as I sank deeply into it, trying to remain inconspicuous.

"You have forced this family to move a number of times in the past." The tone of his voice began to rise at the memories, but he quickly controlled it. "You must understand my apprehension. This is our real home and we can't afford to have you lose control here."

"I am well aware of that," Will answered through clenched teeth. He was trying to keep his composure, despite the interrogation from my father. "I'm telling you that I want to try. I thought this is what you always wanted me to do. I can't explain it; I just really need to do this."

Will stopped and seemed on the verge of actually telling our father about Julia. His gaze met with mine, and I could see the conflict on his face. I smiled in encouragement, reminding him that I did believe in him. Then he turned back with intensity and resolve.

"I want this."

The ticking of the clock echoed and counted down time while our father contemplated. I really hoped that he understood. This is something he had wanted for so long, but now that the words had been said, I hoped that he would actually give Will a chance. Even I could see that Will needed this now. Finally he spoke.

"Despite everything, you are my son, and I am still your father. I want to believe you Will, so I will grant you this. Perhaps I can help. Maybe I can call in a favor and get you some work at night, just until we are sure. But I have to trust you, Will. If there is any sign of trouble, you will have to leave as I can't wait around for you to lose control."

"I understand." Will relaxed, the hint of a smile playing across his face. "Thank you," he whispered and slipped quietly from the room.

Chapter 3
Julia

THE BUZZING OF THE ALARM jolted me from my sleep. It was still dark outside and the sun wouldn't rise for at least another hour, but my alarm went off at 5 a.m. every morning to allow me to get in a run before I needed to be at school. My feet hit the cool floor, waking me up a little and encouraging me to move. I slid on my running pants, t-shirt, track jacket, and running shoes and stepped outside into the chilly autumn air.

My breath floated in foggy wisps around me as I stretched briefly on the porch and turned on my favorite running playlist. My legs still ached from sleep, but I began to run, willing them to move forward. The dark air engulfed me like a blanket, smelling faintly of cinnamon and dried leaves, and I pulled it deeply into my lungs. I allowed myself a glance at the magnificent Bradley estate at the end of the road. A faint light shone through one of the windows making me shudder slightly. The old Victorian had me entranced since I was a child. It was beautiful, with its English gardens and perfectly manicured grounds, but there was something innately creepy about its turrets and the windows that seemed to smile in the dark. The house had been the topic of much speculation over the years. Some people even claimed that it was haunted. It had been uninhabited, although it had always been well cared for. Then Celia Bradley, a student of mine, and her father moved in a few years ago. Apparently, they were relatives of the original inhabitants of the estate. They stayed to themselves and Celia was a quiet student who never offered up much information about her home life. No one bothered to ask her about it either.

As I turned out of the subdivision, my breathing became regular and even as my legs found their pace. I liked to run. I felt stronger when I could feel my muscles pushing to their limits and I liked having uninterrupted time to think. The day planned itself out neatly in my head as I thought about everything that I needed to get done. Today's task was something as mundane as making copies and writing a test. Did I have a meeting this morning or was that tomorrow morning? In what felt like no time at all, I was turning back into my neighborhood, five miles under my belt.

Dawn was just breaking over the horizon and a few seagulls squawked overhead, reminding me that the lake wasn't too far off. I slowed my pace and walked the last quarter mile to my house. It was modeled after an old farmhouse, with its wraparound porch and floor to ceiling windows, but it was only twenty-three years old. My parents built it when I was just three years old. We lived here together for sixteen years until . . . I hated to think of the events that had taken place in the past several years and did my best to keep them locked away. Now I was living here alone, trying hard to focus on the future while trying desperately to bury the past. Images warred within my head, but I wouldn't think about such tragedy today. It was a good day when I could push them aside easily.

After a shower and breakfast, I set out for work. The school was only a mile away and was close enough to walk, but I liked to get there early to get a few extra things done. Today, I managed to pull into the school parking lot thirty minutes early. With any luck, I could get a few papers graded before the first bell. Keys in hand, I hurried to my room and almost ran into the blond student waiting for me at my door.

"Ms. Cavallo?" It was Celia Bradley, her curls looking perfect as usual and a bright smile on her face.

"Oh, good morning, Celia. You're here awfully early. Is there something I can do for you?" Seeing her reminded me of the light on at her house. I wanted to ask her if she had been up, then decided against it... not really wanting to open the door to a conversation. She was highly intelligent and very beautiful, but there was something about her that set off alarms, almost like a warning not to get too close.

"I just wanted to get the vocabulary list for this week. I think I forgot to grab it." She looked at me through veiled lashes, and I felt that her early arrival actually had a dual purpose. Considering she could easily get the list during class and the test wasn't until tomorrow, I began to wonder what else she wanted.

"No problem," I shrugged. "The list is in the basket on the counter." I watched her for a moment as she walked to the other side of the room to rummage around in the basket for the list, humming lightly to herself.

"My brother moved home for a while," she called out casually, and I couldn't help but think that this is what she actually had come in to tell me. Great. That's all I needed. Students were always trying to set me up with their relatives. I definitely wasn't interested. There was no room for anyone in my solitary life right now. Thinking that far into the future seemed a little premature when you were just trying to get through life one day at a time.

"Oh, that's great. I bet you like having him back at home," I responded casually.

"Yeah, he was away at school and then living in Chicago, so I didn't get to see him all that often. It will be nice to have him at home for a while." She found the list and began walking back toward my desk with catlike grace.

"I'll bet. Well, I have to get a few things done. I'll see you in sixth period," I said, trying to kindly dismiss her so that I could get some work done, but by the time I looked up, she was already halfway through the door. I stared at the empty doorway for a minute. What a strange conversation. What a strange girl.

My eyes refocused on the stack of papers in front of me, but my mind wouldn't focus, again drifting to thoughts of the Bradley's. There was much speculation surrounding them, and their story had become somewhat of a local legend. Apparently, my neighborhood had originally been part of the Bradley family estate; some sort of farm. In 1910, the Bradley family, who must have been Celia's great-grandparents, was caught in either a hotel fire, or train accident, or something while in Chicago. According to reports, their bodies were never found. Mr. Bradley and his two children were killed, while his wife survived. She was found dead a few years later, or so they say. Some say she died of cancer or in a fire, but I always thought she died from a broken heart and the pain of losing her entire family. Regardless, it was such a sad story. Sometimes, I couldn't help but stare off at the house and its oversized windows and wonder about how she must have felt during those last few years. In a way, I could relate to her. I knew what it was like to be alone. Before the Bradley's moved back to the area, rumors circulated that the house was haunted and that a woman could be seen walking past the windows from time to time.

A shiver crawled down my spine. I don't know why I had suddenly thought of this. I didn't want to think about the sorrow of the Bradley family now. Today had started out well, and I didn't need to let dark thoughts bring me back down.

"Hey, are you ready for Monday?" said a voice that bounded through the door. My best friend Kara, who also happened to teach across the hall, was one of the few good things in my life.

"Monday?" My mind anxiously thumbed through my mental files. What did I need to remember about Monday? Auditions! "Oh yeah, auditions! Um, I think so. I'm planning on having Steve help me out, but I haven't talked to him." It may be my first year here, but that didn't stop them from asking me to direct the school play. Steve was another English teacher who I had hoped would help me out. The idea of being on stage again was exciting, but anxiety was growing in me as I wondered if I would really be able to direct something. Although, it would give me something to do at night for a few months out of the year. This year, we were attempting Shakespeare's *As You Like It.*

"Well, I know that I'm not much of a thespian, but I can help you if you need me to."

She laughed, knowing that I would never ask her, and then went back to her own classroom. She actually was quite a drama queen. She just didn't realize it. Maybe I should ask her just to shock her.

First bell rang and my students began to trickle in, forcing me to focus on the task at hand. The rest of the day was uneventful as I continued through my normal routine. Discussions, reading, writing, etc. Ah, the life of a teacher. Finally, what seemed like days later, the sixth period bell finally rang. I could see Celia watching me casually, her blue eyes surreptitiously glancing through her curls, as I made my end of the hour announcements.

"Don't forget to read the next chapter in *Pride and Prejudice,* and remember you have a vocabulary quiz tomorrow." My announcements fell idly on the backs of the students as they left my classroom. Within seconds, the classroom was completely empty and quiet and I was alone. Good. No one wanted to stay and talk. I flopped down into my chair and sighed deeply. There was always grading to do, and then perhaps, I would go to the auditorium and play for a while.

I lived to play the piano. I had taken lessons from the time I was in elementary school, all the way through high school and had even been in the school orchestra. Now I just played for me. The sound of a piano is always very calming. There was a piano at home, but there was something about playing a big grand piano on a stage that reminded me of what it was like to play in front of an audience. The sound reverberated through the empty space and danced off the walls, sending a small thrill through me. A concert pianist would have been a logical career choice, but I never had the guts to go through the pressures of practicing to perform.

By the time I had finished grading papers and getting the vocabulary quiz ready, the school was nearly empty. Only a few staff members remained and the auditorium was vacant, as I had suspected. I flipped on the stage lights and immediately felt the heat radiating from them. I was momentarily blinded as my eyes adjusted until the auditorium seats were a haze before me. The sound of the bench sliding across the wooden stage echoed loudly, and I sat gingerly. The ivory was cold and silky under my fingers. If I closed my eyes, the music would find me. I never knew what song would come, but it would be one of many I had learned over the years. I had never been very good at writing my own music. Today, it was Pachabel's "Canon in D," a favorite of mine. It was like an old friend, its melody falling easily from my fingers. I let it grow and crescendo and then fade again, feeling the tension leave my body. When I played, I became someone else, and I was happy. Everything felt right, and I was able to forget. It was one of the few things that still made me feel alive.

Suddenly, I had the feeling I wasn't alone, and stopped playing abruptly. My eyes desperately searched the auditorium expecting to see someone, but with the stage lights on, it was impossible to see.

"Hello?" I cried out tentatively.

No answer.

"Is there someone out there?"

I scanned the empty chairs but could see no one. Then, just like that, the feeling of being watched was gone, and I was once again alone. Unnerved, I gathered my things, stood up and quickly left, barely remembering to turn the lights off as I walked out. While people listening to me play did bother me, knowing someone was there and not being able to see them alarmed me even more. Probably just a student who was embarrassed that they had been caught listening. No big deal. Wow, my imagination was really overactive today. Perhaps it was a thought that hadn't left my mind all day unnerving me. The thought of Mrs. Bradley walking through her empty house all those years ago.

Once home, I immersed myself in thoughts of all that I needed to do to get ready for auditions, and I was able to forget about the incident at school. Takeout made for an easy dinner and would allow me to keep working. It was getting dark out and the house seemed all the more empty, making me jump when the delivery person rang the doorbell.

After dinner, I went out to the porch to take in what was left of the sunset. Pinks and oranges painted the thin clouds that hung over the lake, while the sun had just begun to dip into the water below. I loved to sit on this porch and just watch. A faint glow from the lights at the Bradley estate down the road served as an eerie illumination. I thought back to my conversation with Celia. She really was an odd girl. I started to think about the fact that she had an older brother and caught myself wondering what he was like. Was he tall and blond? Was he a little more social than she was? What did it matter? Was I jealous that she had a brother, and I no longer did? *No, not now.* I pushed those thoughts deep into the crack that I felt just beneath the surface, and mentally tried to patch it. Today had been a good day. I didn't want to think about my family tonight. I just wanted to make it through one day without calling on the sadness that was intertwined with my life now.

Within minutes, the sun was gone, and I felt the call of the piano. I went inside and sat down on the bench. Perhaps, I would play something new tonight. I pulled out some new music I was working on and practiced diligently. Finally, I felt my mind shut down and a different song came out. I wasn't surprised to hear Mozart's "Fantasy in D Minor" erupting from the keys. It was melancholy, which was how I felt now. I played for several minutes, letting the music further deepen until again, I couldn't help but feel like I was being watched. The shades on the living room window were open, but when I looked outside, all I could see was my own startled reflection staring back at me. I reached for the shades and quickly shut them, trying hard to shake the feeling that there was someone or something out there. I reached forward and turned the light out, peering again between the shades into the darkness. My eyes could pick up nothing out of the ordinary. This was the kind of night that made me wish I had gotten that dog, or made Kara move in with me. Living alone sort of unnerved me at times, and it was easy for my imagination to get away from me. I went through the rest of the house locking the doors and shutting all the blinds, working my way upstairs. Sleep did not come easily, and when it finally did, there were dark dreams about glistening eyes watching from the dark.

THE NEXT MORNING, THE RAIN was drumming softly outside my window when my alarm went off. I suppose today would be as good as any to take a break from running, I thought, not wanting to emerge from my warm cocoon. My dreams from last night resurfaced and I was instantly glad that I wouldn't be venturing out in the dark. The thought of all of those eyes watching from the shadows was unsettling.

I squeezed my eyelids together tightly and tried to think of happier things. Fortunately, the comfort of my bed allowed for several more minutes of snuggling underneath the covers. I faded in and out of sleep until finally, the need for breakfast encouraged me to get out of bed. I took my time getting ready, but I still managed to arrive at school forty minutes early. I might as well get some things done. It was Friday and if I got enough done, there would be far less work to do over the weekend.

"Oh Julia, just the person I wanted to see. Could I talk to you for a few minutes?" John Mason, the principal said. I had stopped in the office to get my mail and nearly ran right into him.

"Sure. I'll be right in," I replied, a bit worried. It's funny how on edge I was about being called into the principal's office even though I was no longer a student. I had to remind myself that I had done nothing wrong as I grabbed my things and took a seat across from him in his office.

"How are preparations coming for the play auditions? Is there anything I could do for you? Do you need anything else?" My body instantly relaxed at his questions. He was a small, balding man who had been principal of this school for several years. While his tone was always harsh, he was a kind man who went out of his way to make sure both staff and students were happy at the school.

"Actually, I think I'm doing okay. I still need to find someone to act as an assistant director," I said, suddenly remembering that everyone had said no. When I had asked Steve the day before, he said he didn't have time to help this year, leaving me slightly panicked.
No one else seemed to want to give up their nights and a few weekends. Nothing like abandoning the new girl. "If it's okay with you, I might have Mallory Marshall do it. She's a senior, and has been in all the shows before."

"Oh, that would be fine as long as you think you can handle the logistics. I think she would be a great help to you." He grinned back at me in a fatherly way.

"Well, I suppose that I should get back to work." I stood to leave. "Unless there was anything else you wanted from me."

"No, that was it," he said, and began shuffling papers on his desk, signaling to me that we were finished.

"Thanks for the heads up. And I'll let you know if I need anything for the play," I said walking toward the door.

"Actually, there is one more thing I should mention," he said, stopping me. "I hired a new maintenance guy for after school and evenings. His name is William Bradley. He's Celia Bradley's older brother."

"Oh?" I tried to stop any emotion from showing on my face, although I could feel the warmth spreading though my cheeks.

"Their father has helped the school out financially over the past few years," he continued, "so I owe him a favor, I suppose. Apparently, his son is home for a while and needed a job. He won't be in your way, but I didn't want you to be surprised if you saw him around during rehearsals." He went back to the pile of papers on his desk.

"Thanks for letting me know. If I don't see you, have a great weekend," I replied and slipped out the door in a slight daze. I had been thinking about the Bradley's far too much lately and knowing another one of them would be around was intriguing.

"You too, and don't forget... let me know if there is anything I can do for the play," I heard him add as I was walking down the hall.

I was definitely preoccupied as I went back to my classroom. Celia's brother would be working at the school. She must have known that when she told me yesterday morning that he was back. Boy, some students really tried hard to find someone for me. One thing was certain, I needed to get the Bradley's out of my head and focus on my own life.

There were only a few minutes left before the halls began to fill, and students started to trickle into class. Of course, this meant I wouldn't get much done again this morning. So much for that extra time I had given myself. By the time I had helped the steady stream of students with various questions about the reading or the writing assignments, or those that just came in to chat, the first bell rang.

The day came and went in a whirlwind, helping me push aside the mess in my mind. That is why I liked teaching. It was easy to immerse yourself and forget about life. I could get wrapped up in the lives of the book characters or focus on my students and keep my mind off of everything in my head. There was just too much to deal with.

By sixth period, I was really ready for the weekend and kept glancing at the clock, counting down the minutes. All that was left was to give out the vocabulary quiz and I would be free. As I handed them out, Celia kept on glancing in my direction, a quizzical look on her face, as if she was studying my every move. Our eyes met briefly and she grinned at me. My own smile back to her was meek and small. She was definitely up to something.

Finally, the bell rang and I felt as free as my students. Celia lingered a little, and I worried that she would stay and talk, but I began to pack up my things, making a show of leaving, and she eventually left without saying a word.

The rain was coming down hard when I went to leave. The buses had all gone and the last few students were making mad dashes for their cars, books and jackets covering their heads. Making a run for my car just didn't sound all that exciting. Perhaps I could just wait a few minutes for it to lighten up. Maybe I would just go check the auditorium to make sure that everything was set up for Monday's auditions. Besides the few scraps of paper on the floor, which I picked up, things looked great. I brushed a small amount of dust off the top of the piano and sat down, arching my fingers over the keys. The rain hummed steadily on the roof of the auditorium and almost sounded like an audience applauding in appreciation. Closing my eyes, I let the song find me. They seemed to know which one needed to come out to help me feel better. I wasn't surprised when Rachmaninoff's "Rhapsody on a Theme of Paganini" came out. It had always been one of my favorites and I let the music ebb and flow through my soul. I could almost feel the orchestra playing right alongside of me. It grew into a crescendo and then fell again. When the song ended, I left my fingers lightly on the keys, waiting. Then I froze. Again, the feeling I wasn't alone.

The creak of a chair was enough to make me jump, and I felt my heart leap into my throat.

"I'm sorry. Don't stop on account of me. I just heard

someone playing, and I followed the song in here. Please go on," a deep but soft voice called out.

I turned toward the silhouette hidden in the shadows and breathed a small sigh of relief that at least I wasn't just imagining things. There actually was someone there. I didn't know what to say, so I turned back to the piano and tentatively began to play again. All the while, I could feel him slowly coming closer toward the stage. Toward *me*. I normally didn't like to play in front of others unless it was on a stage. There was something about the stage lights washing out the faces in the audience that helped. But this was different. I knew he was there, yet I still played and it didn't seem to bother me. It only took me a moment to all but forget that he was there as I got back into the melody.

By the time the song ended, he was standing on the stage at the foot of the piano. He looked to be about my age. Dark, wavy hair framed a pale complexion and his eyes were almost silver. I had to really look up to meet his gaze, as he was over 6 feet of muscle.

"I didn't mean to startle you. I was just passing by when I heard you. I'm Will, Will Bradley. I'm the new evening maintenance guy. And I think we're neighbors." He introduced himself, but stayed where he was at the end of the piano. So this was the new hire, Celia's brother. We stared at each other, the grand piano between us, an energy swirling in the air around us. Oh my, he was extremely good looking. I should have been polite and introduce myself as well, but my breath caught and I couldn't get a response out. Fortunately, he didn't seem to notice my hesitation and continued.

"You are an amazing player. I can feel every emotion that you play." His voice pierced through me and his eyes held mine.

"Thank you," I finally stammered, trying to swallow the breath still caught in my throat. I looked down at my hands lying on the keys just to avoid looking into his eyes. I was used to compliments, but somehow it seemed more genuine coming from this divinely gorgeous man. At last, I remembered my own manners. "Sorry, I'm Julia. Julia Cavallo," I said, taking a breath to calm myself. "I teach and direct the school plays here." I threw that last bit in just to let him know that I had some authority to be in here.

"How long have you been playing?" he casually asked. For as deep as his voice was, it had a softness to it that I just couldn't figure out.

"For about 18 years." I tried to keep my tone nonchalant even though my heart was racing. Absentmindedly, I began to play again. "My parents started me when I was young because I kept begging them. I think my pounding on the piano was annoying them. At least then I would be pounding out something that sounded like a melody." I didn't know what else to say, so I looked back down at my hands.

"You play with such passion. My mother used to play and she once told me that passion cannot be taught. It comes from experiences within. Is there a reason?" His eyes flashed with something for a minute and then returned to a stormy grey. "I mean there is sadness. A longing there."

I know he was just making conversation, and maybe he didn't really know about my past, but I stiffened. I didn't want to talk openly with someone I hardly knew.

"I'm sorry, I should go," I stood up and gathered my things.

"Did I say something to upset you?" he was at my side instantly. "I didn't mean to pry." Once again, I was trapped by his eyes and left with my mouth hanging open wordlessly.

I turned away and regained my composure, better able to think straight when I was not looking at him.

"No... it's just that... I think the rain let up and I really need to get home. It was really nice to meet you."

I grabbed the rest of my things and hurried out of the auditorium and straight to my car. I didn't realize I was shaking until I got home.

Chapter 4
Will

T HE SUN FLOODED THROUGH THE windows way too early. I blinked and rolled back over, letting golden rays stream through the window and warm my cold skin. Unlike our mythical counterparts, immortals could tolerate the sun. The disease created a lack of blood flow, which didn't allow body temperature to regulate properly. Essentially, I was cursed with being cold-blooded, my body prone to absorb the temperature around me. Too much time in the sun would result in overheating; not enough sun could result in freezing skin or frostbite. As a rule, immortals tried to stay out of extremely cold climates and tended not to linger in the sun's heat for too long, but I loved the feel of the early morning sun and how it made my skin feel.

The house was quiet. Celia must already be out and a quick glance outside revealed my father working out in the greenhouse across the yard. I sat up and cupped my hands over my eyes trying to block out the day. I thought back to last night and to my encounter with Julia in the auditorium. She seemed guarded and... scared. It seemed as if she had sensed that there was something very different about me. Rightly so, I suppose. She should be cautious. The disease wasn't totally under control, and I was still toying with the idea that there might be something else. My chest ached at the thought, and I decided that a drink should ease the pain. I rolled out of bed and sauntered down to the kitchen. This donated blood thing wasn't bad, but it didn't take the place of fresh blood, which felt more real in my veins. Perhaps I could sneak out and find something else.

My thoughts drifted back to Julia sitting at that piano, playing. She intrigued me. Her music was enchanting and I could tell that there was something behind it. Something more behind *her*, which only made her all the more interesting to me. For a strange moment, I had a vision of us sitting under the trellis in the yard. We were laughing together and talking, and she was confiding in me all of her secrets. I shook the scene away, startled by the appearance of such normalcy and the fact that I didn't know what it meant. Before I had heard her play, I had only thought of people as a way to satisfy a need. With her, perhaps I was considering more.

I shook my head to empty these strange new thoughts. I was so confused now. For years, I had thought that I knew what and who I was and what kind of life someone like me could live. I was a soulless creature who lived off others... thrived off them, actually. Or was I? This would be so much easier if I had someone to talk to. My phone vibrated in my pocket and I grabbed it, thinking instantly of Chris. I could talk to him, couldn't I? Maybe he knew these feelings and would know what to do. The caller ID flashed his number and I answered immediately.

"Chris! What's up?" I greeted cheerfully.

"Oh, you finally decided to pick up the phone," he snapped. "I have been calling you for a few days now. When are you coming back, Will? Haven't you had enough of your old man yet?" There was music in the background, and I was guessing that they had brought the party back to the brownstone and were continuing into today.

"Coming back?" I questioned. The memories were all crashing around me now as I remembered the events of my last night in Chicago. The one that made me hop on my bike and head back here. Did I really want to go back to that now? And now this thing with Julia, whatever it was. Things had become so complicated. "I don't know," I answered truthfully. "Ahhh... I actually had something come up here. Something I want to talk to you about. Some things have been happening here in the last few days and I have been talking to my sister and I think..."

"Oh, come on, Will. Don't tell me you're actually buying into your family's bullshit! What could you have possibly found there that you can't have in Chicago? All those two do is blather on about being human and having a soul. They are delusional. You know this is where you belong. We both know who you really are. Besides, I need you here. I'll come back there and get you," Chris interrupted before I could even begin to tell him about Julia. I shifted slightly and found myself gazing out the window at the lake, not sure of how to continue.

"Yeah, I know. Well... it's not that. It's just... something else," I tried again, but something told me to stop. He was never going to understand. He was annoying me and I wanted nothing more than to get off the phone. Perhaps it was the fact that he spoke a bit of the truth as well. "You know what, never mind. I'll be back in a few days." I hung up abruptly and turned my phone off, pushing Chris and my life in Chicago to the back of my mind. I could already see that he had been calling from the number of missed calls that popped up. If anything, he made my head foggier than it already was. One thing was for sure; Chris's call reminded me of the dark life I lived. I threw my phone down on the counter and stormed outside, intending to walk down to the beach or anywhere away from here.

To an extent, he was right. That was who I was, but for once, I was hoping that I didn't have to be. Could I really change? I needed time to figure things out. I know now that Chris wasn't the person to talk to about this. Who is he, of all people, to talk to me about who I am? He would come for me, or send someone else to do it. I only had a few days to sort things out before I was sure someone would come looking for me.

The air was cool, despite the sunshine. I started walking through the garden more confused than ever and wondering what to do. Perhaps it was time to talk to my father. It seemed like my body had already made that decision for me as I found myself walking into the greenhouse to where he was.

"You know that you can't sneak up on me." He was

finishing repotting a rose bush. "You aren't exactly quiet." I settled myself against a pillar opposite him and just shrugged.

"I wasn't trying to be quiet," I said.

"How was your first night at work?" he asked, getting right to the point. "I trust there were no issues."

He turned to look at me, his gaze set intently on me.

"It was fine." I hesitated, contemplating exactly how much to tell him, and while I could talk to him about my confusion, I decided that it was definitely too soon to tell him about Julia. I didn't want him to be angry. It was clear he still didn't believe that I would behave myself while I was here. This was all so new that I would have to keep it to myself. I still needed to prove that I could stay in control. He would surely mistake my restlessness for something it wasn't, and right now, restless didn't even begin to describe what I was feeling.

"There were more deaths in Chicago last night. It was on the news today." He was calmly clipping the dead heads off the bush he was working on. His tone, like his hand, was incredibly controlled.

"I didn't hear that," I said although wasn't surprised. "Besides, that has nothing to do with me considering I was here last night." I shifted and turned away, trying to sound obscure. Chris hadn't mentioned anything on the phone, but I could only imagine that is where our conversation had been heading. Part of the reason he needed me. He needed someone to help clean up the mess.

"This is exactly why I requested you come home for a

while. It's only a matter of time before the immortals in Chicago are caught and discovered. Their behavior is just too reckless. You know how that will end. Do you remember the incident in New York a few years ago? Authorities had to work for weeks to cover that up. Until people are willing to recognize the fact that this curse does exist and that we aren't all bad, it is imperative that you stay hidden like the rest of us." He had stopped clipping and turned to look upon me with blazing eyes.

This was a long speech for my father, but it was far from being the pep talk I had been hoping for. On some level, I understood his fear, but hiding wouldn't make it go away. I could feel the anger building in me. His smug confidence in his own righteousness and lack of belief of mine was one of the things that we argue about the most. He wouldn't even listen to me or try to see my side. His constant unwillingness to recognize us for who we are, set me on edge, and I immediately became defensive.

"But we do exist!" I shouted, my relaxed stance gone as I took a step toward him "Don't you get it? We are diseased. You and Celia never seem to understand. We are immortal and this is what we do. We need blood to survive. Death is just a side effect of our survival. You know, it must be difficult to keep hiding from what you really are and pretending to be something you aren't," I turned away from him abruptly clenching my fists at my side. I hadn't come out here to argue, yet I couldn't seem to control my ire. He was so quick to dangle his trust in front of me, only to snatch it back up. I thought he wanted me here, but I didn't come back for a lecture. I hated that he constantly believed the worst of me, all the while telling me that he hoped for the better.

"Just because you need blood to survive, doesn't mean you have to kill to do it," he answered back. "This disease doesn't mean you aren't human anymore. Damnit Will, when are you going to understand that?" he glared back at me, daring me to continue. We stared at each other for a moment before he turned back to his roses.

I sighed and settled down on the wooden bench. He made it seem so simple, but he was wrong. Of course, we weren't human anymore. Humans were born. They died. They lived a life somewhere in between, which is something I was definitely not doing. It was so damn easy to turn my back on any part of humanity left in me. Sometimes I wanted to be out there doing what the disease told me I needed, but then there were times like the last few days, when I had to admit something had begun to stir in me. I didn't want to be in Chicago, but I still wasn't sure I wanted to be here. Turmoil flowed through me as I thought about her. I could actually think about something other than being a soulless monster when I thought of her. Perhaps I could actually see my father's rationale.

He looked up at me again, and I hoped that maybe for once he could see the conflict in my eyes, yet even though something in me was changing, he didn't even notice. I turned away gazing off at the lake in the distance, not wanting him to search too deeply. I had too many secrets that weren't ready to be revealed.

"It doesn't have to be that way, Will," he continued quietly, while turning his attention back to the rose bush. "You can't let this condition get the best of you. You only lose if you let go." If he only knew the truly dark things I had done in this new life. I don't think he would feel the same way. Could I really forget all of that?

I wanted to believe him. Especially now. But despite my new found feelings, I was still afraid that it was too late for me. I had been in a dark place for far too long.

"Whether you believe it or not, I am trying while I'm here, but I fear it could be too late for me. I can't go back and change what I have done," I said and walked over to a red rose bush. A single rose bud was trying to open in the morning sun. In another day, it would be fully open. Thorns stuck out from the stem. How could something so beautiful be surrounded by something that could cause so much pain? That's when I realized what my father and Celia were trying to tell me. The two could coexist. I just needed to learn to see the beauty.

"I know that you and Celia believe there is something else out there," I continued, "but I'm not sure I can. I'm not sure there is anything left of the old me. Just face it, perhaps I was never really good at being human to begin with. Maybe this is who I was always supposed to be," I said, grasping a rose stem tightly until I felt the thorns poke through my flesh, the pain it inflicted helping to hide the shame. "I wish it was different. I wish it more than anything, but I realized long ago that there is no hope left. I have no soul left to save."

He walked toward me and placed his hands firmly on my shoulders. He and I were the same height, and his eyes were intense as they stared right into me. He wouldn't let me breakaway as he searched for what I didn't want him to find. I could feel the ache growing inside my chest again.

"If that were true, you wouldn't have come back here. It's not too late." His hands slid limply from my shoulders, and he turned back to his pruning. "You came here because there is still something left in you. Some sense of humanity and attachment. I can see it. If your soul were completely gone, you would have stayed with the others. You can't let this disease get the best of you. It will only take what you give it."

I desperately hoped that he was right and that my soul wasn't completely gone. He thought it was never too late if there is a sliver left. I did not have to let this disease take over. I did not have to give in to the monster within. I pushed the thought deep down. It was a moment before I spoke again. There was more to say, but I wasn't ready and let everything still unsaid hang in the air.

"Thank you. I will stay here as long as I can." I said quietly. With that, I walked back out into the sun and headed down the path to the lake.

Once I was clear of his vision, I ran to the shoreline. I found a spot on an old log and gazed out at the light playing upon the waves. I felt the cool breeze blow across my skin while a lone seagull fought against the wind above me, calling out in search of food. Despite the coolness of the autumn air, the sun's rays were heating up my skin. I would only be able to last out here for a short time before I would need to go back. I looked down at my arm in the sunlight. The skin was almost translucent, the bloodless veins running through my arm, a purplish grey.

My father's final words swirled around in my head. *It will only take what you give it.* I could be as good or as destructive as I allowed myself to be. He thought I could just choose what I wanted to be. I chuckled to myself at the thought. Funny, but when I began this second life, it didn't seem like I had much of a choice. I had never seen how it could be anything different. I never understood what it meant to choose, but for the first time, I began to feel that if given a chance, my decision could have been different. I thought about Julia and about the fact that she made me feel something, even if I didn't know what it was yet. Could this help? Could she make me want to be better? To live like my sister and my father? God, I hoped so, but it was too soon. At the very least, it made me wonder. But for now, I just didn't know.

I sat for a while and just listened to the simplicity of the waves crashing on the shore, steadily swelling and then receding. Eventually, the heat was too much and I made my way back toward the house.

"SO, HOW WAS YOUR FIRST day on the job? Did you get to meet Ms. . . . I mean Julia?" Celia said, blocking my way inside and making it clear there was no way I was getting out of this discussion. I contemplated how to answer for a moment, but the determination in her eyes convinced me to just tell her the truth.

"Actually, I did. She was in the auditorium and I went in and introduced myself." I could feel the ache as I talked about her, the excitement coursing through me. My mind was still jumbled though, so I tried to remain my normal stoic self, not willing to give my thoughts away. A difficult feat in front of someone as perceptive as my sister.

"Uh-oh, things didn't go so well, did they," she said, concern crossing her face. She gazed so intently at me that I had to give up hiding. It was much too difficult, and I did need to talk to someone. I sighed deeply, my shoulders sagging in defeat while my hardened expression melted and the words began to tumble out.

"She was playing the piano," I began, as I pushed past her to slump into the worn leather of the overstuffed chair nearest to me. "We talked for a few minutes and then she left rather abruptly. I thought things were going okay, but then... it was like I did something wrong and I don't even know what!" I had been trying not to over think last night's events, especially after my reality-check discussion with Chris. My conversation with my father had made me think about a different life. After today, I didn't want to think. I was done with thinking. But, as I told my sister what happened, I began to doubt everything. Maybe I should just go back to Chicago and live my life. It was so much simpler. I knew my place and never had to worry about emotions. And there was no thinking. No need to contemplate my actions or my existence.

"Well, you can be a little intimidating!" my sister said.

"Did you ever think about that? Did you use your normal tone of voice, because that can be pretty scary sometimes?" She sat down on the chair next to me trying to work out where I went wrong.

"I don't know, maybe. This is not exactly something I worry about on a daily basis. I didn't know that I needed to be careful of something like that," I glanced at her sideways, still afraid to truly give all of my thoughts away.

"Of course you do! People are very sensitive to things like that!" She threw her legs over the arm of the chair and tossed her hair back. "I guess that we will just have to work on things."

Confidence constantly poured from her. She knew who she was and wasn't afraid.

"You're enjoying this, aren't you?" I groaned, burying my head in my hands.

She looked at me excitedly, and then bounced up and grabbed my hand, taking my actions as giving in to her.

"I can help you, Will. If you will let me," she said quietly, all humor gone.

I studied her face for a moment. She had a glimmer in her eyes. A light. I have been told that it's one thing that distinguished our kind from our human counterparts. My father and sister both shared the same glimmer. A part of their soul, he had said. They say it was because they had never lost touch with their humanity. They had never fully given in to the nature of the disease that fed off of darkness and turned the infected into soulless creatures. They had managed to hold on and maintain a remotely human existence. Those who held on to the light never fell to the dark. I saw the excitement, the life, radiating off her and began to hope for a moment that I, too, could be like her.

"Cee, can I ask you something?" I questioned tentatively, momentarily letting my guard down. She drew back slightly then nodded.

"Do you think... I mean... is it possible that I still have a soul?" I turned away from her, not wanting to meet her eyes for fear of what she would see. When I did look, I felt the now constant pressure in my chest grow. Her eyes narrowed and she looked intently at me. Her mouth turned down at the corners and her brow furrowed. Suddenly, her face relaxed and she smiled.

"Yes. There is... something." She held my hand tenderly, excited by the prospect that she hadn't totally lost me either.

I breathed a deep sigh of relief and closed my eyes, feeling a tightness in my chest.

"Maybe I can try to help you get it back, you know. I can help you truly feel. There is so much more out there when you open yourself up to the possibilities." Her voice was soft and my chest nearly exploded as the ache consumed me. Weakness overcame my body, and I nearly crumpled to the ground. Images of Julia at the piano flashed through my mind. Her dark hair cascading over her shoulders, fingers arching delicately over the keys, a smile playing at her lips. And then, I imagined myself standing behind her, my hands on her shoulders while she played. It was a possibility. A glimpse into a conceivable future for me, and I suddenly wanted it so bad. I didn't realize until now how much I was missing. For decades, I had given in to my urges and let myself become the monster that I thought I had to be. My father said he had never given up hope. Celia had never given up hope. No matter how bad it got, no matter how much trouble I was in, she always stood beside me and brought me back when I was at my darkest. Perhaps it was her belief in me that kept me holding on to a tiny part of light for all these years. My subconscious secretly hoped for a change.

Suddenly, I knew how I would gain it back. I knew what it was that had reawakened me to this point. Julia. I thought that I had been drawn to her blood. I thought that I wanted to kill her. It was just the opposite. I needed her to make me whole. She is what I had been waiting for.

"It's Julia, isn't it? That's why I'm drawn to her. I mean I've been having strange visions and haven't been able to stop thinking about her all day." I glanced back to my sister.

"I don't know," she answered. "It could be. And if this is what will bring you back, I definitely think you should find out."

I hugged my sister and felt relief wash over me. Relief that I could change. Relief that I wasn't just a bloodthirsty monster. Relief that there was hope. Maybe immortals could change. Maybe this disease could be controlled. I certainly was determined to find out.

ELECTRICITY COURSED THROUGH MY BODY as I waited for nightfall to try to see Julia again. I didn't want to show up at her doorstep after our encounter in the auditorium, but it was only Saturday, and I wouldn't see her until Monday. I was standing at the window looking at the streetlights go on one by one down the street, a signal to me that I could leave. When the last one blinked on, I hurried toward the door.

"Where do you think you're going?" Celia was blocking my exit.

"I'm just going out. I'm a little thirsty and I need to take a walk," I said jokingly, but still painfully aware of our earlier conversation.

"There is plenty of blood downstairs, there is no need to go out while you are here, you know. Are you forgetting about what we talked about already?"

"I know, it's just that I prefer it fresher." I smiled weakly. Despite everything I had told her, I remained guarded. I was barely able to admit this new need to myself, let alone to her, but the look on her face told me that she wasn't buying my excuses. "Besides, it's nice out and I thought I would stroll through town. I need some time to think." I tried to push past her nonchalantly.

"You can take a walk in the garden. Or down to the lake," she replied, crossing her arms as she stood her ground in front of the door. "Quit trying to joke with me, Will. You're going to go to *her* aren't you?" she said sweetly. It wasn't really a question because she already knew the answer. I guess I couldn't hide anything from her or at least not for very long.

I hesitated before answering her. "Yes, well, I suppose I am. I mean, I was going to go out anyway. Maybe I would wander to her house." Just thinking about Julia was making the pressure in my chest worsen.

"I know we think that she will be the one to help you, but I have to ask. Do you think you can control yourself around her when you're like this?" Her tone was serious. "I mean, you said that you were drawn to her blood. Maybe you shouldn't go alone."

Part of me knew that she was right, but I was still hurt by her accusations. "I can control myself. I was fine when I was alone with her in the auditorium." I was becoming confident that the mystery that surrounded her — and my attraction to her — would keep her safe. I needed her now to help me figure myself out. "I know that you want to help me, but you don't need to go with me like a babysitter. This is something I have to do by myself." I stormed past her and out into the night.

The neighborhood was quiet. It had never been very active, which is part of the reason that my family was able to stay here after all these years... no nosy neighbors who tried to learn too much. The houses sat back from the road a bit, each one situated on large sprawling lawns. It wasn't like the city, where the houses breathed on each other. The streetlights created eerie shadows that played on the asphalt and the grass. I walked quickly, trying not to draw any attention. Just someone out for an evening walk. Within a few minutes, I had reached her house.

There was a solitary light on, but it wasn't in the living room. She was not at the piano tonight, which made me painfully aware of the gnawing in my chest. It must be her bedroom light, because she was standing in front, gazing out. I stood by a tree, just out of range of the lamp light spilling on the lawn. I was struck by her beauty, even in her t-shirt and sweat pants. Her hair was pulled up in a ponytail, save for a few strands that fell in front of her green eyes. I could sense her sadness.

"She does have a certain appeal, doesn't she?" Celia was beside me and I turned, startled, to glare at her.

"That doesn't help. What are you doing, following me? I told you I don't need a babysitter." I couldn't hide the annoyance in my tone.

"Stalk much?" she said lifting an eyebrow in accusation. "I was only kidding. And no, I am not babysitting you. Just curious," she chided.

Julia squinted out the window and we flattened ourselves against the tree, hoping to disappear as we became one with the shadows. She looked quizzical for a moment, rubbing her hand across her wrinkled brow. Suddenly, she turned on her heel and was gone. I could hear her tread through the house as she walked. Then, I heard the piano bench pull out softly. She was going to play. This is what I had hoped for.

She sat in the dark, but my vision made it possible to see her silhouette as she sat at the piano. She placed her hands upon the keys and began to play, slowly and quietly. The song gradually grew in intensity, and I could feel her emotions swirl around her as they changed. She was content. She was happy when she played. This must be the cause of the turmoil I sensed within her. She may feel sadness, but when she played, the feelings were replaced by joy. I felt the same. When she played, she made me happy as well. My cold heart warmed, and I suddenly longed for another existence so different from the one I had been enjoying. My mind went back to the scene that first entered my mind this afternoon of Julia and me at the piano. Celia was right, I did want more. Julia made me want to be better. She made me want to reawaken my soul. I finally began to realize why my father and Cee were always so happy. Being human meant so much more.

Julia's song stopped, but she didn't get up. She stayed at the keys and flexed her fingers lightly over them. A deep sigh escaped her lips, and I could sense her contentment. The bench creaked lightly when she finally got up and walked back through the house. I sat back against the tree not wanting to move.

"Will, I think you're okay here," Celia's voice was barely above a whisper. "I will just meet you at home." She placed her hand on mine and squeezed.

I barely heard her leave, as I was too distracted. I couldn't tear my eyes from the girl who had gone back to her bedroom. It only took a few moments for her to settle into bed and fall asleep. I could see her through the open curtains, and the rising moon made shadows play across her face, which began to soften with sleep. I wanted nothing more than to go into her room and hold her while she slept. I wanted to let her warmth heat my cold body. I wanted to caress her cheek and feel her hair play across my skin. Most of all, I wanted her to play for me. I wanted all of this more than anything in the world; I just didn't know how to get it. I didn't know how to fight the darkness inside of me. How could I stop what had become second nature to me? I couldn't do any of the things I'd envisioned because she hadn't invited me in. She hadn't given me permission to be in her life. I could only hope that someday, she would.

CELIA WAS WAITING UP FOR me when I got back to the house, as I knew she would be.

"How are you," she tentatively asked.

"I don't know." The words tumbled out, and I ran my hands nervously through my hair, feeling restless while pacing back and forth.

"Just sit, Will," Celia commanded. "You need to stop pacing... and I have something to say." I stopped and sat on the sofa across from her.

"What?"

"I don't know why, but I can see what she does to you. You were different there. I could feel you were at peace. And the light in your eyes... it's a little brighter."

"I am so frustrated. I don't even know her and she has affected me in so many ways. I guess that I'm just confused with who I am. I don't know how to become a better person." I could feel the anger at myself begin to rise up again. A hand squeezed my shoulder and I reached up to touch it. My sister was so good. I couldn't help but envy the control that she had. She never had been and never would be a monster.

"I don't know how either, Will. I can try to help, but I can't tell you how to feel. Does that make sense? I want this so much for you, but I can't make these choices for you." She wrapped her small arms around my shoulders for a quick hug. "I'll never give up on you, Will."

"I know, Cee. I know." This I believed. I knew that no matter what, she would always be able to see the good in me. She always had. It was probably the reason that I stayed in contact with her through all these years.

After I was alone, I stared out into the darkness. I could still hear the music in my head. The ache in me was powerful. I thought seeing Julia would help, and it did at the time, but there was now an empty void to fill when I wasn't near her. I had barely said three words to her, yet I couldn't stop thinking about her. I wanted to know everything I could about her. However, I would have to wait until Monday.

Chapter 5
Julia

TODAY WAS SUNDAY, AND IT was a day that I dreaded. Not because it was Sunday but because it was *today*. The anniversary of the day my life began to fall apart seven years ago. Seven years since my life changed forever. I shook my head of the memories and reached for the TV remote. I needed to find something insignificant to fill my mind, in order to keep my thoughts at bay. If only I could just sleep the day away and avoid it all. I wouldn't be able to, though. I had tried before. There were just too many jumbled memories in my head for me to sleep them away.

I mechanically flipped through the channels, looking for anything that would serve as a distraction. Mundane infomercials and old reruns of cheesy talk shows where they search for the true father did nothing for me. Neither did the news, so I switched the TV off in a huff and tossed the remote down on the bed. And the news was always so depressing. There had been something about a boy found after being lost in the woods for two weeks and another story about all the murders happening in Chicago. It made my head spin, and made me happy that I lived across the lake in a sleepy little tourist town. Big cities did nothing for me.

Eventually, I crawled out of bed, knowing I should get up and do something despite my inner turmoil. If I tried to focus on daily tasks, maybe I could ignore the bubble of emotion that lay just below the surface. *Push it down, just don't think. Don't think. Don't think.*

I hopped in the shower. The air was chilly and I let the hot water run over my skin, warming me. *Don't think.* Steam swirled around and enveloped me. *Don't think.* But I couldn't help it. Even standing in the hot water with my eyes closed tightly could not stop the emotional fissure in my heart. I tried to hold them back, but the tears came anyway. Within seconds, I was leaning against the wall, sobbing. I pictured his face. My brother, Aaron. He was 18 when he committed suicide. My mother had blamed everything on my dad, claiming that he was constantly pushing Aaron to succeed and was too hard on him when he didn't. She said my dad wasn't letting Aaron be a teen, and that's why he had been so depressed all the time. Of course, no one ever saw the signs, and those that did, chose to ignore them. After Aaron died, my parents began to grow apart, until eventually, my father came home and announced that he was leaving us. He had been having an affair and was leaving to be with her. He abandoned us to start a new family because ours was so broken. At least, that's how I saw it. My dad was an asshole for leaving us. I had even begun to side with my mother, believing that he had been the reason for Aaron's suicide. After that, my mom had been in an inconsolable stupor. She went through the motions of being a mom, but I knew that she wasn't the same. When I graduated from high school, I left home for college and never looked back. A year later, my dad and his new wife died in a car accident. Not long after that, my mom was diagnosed with cancer. She was relatively young but died six months later, her body never responding to treatment. I think she was consumed with grief over her lost life. I never forgave my parents for what they did, and as a result, I rarely spoke to them from the time I was 16 until the day they each died. And just like that, within a few short months, I was completely alone. My entire family was gone. Both of my parents were only children, leaving me no kind aunts, uncles, or cousins to live with. All of my grandparents had been gone for years. These feelings of loss, feelings of abandonment, and feelings of anger were constantly being stuffed down to a place that I didn't want to acknowledge. When it all came out, I didn't know if I was sobbing out of anger or sadness. The tears were all the same lately.

Eventually, the hot water ran out and I was forced to get out, my fingers and toes as wrinkled as prunes. My skin was steaming, and I knew that my eyes were red and puffy. I was exhausted and it wasn't even noon! Slowly, I dried myself with a towel and wrapped myself in a robe. Suddenly, the phone rang, making me jump.

"Hello?" I answered tentatively, wishing I hadn't gotten rid of the caller ID.

"Hey, how are you doing?" A sigh of relief. It was Kara. "Do you need anything today?" My best friend always remembered the important things, today being one of the days when I needed a friend the most. She never needed to come right out and say it. I knew what she meant.

"No, I'm okay. I just got out of the shower. I think I will go to the cemetery and then maybe go to school to get things ready for tomorrow. I just need to keep busy, you know?" Sitting at home would not be an option for me. I needed to keep my mind occupied, so going to school seemed like the logical choice. Anything to distract me. And I wouldn't need to interact with too many people.

"Would it be okay if I came over later? I can bring you dinner." I didn't think that she was asking me and it would be nice to not be completely alone all day.

"Yeah, that would be great!" A little girl time would help keep my mind off of things as well. "How about six? I should be done with everything by then."

"Okay, I'll call you in a while."

I waited until I heard the click of the phone hanging up, and then I gently placed the phone back into its cradle. My eyes wandered to the living room where the piano was calling me, and I couldn't help but sit down to play. Music had been in my blood since I was a child, but after Aaron died, it had been hard for me to play because he had always loved to listen to me. Music was what tied us together. He played the violin and I played the piano. We were going to be a famous duet someday, playing concerts all over the world for sold out crowds. We had big plans. For a while after he died, just looking at a piano would make me cry, but after a few months, when everything started to happen with my parents, I couldn't stay away from it. I needed music to heal. When I *did* finally play, I avoided *his* song, the song he had written for me.

I stared at the keys for a long time before I placed my hands on the smooth ivory, just waiting for the right song. Closing my eyes, I felt myself leave my body for a moment and the melody I had been avoiding for months found me. A memory flashed in my mind. Aaron was smiling and looking at me, asking me to play his favorite song. There was a light in his eyes and he laughed. He danced around the living room as I played. I was only 10 years old at the time. The vision left, and I was pulled back to the present. Tears streamed down my face, and I was shaking. My breath came in short spurts as I stared blankly. I didn't know what made me want to play it, but I wasn't sure that it had been a good idea. I placed my hands on the keys again and tried a different melody. This one was more relaxed, and I let its sound take me. My fingers moved effortlessly over the keys, and I let my heart lead the way. When the song finished, I felt much better. I believed that I would have the strength to make it to the cemetery.

It was a nice enough day so I decided to walk. When I reached the end of the road, my eyes were drawn to the Bradley's once again, and I was immediately reminded of Celia's brother, Will, and our chance meeting in the auditorium on Friday. I would be lying if I said I wasn't attracted to him. His grey eyes drew me in, but there was also something else about him. I had played in front of him. I didn't play in front of anyone, let alone a stranger. I felt at ease with him around. And then I ran away like a coward when he asked me a question. The strange thing was, it wasn't because I didn't want to answer him. It was because I felt comfortable enough *to* answer him and that scared the hell out of me. Now, I was embarrassed by my reaction and knowing that I would see him again made me really feel like an idiot. At least thinking about him had taken my mind off of my own problems for a short time.

I realized that I hadn't been watching where I was walking, or how far. I looked up suddenly to see where my feet had taken me and realized that I was already at the iron gates of the cemetery. I looked around, sadly sighed, and pushed the gates open.

The cemetery was very large and very old. It had a gothic beauty to it. Old family crypts dotted the rolling hills. Angels and saints and gargoyles stood watch over the tiny structures. Solitary gravestones filled in the spaces in between. I meandered through the various plots on winding trails, trying to take my time, but it still only took me minutes to get to my destination. The wind swirled in the branches above, sending red leaves tumbling all around me. The ground was damp but I sat anyway, hugging my knees to my chest.

"Hi Aaron," I whispered to the cold stone in front of me. "I miss you." The tears began to flow freely now. It was much harder to keep up my wall when I was here. I missed my brother so much.

"I wish you were here so that we could talk. I just wish… I wish you were here."

I told him all about my life and what was going on now. I could almost hear him answer me in the silence. I talked for what felt like hours, and when I ran out of things to say to him, I lay down in the wet grass, my cheek touching the cold hard ground to feel close to him. I closed my eyes and breathed in the autumn air deeply. I felt drained, like I had nothing left to give.

I don't know how long I lay there before I got up to walk home. The cemetery was getting dark. I glanced at my watch and saw that it was 5:30pm. I had been here all afternoon. Kara would be over soon. So much for going to school and getting any work done today. The evening air was growing colder, and I wrapped my arms around myself. Somewhere in the distance, an owl called out. Shadows began to play across the stone crypts and their guardians. I shivered a little and glanced around nervously, hastening to the entrance. The iron gate clanged loudly behind me and I hurried home, sticking to the brightly lit sidewalk.

I only beat Kara by fifteen minutes. Just enough time to put my comfy sweats on, grab a blanket and book and head out to the porch. It wasn't until I saw her that I remembered that I was supposed to call her.

"Knock, knock, anyone home?" She was on the porch smiling at me a few seconds later. "I tried calling, but you never answered. I just assumed that you were busy and that I would get to pick our dinner," she teased.

"Hey! Thanks for coming over tonight," I said standing up to hug her. Her moods were infectious. She was always able to bring me back from the darkest of places. "I know, I'm sorry. I actually spent the entire afternoon at the cemetery. I totally lost track of time and never made it to school. So, what did you bring me for dinner?" I grinned back.

"Chinese. And it's from your favorite place!" She held up two brown paper bags and the scent of deep fried deliciousness swirled around them.

"Did you make sure that they gave you enough sweet and sour sauce?" I asked, digging into the bags.

"Of course! What kind of friend would I be?"

We went inside and set up our dinner. We talked about school for a while and then Kara prattled on about her latest dating disaster, all the while avoiding the untouchable subject; the reason she was really here tonight. Kara and I had known each other for years. She had known my family back when we were whole. She had stuck with me through it all. Kara would let me talk about Aaron and my parents if I really wanted to, but I didn't want to talk about them. She already knew the whole story. She knew how I felt without me having to remind her. Besides, there was something else that I had been thinking of. Or someone, I should say.

"So you have anything to tell me?" Shock must have registered on my face. Clearly, she knew that something besides my brother had been on my mind today.

"What do you mean?" I tried to be coy, as I wasn't really ready to talk about the cute guy with the dark hair and gorgeous eyes yet. I was still trying to sort things out in my head.

"Oh come on, you know what I mean. You're hiding something. I know you better than you know yourself. Something is on your mind. I can see that you've been thinking all day and it isn't the something I would expect on a day like today." She was trying to be nonchalant, but her eyes reflected her enthusiasm. She was dying to know whatever it was that I had to tell her. I sighed loudly, guessing I had better just get it over with. I could unload it all. Maybe she would give me the badly needed advice I was seeking.

"Okay." I paused for a minute, not really knowing how to continue. How was I going to tell her that I couldn't seem to stop thinking about Will Bradley, a guy that I had only talked to once and who I had run away from? "Do you know who Celia Bradley is? She is one of my students."

"Yeah. Why?" Kara furrowed her brow trying to figure out where all this was going.

"Well, her older brother just moved back to town and is working at the school in the evenings doing odds and ends. I ran into him Friday night." I rolled my eyes and tried to act like it was no big deal, as if I talked about boys like this with her all the time.

"Oh, I just knew that it was boy problems!" She squealed in delight, and I began to see the inner working of Kara's mind as her overactive imagination began to construct the entire scenario. I could see where this would lead. If I didn't explain fast, she would be naming our unborn children and planning house colors in minutes.

"Just wait, it's not like that!" I stood up and held my hand up in front of her, trying to bring her attention back to me. "It was late after school, and I was in the auditorium. It had been raining, and I was just passing some time until it let up, you know. I felt like playing the piano, so I sat down and just started to play. All of the sudden, I wasn't alone; he was there, listening. It was dark, and I could barely see or hear him come up to me. Then, he was in front of me. It felt strange to have him there listening while I played, but I didn't stop." I hesitated, unsure how to continue. "He started talking to me and asking me questions, and I freaked out and left. Now I feel so dumb." I sighed loudly and threw my head into my hands.

"Is he hot?" A snort escaped, and I laughed loudly. Leave it to Kara to miss the important things and focus on his looks.

"He's really good looking, but that's beside the point!" I dismissed her question and tried to bring her back to the problem. "I am so embarrassed by how I acted, and I'm sure that I'll see him again. He probably thinks I'm a total idiot." I swirled the last of my egg roll absentmindedly in the sauce.

"What did he ask you?"

"Well, he complimented my playing and then pointed out that I play with a lot of emotion. He wondered where it came from." I sat back down and buried my head in my hands.

"Oh."

"It hit too close to home. I'm not ready to tell a stranger

all about my troubled past. But I know he had no idea what he was asking. I think he was just being polite. Besides, I thought everyone knew all about my problems. I mean come on; everyone thinks I'm a ticking time bomb!" I paced around the kitchen nervously.

"You know that isn't true. So maybe you should apologize next time you see him. I'm sure he wasn't offended. And not everyone knows the story of your life."

"Yeah, maybe you're right."

Kara dug in for another bite of fried rice and shrugged it off. I pushed my own dinner around my plate and finally shoved it away.

"That's not everything, Kara. There's just something about him. I'm usually so cautious with others, but I felt so comfortable with him, despite the fact that I ran off." My thoughts took me back to Friday night. There was something unusual about him. I could have sworn that his steel grey eyes could see through to my soul. I got up and walked to the piano bench. Kara followed me into the living room.

"What do you mean you felt comfortable?" she asked.

"Well you know how I am. I'm not exactly the world's most social person. I don't walk around screaming for attention." I cautiously lowered my eyes. I was glad that I didn't have to speak about some things with Kara. She knew how difficult it had been for me after Aaron's death and then my parents. I felt like a fish in a bowl in this town. Everyone always looked at me with pity. Everyone except Will. Of course, I feared that it was only a matter of time before he found out and started treating me like something fragile and ready to break.

"When he looked at me," I continued, "I felt a sense of calm come over me. I can't explain it."

I looked over at her, only to see her staring at me. The incredulous look on her face was discouraging.

"You know what, never mind. Just forget I said anything." I waved her off and turned toward the piano, my fingers absentmindedly toying with tapping out random cords.

"What do you mean, forget about it? Jules, this is big... no this is more than big! You have to talk to him again! If there is something about him, you have to find out what it is. You haven't had a date in like, forever, and if you feel something for this guy, you should go for it!"

I shrugged and continued to play some random melody, trying to give her the hint that I didn't really want to talk about it anymore. After a few minutes, she looked at the clock and stood to leave.

"I should probably go. We can talk more tomorrow if you want."

My fingers stopped for a moment.

"Thanks. I mean it Kara. I guess I just have some things to sort out."

"I know. And all I'm saying is that maybe you should give this hottie a chance," she smiled supportively. "I'll see you tomorrow."

The door shut quietly behind her, and I watched her pull

out of the driveway from my perch on the piano bench. The day was almost over, and I had survived it yet again. All in all, it wasn't that bad of a day. At least it ended well. Sometimes, I could almost feel myself getting stronger, getting ready to rejoin the real world and do more than just work, run, and play music.

My head was still filled with everything I had going on. I decided to go to my bedroom and read to give my brain something else to think about. I shut the door behind me and leaned against it for a moment before grabbing my book and sitting in the chair. I was still bothered by the images that were going through my head when I played Aaron's song earlier, and I could still see a pair of grey eyes gazing at me when I closed my own. The words on the pages were beginning to blur. Clearly, reading wasn't working. I found that I kept reading the same sentence over and over again. It didn't take me long to give up and put the book down. I got up and paced around my room, humming.

"You really need to pull yourself together, Jules. Today was just a day and Will is just a guy. Nothing special. Great," I sighed, "now you're talking to yourself. If that doesn't prove that you're a head case, I don't know what does."

It was obvious that I couldn't concentrate. I needed to get my mind on something else. I went into the living room again and sat back at the piano. Lightly, I ran my hands over the keys until they found their way into a song. The notes seemed to find me and I played, letting the music flow through my entire being. It was only then that my head began to clear. Ah, this is what I needed; this is when I felt like myself. I played late into the night, until my tired brain told me to stop. Reluctantly, I did stop and forced myself to stumble up the stairs and into bed, where I fell into another night of fitful sleep.

Chapter 6
Will

MY PHONE RINGING IN THE middle of the night woke me. I reached onto my nightstand and grasped for it blindly. I couldn't believe I had forgotten to turn it off. Was I ever going to get to sleep in this damn town?

"Yeah?" I didn't even try to hide my annoyance.

"Hey, Will, where the hell are you? It's been a few days. I thought you would be back in the action." It was Chris again. I shouldn't be surprised he would keep on me, after our last conversation. He was my closest friend, in theory, as I didn't really consider myself to have friends, and self-appointed leader of the group in Chicago. He was out at some bar. I could hear the noise in the background.

"I'm still ho-... in Michigan." Home, I had thought to myself, which was strange because I hadn't considered this small town home in many decades.

"What are you doing there? I thought you were going out

with us tonight."

"No, I told you I would be gone for a few more days, and that I would call you when I was heading back. Don't you remember our conversation? I uh... need to stay here for a while... take care of some things." I rolled over to look at the time. One a.m. I assumed he was just getting started for the evening.

"And I thought I told you that I needed you back here," he said impatiently. "Besides, since when have you cared about your family? It's not like you have ever given a shit about them, besides maybe that little tart of a sister you have. You've already spent a lifetime with them so why don't you tell them to fuck off and get back here. There are lots of willing victims in this city, and no one will miss them. And I know your daddy doesn't attend to your needs like we do here. "

"You're a little vulgar, you know that?" I don't know if it was because it was the middle of the night, or if I was just realizing this about him, but he was grating on my nerves. Normally, I wouldn't hold anything back about the "boring" time I was having here, but now his questions just seemed intrusive. I knew he would never understand why I would stay here. My time was up. His incessant calling was making that very clear.

"Never bothered you before. Maybe you should watch the news to see exactly what you've been missing. Last night was a big night." I had been watching the news, as had my family. I knew what was happening in Chicago, but I didn't know how I felt about that anymore. Chris would never understand that was part of the reason I needed to stay away. I needed time to clear my head and make a decision.

"Yeah, well. I'm still going to be here for a few more days." This conversation was clearly going nowhere and was not helping me at all. "Don't worry; I'll let you know when I come back." I clicked the phone shut before he could answer.

I sat up in bed and put my head in my hands, confusion surrounding me. Why did he have to call and bring this argument up again? It was making me doubt again. Maybe Chris was right. What was I doing here? A few days ago, all I wanted to do was go back to Chicago; go back to the life that I thought I wanted. But now, things felt different. I wasn't totally sure what that was anymore. I could now see how my father and sister had found peace in this small town. When I was around Julia, things were very clear, but there were times like this when I felt the lure of my former life and I wanted to be back in Chicago. The only thing I did know was that my two worlds could not coincide. Eventually I would have to choose.

I rolled over and hid under my pillow, content to try to avoid figuring things out right now and instead, hoping for sleep. It felt like only a few minutes before my phone rang again, but I could see the dawn pushing through the windows and a glance at my clock told me that several hours had passed. Chris just wouldn't quit!

"What?" I answered, trying to hide my frustration but failing miserably. I could barely contain the venom in my voice.

"Is this Will Bradley?" the voice answered. It wasn't Chris again as I had suspected.

"Oh, hello. Yes, this is Will." I sat up, interested in who was calling me.

"This is Mr. Mason. From the school." Oh shit. My new boss. Had I done something wrong? Was I getting fired? My father would never let me live it down if I was.

"I have a favor to ask you," he continued. "Have you met Miss Cavallo, the director of the school play?" Julia. If he only knew. I sat up straighter now, no longer half asleep at the mere mention of her name.

"Yes actually, I met her on Friday." I couldn't contain the smile that crept across my face.

"Well apparently, she's in need of an assistant director for the school play. None of the other teachers want to do it, and I don't like the idea of her being at school alone every night. It's her first year. Do you know anything about theater or Shakespeare?"

"Well, I've never done any theater, but I did study Shakespeare." Shakespeare had been one of my obsessions many, many years ago. You wouldn't guess it just by looking at me, but I had read and studied every play and sonnet that he ever wrote. When you have lifetimes to look forward to, you look for different things to occupy your time.

"Great. Do you think you would be able to help her out? I know that I just hired you for odds and ends, but it would be great if you would do this instead. Rehearsal will go for 3 months. If you are still around after that, we can talk about other kinds of work."

"No problem, I would be happy to help." Working with Julia on a daily basis was more than I could hope for. I had answered without thinking.

"Excellent. Auditions start tomorrow night. I'll let Julia know that you will help her out." I heard the phone click and could barely contain myself. I would be able to spend so much more time with her. Then it hit me. I would be alone with her. Would my father approve? Did I really believe I had things under control? I would have to. If I couldn't, it would give everything away, and I just couldn't do that to my family... or to her. I could feel the strange heaviness in my chest again. I needed nourishment, but I knew that it was a feeling I would have to overcome if I wanted to be around Julia. Drinking donated blood would have to be the only answer. I didn't want her to think . . . I didn't know what I wanted her to think, but I knew I wasn't ready to tell her the truth about who I really was.

I lay back down and threw my arms over my face, letting out a deep breath of air. No matter how much I tried now, I wouldn't be able to get back to sleep. Eventually, I was forced to roll out of bed when the morning sun warmed my bare skin too much. I needed to find Celia and tell her my news. Maybe she would help me figure out what my next step should be.

The house was quiet when I made my way downstairs, but I knew Celia was up because her door was open and her room was empty. She was probably outside or out for a walk. A quick walk through the house confirmed my suspicions that she wasn't here. Maybe I should just sit and wait for her to come back.

Our bookshelves had always been well stocked, as we had always been a family of readers. I could see a few new titles had been added as I ran my fingers along their spines. Finally, I just grabbed one — some new crime novel that I hadn't read yet, and sat in the comfy chair my father often sat in to read. Within the first few pages, it was clear that I wouldn't be able to focus. The words before me blurred on the page and I found myself having to reread every other paragraph. With a frustrated sigh, I shut the book and tossed it on the table next to me. Who was I kidding? I couldn't sit still right now. My body felt electric, and I knew that I would be better off just trying to find Celia myself. In less than a minute, I was out the door.

I briefly glanced down the street in the direction of Julia's house. The neighborhood was quiet, other than a dog barking a few houses away. I started down the garden path figuring I would try around the house first. It was a warm autumn morning so I shouldn't have been surprised to see her sitting under the gazebo reading.

"Hey," I tried to sound casual. "I wondered where you went off to. The house was quiet this morning."

"What's up?" she said, closing her book and placing it next to her. "You look like you have something on your mind." I leaned up against the railing and looked at her.

"Well, Principal Mason called to talk to me a few minutes ago," I started.

"Um, you didn't do anything wrong, did you?" A look of horror crossed her face for a second before she composed herself again. It always bothered me that my father was constantly jumping to the wrong conclusion, but I didn't expect Celia to question me. She had always reassured me that she believed in me. Maybe they were both waiting for me to screw up, despite what they said, and I couldn't say anything to dissuade them. I probably deserved it, considering my behavior over the last few decades.

"No, it was nothing like that. Actually, he called to offer me a different job." I waited for her response, but continued talking when she didn't answer. "He wants me to be the assistant director of the play." Again a pause. "With Miss Cavallo." I smiled lightly, trying not to show how happy I was.

I could see her turning over the phrases in her mind, trying to find the significance, until it finally dawned on her what it meant.

"Really? Oh Will, that is great! I am so happy for you! I mean, this is wonderful for you. This is just what you need! " She jumped up and grabbed a hold of me so forcefully that I nearly fell.

"Yeah, I think so too. I know now that there is something about her. Something that draws me in. I just can't explain it, but I feel that I'll be able to find out if I work with her every day." She released her hold, and I stepped away, sitting on the bench across from her. "I mean, I'll be able to see her, get to know her, unravel the mystery."

The happiness on my sister's face began to fade. Without a doubt, I knew she was thinking of my own worst fear.

"Will, will you be able to handle it?" she asked quietly. "I mean, do you think that you are strong enough for this much contact? You've barely been here a week, and our world is so different from the world that you live in. This is just so soon! I know that you want this. Hell, I want this for you, and I see that you have already started to change. I'm sorry that I even have to ask, but... will you be... okay?"

I rested my hands on my knees and looked up at her. Her concern was genuine. Not just for Julia's safety but for my well-being. It was a question I had been asking myself over and over. I couldn't be angry with that.

"Thank you for your concern, Cee. I'd be lying if I said I wasn't a bit worried myself, but I really believe that I'll be okay." I stood back up and walked toward her, my arms hanging limply at my sides. Suddenly, the conversations with Chris came back to me, and what I wanted was crystal-clear. "I have been thinking a lot, and I really want this. I want to change who I am, and for the first time in my existence, I feel like I have a chance to get away from the monster I've become."

"Oh Will, that's what I have always hoped for. I just want my brother back." She hesitated for a moment and then scrunched up her brow. "I think we should keep this from father, just in case. For a little while, at least. Prove to him that you have changed before asking him to accept it. We wouldn't want to give him unnecessary concern."

I had thought that we should tell him right away, but Celia's logic prevailed, and I decided she was right. The fewer people that knew about this, the better. Maybe after a week or so, I could tell him. He wanted this life for me so much; it would be so great to show him my choice, once I was really strong.

"Alright, thanks for the talk, Cee. I guess that I had better go study up," I said as I turned to walk back inside.

"Study for what?" she called after me.

"Shakespeare, the play is by Shakespeare." I could hear her laughter echo after me.

THE NEXT NIGHT, I ARRIVED at school early. I walked instead of taking my motorcycle, needing to get rid of some excess nervous energy before I would be around her. Besides, school was close enough. Julia was on the stage at the piano, exactly where I hoped she would be. Cautiously, I walked down the aisle, slowly stopping when I was about halfway. I did not want to scare her away this time. We needed to work together, after all.

The music came to her easily tonight. It was as if she were a conduit for a higher power. When she finished, she sat there gently resting her hands on the keys and sighed. I clapped lightly to make my presence known.

"Jesus, you scared the crap out of me." She jumped up, the piano bench scraping loudly against the floor. She nervously tucked a strand of loose hair behind her ear. As usual, I was struck by her beauty; her cheeks were flushed and her eyes, a storm of emotion.

"I didn't mean to startle you again, but I was afraid if I spoke sooner, I would disturb you." I didn't know how to proceed as she was eying me suspiciously from behind the wall the piano created. Hesitantly, I began to walk toward the stage, my hands up as in mock surrender.

"No... it's okay. I just didn't think anyone was... I thought I was still alone." She stumbled over her words and looked down at her hands.

"I'm assuming that Principal Mason spoke with you about why I'm here tonight." I continued walking down the aisle to the first row and then sat directly across from her. "He thought you needed the help. I don't have theater experience, but I do know Shakespeare. Don't worry, though, I won't get in your way." I smiled warmly.

"Thanks. That would actually be nice. I could use an extra person here. Everyone I thought would help has pretty much backed out." She paused, as if she was struggling to form her next sentence and then tensed up. "Listen, I wanted to apologize for my rudeness the other day. I didn't mean to up and leave. Sometimes I'm not very good with people. Your questions just surprised me, that's all."

"No it's my fault for being intrusive," I apologized. "I've been told that I can be a little forward. I am sorry." Her green eyes carried the hint of the sadness that still eluded me. She situated herself back on the bench and turned to play.

"So, you are Celia's brother? She said you were home from grad school or something." Small talk. Her hands were busy on the piano keys, but I could still see them shaking slightly. Was it from being startled or did it scare her to be alone with me? I really hoped it was the first. I never wanted to frighten her.

"Something like that. I've been gone for a while. I don't get much time to come home." I tried to sound casual but didn't want to go into my life too much. She didn't need to know the real reason that I was here. She would run screaming in the other direction. Then again, that would be the smarter thing for her to do, even thought I was convinced that I would bring her no harm.

We sat without talking for a moment, the music floating in the air between us as her full attention turned back to her song. I leaned back and closed my eyes deep in thought, letting the music run through me. The ever present ache subsided when she played. That much I knew. It was like I could breathe again, relieved of the pain. Whatever it was about her, her music soothed a part deep within me. When she finished playing, I sat there taking a few moments before I reopened my eyes.

"You really do play well, you know." My voice was barely above a whisper. She was slumped tiredly over the keys when she turned to look at me; any barrier I had imagined existing between us was gone. I looked at her, trying to read the sadness within her eyes, all the while being drawn to it. Our eyes locked for a moment and I felt a deep stab in my gut. Finally, she turned away.

"Thank you." She folded and unfolded her hands in her lap. "I guess that we had better get things together. The students will be here any minute."

She stood up, straightened her shoulders and began to walk across the stage, our moment over. I watched her surreptitiously as she gathered her things. We moved chairs and set up the stage in silence, ever aware of each other's movements. Within minutes, the auditorium was buzzing with excited students ready to go. A few quick introductions and instructions about the process and we were ready. I sat down, leaving a seat between us, giving her some space and trying not to seem too eager. She glanced over at me smiling as the first student took the stage and I could no longer pretend that she wasn't all I needed.

Chapter 7
Julia

"OKAY GREAT, ANDREA. CALL BACKS will be posted tomorrow afternoon outside my room. Good luck." The gangly girl walked off stage, a nervous smile on her face. She was the last audition of the night. I had tried to forget about the person sitting next to me all evening, but I was ever aware of him. I stole a glance sideways and caught a glimpse of him biting a pencil in concentration. I just couldn't figure him out. Where did he come from? Why was he here? One thing was for sure. He seemed to know a thing or two about theater... or at least Shakespeare. I turned toward him, deciding to be the one to break the silence. He was still taking notes about our last audition and I could see the muscle in his jaw flex in concentration.

"So, what did you think?" I tried to sound casual. "Do you think we have a chance at a good show? I mean do you think we have some talent?"

"Well, this is no Globe Theater, but I did see some promising actors." He flashed a grin at me and swallowed me whole with his steel grey eyes. I had to turn away to compose myself and hide the embarrassing blush.

"I suppose we should talk about who we would like cast." *Try to stay on task* I kept telling myself. I could not let his looks distract me.

We sat and talked about who we wanted to see come back. After a few minutes, it was clear that he was not only familiar with Shakespeare, but was an expert with the Bard. This, of course, just heightened the puzzle that surrounded him. He knew the characters almost too well, and knew exactly who would be best for each role. We agreed with each other on who to call back for tomorrow. On the surface, our conversation was about Shakespeare but really, it seemed to be about so much more.

"Well thanks a lot for the last minute help. This is my first show, so I really appreciate it," I said, as I gathered my things. "I guess I'll see you tomorrow night."

I started to walk down the aisle when his voice stopped me.

"Julia, wait. Let me walk you out to your car." Within two strides, he was at my side.

"You don't have to. I'm sure you need to get home, and I need to turn out the lights."

"It's not trouble, I can wait." He flashed that charming grin again and my breath caught. "Besides, what kind of gentleman would I be if I left you here alone?"

I laughed in response and began walking back to the stage to shut the lights off.

"Alright, well I guess I can't argue when a knight wants to save a damsel in distress," I joked. "I'll only be a moment."

The breeze stirred the leaves on the trees as he walked me out to the parking lot. Our arms brushed against each other and a shiver went down my spine. I pulled my jacket tighter around me, attributing it to the weather and not to the energy he seemed to carry with him. I walked a little faster. There was only one car in the parking lot, making me wonder how Will had gotten here. I turned to offer him a ride home and almost ran into him. We were standing so close; I could barely get any words out.

"Do you need a ride home?" I stammered. "I just live right down the road from you." He was standing close enough that I should have felt his breath, but all I could feel was a cool rhythmic breeze on my skin. It was hard to admit that I didn't really want our evening together to end.

He looked surprised at my question at first, but then a smile crept across his face.

"That would be nice, if you don't mind." He stepped away from me, as if he was suddenly aware of our proximity, but his stormy eyes stayed locked on mine.

An owl called out into the night air, startling me. The car was still a little ways away, and I briskly walked to it, fumbling with my keys at the door. I didn't know what was wrong with me. I was usually so much more together than this. I was acting like a stupid school girl with a crush! *Pull it together*, I murmured under my breath. *Try not to act like a total idiot!*

Once in an enclosed area, the energy between us seemed to intensify and I could feel my heart beating. It was so loud, I was sure that he could hear it. He sat still next to me, and I wondered if he was feeling the same way I was. Finally, the nearness of him in the car and my nerves got the best of me, and I just started prattling, unable to stand the silence.

"So are you home for a while?" Dumb question. He would be here at least 3 months if he was going to help me out.

"Yes, although I'm not sure for how long. I mean, I don't know how long I will stay after we finish the play." His response seemed measured and cautious.

"Where were you before?" I continued. "I mean, where do you usually live?

"Chicago. I uh, used to go to school there." Yes. Definitely a hesitation. There was more to that response and I couldn't help but wonder what he was hiding. A reminder that I shouldn't be too eager to let him in. "I was going to grad school, but I decided to take some time off."

"Was it not what you thought it should be?" His answer had seemed too calculated.

"That and I just started to miss home." He let out a long sigh and seemed to relax a little. "It had been a long time since I'd been home. Plus, it's a big house for my father to take care of. And my sister and I have always been very close."

The energy in the car began to dissipate a little, making it easier for me to talk. I just wish I didn't feel so tongue tied around him. He shifted a little in the seat and looked out the window, making it easier for me to continue with the small talk.

"Yes, Celia is a wonderful student. She's in one of my English classes. Your father must be very proud of her." Suddenly, I realized that he must be around my age, yet I don't remember seeing him in school. "Where did you graduate from high school?"

"I went to high school in a small town in Massachusetts. We lived there before my father and sister moved here." The more I tried to decode him, the more the enigma kept growing.

"Where is your mother, if you don't mind my asking?"

"She died a long time ago." His voice was cold and his tone was even. I shivered a little and decided not to push the topic anymore. I could see it was not a conversation that he wanted to continue.

"Oh. I'm sorry."

We pulled into the subdivision. The ride was too short. My eyes were drawn to a solitary light on at his house. Before I could turn down the driveway, he interrupted me.

"You don't have to drop me off at my house. I can walk from yours."

"Are you sure? It's no trouble?" I slowed the car, preparing to head down the dark driveway.

"No, the driveway is hard to see at night. Besides, it's a pleasant walk."

"Okay." I turned into my driveway instead and turned the car off. He unfolded himself from the front seat.

"Goodbye, and thank you for the ride," he said from over the top of my car. Even in the dark, I could see his grey eyes clearly.

"It's not a problem." I bit my lip nervously. "You know, I can give you a ride home again, if you need it." The words tumbled out of my mouth before I could stop them.

"That would be great." He flashed a smile at me. "I guess I'll see you tomorrow night." Within seconds, he disappeared into the night.

I stood on the front porch for a few moments, staring out into the darkness after him. At least I didn't freeze this time. I had actually managed to hold an intelligent conversation with him. Well, I think it sounded intelligent. Not only that, we would be working together every night. Nothing could stop the smile from erupting on my face. If I didn't watch it, I could find myself falling for this boy. I did know one thing. I couldn't wait until tomorrow night.

WINTER WAS JUST AROUND THE corner and the air had a chill to it when I got up for my morning run, but it only energized me. My mind was clouded with thoughts of Will and the auditions last night. There was definitely something about him. He intrigued me. When he smiled, part of me wanted to run and part of me wanted to melt into his arms. I shivered at the thought of seeing him again, and picked up my pace a little, letting my muscles stretch and warm in the morning air.

It didn't take long for me to run three miles and before I

knew it, I was home. My body felt good, but my head wasn't any clearer. What was I doing thinking about him all the time! I just met him. If I really thought about it, the whole situation was strange. I mean, he was polite, too polite. And the way he moved. It was as if he never made a sound. He was just there. Plus, he was the brother of one of my students. It was just too weird. I needed to forget about him in that way. It would be good to have the help with the play, but I needed to keep reminding myself that within a matter of months, he could be gone. I couldn't afford to let myself get involved.

I was early getting to school, as usual. A few staff cars took their regular places in the parking lot and the few zero-hour students had already begun to filter in. I posted the call back list, locked my door, and went and hid in the teacher's lounge. I was not in the mood for a bunch of whiny students wanting to know why they didn't get a call back. My head was too busy for that. It was best to stay away until the bell rang.

"Hey, Jules. How did auditions go last night?" Kara sauntered into the room, looking bright-eyed and bushy tailed as usual. I sat at the table playing with my cup of tea.

"They were great." I hesitated, not sure whether or not to add the next part. She grabbed a mug from the cupboard and poured herself a steaming cup of coffee. After topping it off with what must have been ½ a cup of sugar, she took a sip only to make a face, put the cup down, and add more sugar. When she was finally satisfied, she took a seat across from me.

"Ah, John found me an assistant director," I started again

and put my cup to my lips so that she wouldn't see me smile.

"Really, and who might that be?" She set her mug down, her eyes full of anticipation.

"Will Bradley." She raised an eyebrow at me, signaling me to go on. "I guess he's pretty good at Shakespeare. Honestly, I don't think that John wanted me alone in the building at night, so he asked the first available male to help. It's okay, I think it will work out. I mean he seems knowledgeable." I sounded like an idiot trying to justify Will helping me and ended up rambling on.

"Will Bradley? That's the guy, isn't it? The guy you hinted at the other night." She practically shouted his name.

"Shhhh! Keep your voice down. I don't want people to get the wrong idea." I looked around frantically to see who might have overheard. "And don't forget, his sister could be roaming these halls at any minute!"

"Sorry, I just got a little carried away thinking about the prospect of a boy for you. I mean, how could you not be excited?" Kara brought her voice back down to a conversational tone, but the mischievous twinkle was still in her eye. Nothing got her going like good 'boy drama.'

"I am, I think. I... It's just that I don't really know. I can't figure him out. He just doesn't seem like a normal guy. He doesn't bombard me with too many questions and he doesn't know about my past. And I need to focus on the play, not some guy. Besides, he will probably leave after the show anyway." And it was just too soon for me to let someone in.

"Would it be a bad thing if he did know? About your past,

I mean?" she stated matter-of-factly.

"Well, no. It's just easier to not be judged and looked at as *that* girl. I am so tired of everyone in this town looking at me like I'm a leper, just because of my brother and parents. I just want people to recognize me for me, you know?" I shoved the chair out roughly and walked away, staring absentmindedly at the wall.

"I'm sorry. I hope I've never done that to you."

"No, it's not you. You are the only one who *doesn't* treat me that way." Kara sighed, and I heard her get up and walk over to me.

"You know I just want you to be happy," she said squeezing my shoulders. I shrugged and smiled.

The bell rang, warning us that we had better get back to our classrooms. We got up and walked out the door, parting when we got to our rooms.

"See you at lunch?" I called after her.

"Definitely, but maybe we should eat in my classroom today. I don't want to deal with school gossip once those kids see the cast list," she answered pointing to the brightly colored sheet of paper taped to my door.

"ALRIGHT, CLASS. DON'T FORGET TO hand in your compare/contrast essay before you leave." I sighed when I thought the last student had left my class, so I was startled to hear a voice.

"Miss Cavallo?" Celia was standing near my desk. I hadn't heard her come up. She was stealthy just like Will. Very strange. I pushed the comparison from my head.

"Oh hi, Celia. I didn't see you there. What can I do for you?"

"I'm sorry. I didn't mean to sneak up on you like that. I just wanted to see if you were okay. You seemed distracted today." A corner of her mouth turned up slightly, but her eyes were unreadable.

Crap. Had I let on to the students that things were off in my life? Panic crossed my face. Did Will say something about me? Could Celia tell how I felt?

"Oh thanks. I'm just a little tired, you know with auditions last night. I have to remind myself that it's going to be a couple of long months." I smiled meekly at her.

"Yeah, my brother told me about them. He is really excited to be helping you with the play." She paused, a smile on her lips. "Okay, well, have a nice night." Her smile turned into a smirk. Clearly, she had been talking to her brother. And what did she mean by that? He was excited about the play or excited to be with me? I don't know. I was so confused. Seeing her in my class didn't help. The way she always looked at me. It was like she was trying to read me. I needed to stop thinking so deeply into this!

Tonight couldn't come soon enough, and I found it hard to pass the few hours in between school and the rest of the auditions. Reading papers for an hour managed to occupy my mind and my time, but I decided to go home and grab some dinner instead of sitting here trying to waste time. The wind had picked up a little and the grey and fluffy clouds warned of snow. I wrapped my jacket tightly around myself as I walked outside. As I was unlocking my car, I suddenly had the feeling of being watched. I turned, expecting to find someone. Nothing. I looked around nervously and scanned the parking lot. There were a few cars left. Anyone could be hiding behind one and I certainly didn't want to find out whom. My imagination could be pretty wild if I wasn't careful.

Once in the car, I locked the doors and sped away, not wanting to look in my rear view mirror to see if anyone truly was there. As a pulled into my driveway, a body stood up from the front porch and I froze. Tentatively, I inched my car closer, and then my heart skipped a beat. It was Will.

I tried to act nonchalant when I got out of the car. I hoped that my emotions were not written all over my face.

"Hi, Will. I hope you haven't been here for long. I would have come back sooner." Hell, I'd have jumped in my car immediately if I had known he was here!

"I'm sorry that I'm here waiting for you, but I don't know how to get a hold of you. Could I get a ride with you to rehearsal tonight?" His grey eyes deepened and bore right into mine.

"Oh sure. No problem," I replied nervously, fiddling with my hair.

"Thanks, I don't have a car, living in a big city, and I don't want to have someone keep dropping me off." I watched his long fingers play with the zipper on his jacket, mesmerized.

Realizing I was staring, I reached down to get my bags out of the car. He met me in the walkway and reached to take them from me. I always took way too much home from school with the intention of doing work, but somehow, nothing ever got done. He followed me to the front door. I unlocked it and stepped inside. I was a few feet inside when I noticed that he didn't immediately follow me. A true gentleman. I guess it was rude of me to assume he would just walk in like that.

"Do you want to come in?" I asked.

He looked around nervously as if he were unsure.

"Oh. Sure. I guess that I'm sort of old-fashioned. I didn't know if you wanted me to come in." The last part came out hesitantly, like he was covering something up. He walked to the table and set my bag down.

"I was just about to get something to eat quickly. Can I get you something?" I began to pull some semblance of a dinner out of the cupboard.

"No, that's okay. Actually, I think I will just run home quick and get my things."

"My cooking is not that bad," I tried to joke, and a smile broke out on his face. How quickly I had become comfortable with him.

"No, it's not your cooking. I just have a few things I want to get done before we have to go tonight." He walked toward the door, and I followed shyly, hoping that he would change his mind. "I will be back over here in 45 minutes."

"Okay, great." I replied as he stepped out. After waiting a moment, I slowly shut the door, and then peeked out the window to watch him leave, but he was already gone. It was like he had vanished into thin air. I must have waited longer than I thought and he must have jogged home. Yeah, that would explain things. But, somehow, it didn't. That was the thing about Will. I felt that there was so much left unexplained.

"THANK YOU ALL FOR COMING tonight." I glanced quickly at Will sitting next to me. "Mr. Bradley and I think that we will have an excellent play and can't wait to begin work. Final casting will be posted on the door outside my room tomorrow." The quiet auditorium erupted with students talking as they left. Most of the girls eyed Will, taking in his good looks and forgetting he was out of high school. I rolled my eyes toward him as he smiled back at them.

"They are too young for you, you know," I chided, careful to not let him see my own jealous expression. I had spent years building up a tough exterior so as to not let anyone see what I was really feeling. I hoped that Will wasn't able to see through it.

"What are you jealous?"

So much for that. He laughed, flashing that killer smile at me again and I tried not to melt. I smiled back, admitting to myself that his presence was growing on me. There was definitely something about him that was drawing me in. The more time I spent with him, the less skeptical I became. I began to gather all of my papers and shove them in my bag. It gave me an excuse to not look at him, something that I couldn't seem to stop doing.

"No, I just think it's funny that all the girls look at you that way."

"Look at me what way?" he asked innocently. I turned to glare at him. He stood with his arms crossed, the muscle in his jaw flexing as he clamped down a smirk on his face, and a few tendrils of dark hair lay across his forehead.

Looking at you the way I am probably looking you, I said to myself. Our eyes locked for a moment and I felt a fire spread through my cheeks. I turned away still aware of his gaze, unable to answer him.

"Okay, let's get things cleaned up around here and get going. I'm ready for a hot shower and then bed." We cleaned up in silence for a few minutes, but I was constantly aware of his presence. There was more to it than that. Will had been a tremendous help to me over the last day or so. He really was knowledgeable when it came to Shakespeare. He gave the kids lots of hints on their auditions. He may not know a lot about theater, but he certainly understood the play's meaning.

"So why did you become an English teacher?" He finally broke the silence with more questions. I should have been prepared, considering that I had been asking him questions myself. It was only fair.

"Well, my grandmother was a teacher and I really admired her. And I always loved to read and write. It seemed to make sense that I should be an English teacher. I guess it's what I always wanted to do."

"Do you like teaching high school?" He was walking through the aisles, picking up any trash on the ground. I couldn't help but look at his backside when he bent down.

"Yes, I do. I like dealing with the older students. Although, I don't really feel that much older than them, since this is my first year. And I don't think I could work with elementary. They are too moldable. I might corrupt them." He laughed at my response. "What about you. What were you studying in Chicago? Or did you finish college?"

"I started out studying medicine, but I don't think that's for me. That's part of the reason I came home. I don't think I want to do that anymore." He looked up at me with blazing eyes. "In fact, I'm not sure *what* I want anymore."

Surely, he wasn't talking about school anymore. My cheeks flushed again at the thought.

"Hmm." I smiled a little. He was being so open tonight. Last night he didn't seem to want to talk at all.

"What? What are you thinking? Did I say something amusing?" He moved back up the aisle to join me.

"No, it's just that you're giving information so freely tonight. Last night you were so guarded. I like learning more about you." I grabbed the rest of the audition sheets and put them in my bag to avoid his eyes. "I only mean that it's nice to know more about you, since we will be working so closely together." Something in me felt the need to clarify. I didn't need him to think I was some sort of crazy stalker.

"Oh, I guess I just didn't know about you last night. I mean, what you would think of some stranger helping out. You are very easy to be around." I looked right up into his grey eyes. I leaned into the nearest row of seats, suddenly feeling the need to sit down. He seemed to be looking right into me. His eyes were bright tonight, brighter than I had ever seen them before.

"Well, I'll admit, I wasn't sure about you at first. What was I supposed to think about the mysterious night janitor who can help with theater? But you really know a lot about Shakespeare so how could I turn that down."

"There is nothing either good or bad, but thinking makes it so." He smiled sweetly and I laughed. Quoting *Hamlet*. He was good.

"I suppose we should get home. Are you ready?" I asked.

"Sure, whenever you are." He flashed his million dollar grin again. Seriously, I think my heart skipped a beat. I turned the lights off and then locked the auditorium after giving the piano a longing gaze and then we walked to my car.

It was a short drive home, so I drove slowly, never ready for our time together to end. I welcomed the comfortable silence in the car. I could feel him looking over at me from time to time and I resisted the urge to look back at him. Things were falling into place with him. The more time I spent with him, the more comfortable I felt, yet he set my emotions on edge and made me feel like I never had before. How strange that someone could affect me like that in such a short time. It scared me that I felt so at ease and yet flustered. I had been pushing people away for so long, building up an emotionless exterior, so I panicked at the thought of letting him in. Then again, he was so different from anyone that I knew. I didn't really know how to describe it. I suppose it was akin to standing on the edge of a precipice ready to jump. It was equally exciting and terrifying at the same time.

Soon we were pulling into my driveway and saying our goodbyes. I would see him tomorrow night, yet I was anxious to watch him leave.

It was dark out and getting cooler by the minute. I stood on the porch for a few minutes, watching Will disappear. It would only take him a minute to get home, and then I knew what I needed to do.

Once I thought that he wouldn't notice me, I climbed back into my car and drove. I needed to talk to someone... my brother.

The cemetery is technically closed at dusk, but I knew a way in. I liked to come at night since it was quieter and I knew that no one would be here to bother me. Unlike most people, I liked being here alone. There was solace to be found at times, in this maze of stone. During the day when others were around, I felt as if they watched me at his grave, like they wanted to see me break down. Or they felt pity. That was the thing about this small town. I always felt watched and judged. Everyone knew your life story. They knew your strengths and your weaknesses.

The granite headstone shimmered in the moonlight. I was at peace out here tonight; a stark contrast to some visits. Missing Aaron seemed to be a consuming part of my life at times. Some days were harder than others, and I ached with the loss. Some were like today, relatively easy. Still, I visited his grave often. My parents were buried separately, in different cemeteries. I think I came to terms with their deaths long ago, but I had never understood the unfairness of Aaron's death, so his seemed to haunt me more. I had always been closest with him anyway, so he was my first choice when I needed someone to talk to.

"I started play practice this week," I began. I could almost hear him answer in my head, while I prattled. "I think we'll have a good cast this year. We're doing Shakespeare's *As You Like It*. And I have a new assistant director. You remember the Bradley place down the street? Well, Will Bradley, the boy I was telling you about before, I guess he's really good at Shakespeare, so he's helping me." I paused and traced my finger over Aaron's name. The stone was cool and smooth. I breathed in deeply, letting the extra oxygen settle deep in my lungs. "There is something about him that I like. Will. I find myself letting my guard down and... and it scares the shit out of me." I spoke very softly, as if someone else was around to hear my confession. Finally, I had said it aloud. There was something about Will Bradley that scared me, true, but there was also a part of me that liked that about him. And I was definitely drawn to him. The way his eyes pierced through me. The way he flexed his chiseled jaw. The few strands of hair that constantly seemed to fall forward and get tangled in his long, dark lashes. The deep timbre and lilt of his voice, like a siren song, drew me in.

"I don't really know what to do or how to act. I've been pushing everyone but Kara away for so long, that it feels strange to actually meet someone that I'm drawn to. I want to let him in, but I don't want to scare him off. " I sighed deeply and closed my eyes, letting my feelings out. The grass was cool and welcoming as

I lay my cheek down.

I sat up quickly at the sound of something close; a rustling of leaves. My eyes darted around in the darkness. My body froze, but I could see nothing, and then the feeling was gone. It must have been a deer, I rationalized. Who in their right mind would be venturing around a cemetery at night, right? Then again, I was out here, wasn't I?

I shook off the dark feeling and turned back to the cold stone memory in front of me.

Chapter 8
Will

T HE REST OF THE WEEK went by in a blur. My days dragged as I waited for night to come, when I would see Julia again. We quickly fell into a routine. I would walk to her house, and she would drive us to rehearsal. After rehearsal we would part, but I would usually come back to see if I could catch her playing the piano. I longed for time to spend together. The aching pressure in me was still there, but subsided substantially whenever I was with her. We spent so much time together that I became completely aware of her. I couldn't explain it. It was like I had an insight into her mind. If her feeling was strong enough, I could almost get a vision of her. I didn't know what to make of it; I only knew that it was unusual. It was becoming stronger every day, and I knew I would have to tell someone eventually. Tonight, however was Friday; there was no rehearsal. The pain I felt was my own, and it was back with a vengeance. The ache of not being with her for a few days was torture. To make things worse, I was paranoid that Chris would send someone here, looking for me. Or worse yet, he would come himself.

I felt weak with a restless urge, a longing that I had not felt all week. The idea that I would be able to change didn't seem so strange anymore. In fact, I seemed to be doing quite well, hardly able to remember the person I had been before. I had managed just fine on donated blood and actually felt satisfied. I had either been with Julia or knew that I would see her soon, which made me content. Tonight, however, was unbearable. It didn't feel right to not be around her, and this pleased the disease. I stood in front of the mirror staring at myself, trying to see the monster struggling to come out, fighting with myself. My eyes were sunken in and dull. Even my face was greyer than usual. I didn't understand, because things had been going so well, but now I looked and felt horrible. It was becoming clear to me how much I needed Julia. Just then, Celia came bounding up the stairs. One look at my reflection as she passed by caused her to stop in her tracks.

"Are you okay, Will?"

"I feel so restless again, Celia, I can't stand this feeling of unrest. I need to go out or something." I sat on the edge of my bed and ran my hands through my hair.

"But you have been okay all week. Why is it so bad right now?"

"I don't know," I lied, then changed my mind and opted for the truth. Change also meant not hiding behind my old ways anymore. Honesty could only help. Maybe she would know how to help me deal with this. "Actually, I have a theory."

"Let's hear it." She settled against the wall opposite me.

"I think it has something to do with Julia. When I'm around her, I don't feel the urge. I can make it through the day because I know that I'm going to see her at night. Tonight is hard though, because I know that I'm not going to see her until Monday. Have you ever had this happen? Don't you ever feel like the donated blood isn't enough?" I shifted uncomfortably on my bed.

"I used to. I mean I used to feel those urges, but I don't anymore. I never knew why. I just thought that I got used living this way, so I resolved to be content and refused to give in. The feeling is still there, but it's buried deep. It's like I care more about my life now and don't want to ruin it." She looked up at me carefully and then smiled jokingly.

"I'm glad my pain amuses you." I started to push past her, feeling suddenly annoyed, but she grabbed my arm and spun me around, not allowing me to walk out. I really was on edge tonight.

"I'm not laughing at you, Will. Look at me, damnit. How do you feel right now?" I didn't understand where this was going, but I decided to humor her anyway.

"I'm angry," I said, glaring at her. "And if I have to be honest, I guess I'm sad too. I miss her. I know that sounds stupid because I hardly know her, but I miss her. I feel an empty space when she's not with me." I pushed away from her and stood gazing at the mirror again. "But there's more. I'm beginning to *feel* her."

Celia looked at me in a strange way. Concerned and curious all at once.

"No, it's not bad," I said. "You know how I was so drawn to her because of something I felt? Well, it's stronger now, and I sense her mood. I know if she's happy or if she's in pain. I can feel her even when I'm not with her." I walked to the chair and slumped down, letting my head sink back into my hands. The grandfather clock on the wall ticked rhythmically, the only sound for a moment.

"I have never heard of that before. I mean I've never heard of *anyone*, diseased or not, being able to sense mood in others." Her voice was barely a whisper as it floated from across the room. "Are you sure you're not just attracted to her blood? That it's not just the need pushing through?"

"Positive. It's definitely different than that first time. Most of the time, I have a feeling like she's just there. But then, I'll suddenly get an impulse of her feelings if something changes. If it's an intense feeling, I get a flash of her. Like I can see what she's doing. I feel almost as if I'm in her mind."

I only felt a small amount of relief in confiding to her. Celia was looking at me like I was crazy. Of course, I didn't realize how strange this all sounded until I said it out loud. She returned my gaze, squinting a little as if she was trying to see further inside of me. I looked back down ashamed and embarrassed by how stupid I sounded.

"Please don't tell me I'm crazy," I couldn't help but add.

She began to walk toward me, standing in front of me for a moment before kneeling down and cradling my face in her hands. Her gaze was intent and I felt as if she was seeing right into me.

"Your eyes. They are different. There is more life in them. You're changing, Will. Whatever you have with her is changing you." She dropped her hands from my face and grabbed my own hands. "I really think it might be time to talk to father about this. You need to tell him everything. Maybe he knows something you and I don't. "

"No." I almost spit the words out as I stood abruptly. "I'm afraid to hear his disapproval. I'm still not sure that he would understand."

"It doesn't matter, Will. You're in too deep and he's going to notice something is up. He has to find out and it would be better coming from you." She gently squeezed my hand and then slipped from the room, giving me time alone to process.

She was right, of course, and minutes later I was standing outside of my father's study, ready to tell him everything.

"YES," HIS VOICE ANSWERED FROM within. "Come in."

Quietly, I slipped in. My father was standing by the large window of his study, with his back turned. He had a book in hand and never looked up.

"Will, what can I do for you? I trust your job is going well, considering I haven't heard anything negative." He turned to face me, a small smile on his face.

"I have to talk to you about something. Well, I actually have to tell you something. Can I sit down?" I nervously shoved my hands in my pockets not sure where to begin. I needed to ease his suspicions right away. Usually when I talked to him like this it was because I had screwed up and I needed him to help me cover it. At least that's what I used to do before I finally moved to Chicago.

I wasn't sure he would believe the truth, but I had no choice but to tell him. He motioned for me to sit all the while eyeing me cautiously and patiently waiting for whatever it was I needed to tell him.

"There have been some things happening this week, things that I need to tell you about." I looked up to gage his reaction. His face was still, unreadable. "Last Sunday, Principal Mason called and asked me to help out with something other than the odds and ends at school."

"Why, was there something wrong with working at night? Did you do something wrong?" So much for easing suspicions. He didn't raise his voice, yet I knew he was agitated.

"It's nothing like that. I swear I did nothing wrong. He needed me for something else, a special project and asked me for help." Again I waited for a comment, and I pleaded with my eyes for him to let me finish, so he let me continue. "The school play needed an assistant director and he asked me if I would help out. The director is a teacher named Julia Cavallo. She lives just down the street. He didn't want her working alone at night and thought I would be helpful."

"Miss Cavallo, you mean Celia's English teacher?" His facial expression went from concerned to quizzical.

"Yes, I believe so. It's just that...how can I say this," I couldn't let on that I knew so much about her quite yet, but after my pause, he jumped in, not allowing me to finish my thought.

"Does she know? About us I mean. Is she in some kind of danger? Are you okay alone with her? What happened to her?" In two strides he had crossed the room to stand in front of me, his questions turning to accusations and coming fast and furious. I tried to stay calm, reminding myself that he had every right to be so paranoid, of course, based on my past performance. Plus, up until this week, I hadn't been sure that I could be alone with her without endangering her life. Taking a deep breath and calming myself, I said, "She is not in danger. I assure you. I would never dream of hurting her. That's not what I need to talk to you about. It's just that... well... I... " I was stumbling over my words, unable to figure out just how to say it. "We have been spending a lot of time together and... I think I'm starting to *feel*." I held my breath waiting for his reply.

Shock registered on his face, and I wasn't sure if that was good or bad. I was used to getting chastised. Silence and shock were not things I was prepared for. He turned his back to me and crossed back to the window to gaze out over the lake.

"Say something, please," I whispered. The ache in my chest burning, I brought my hand up and began rubbing the ache as the demon I had been pushing down all week warred with my new found need. Talking about her always made it worse.

He turned back to me and his face had softened, but I could see conflict in his eyes. He seemed to mirror the conflict I felt within myself.

"You feel. I had hoped for this day for years. I'm only sorry that it didn't come sooner. Before the change, I mean. You were always such a rebel as a boy, never caring about the consequences of your actions. And now, finally..." His voice faded as he stopped to really look at me. I knew he was taking in my pale skin, the deep circles under my eyes, and the sadness and pain I was trying to keep from my face.

"I can see it now. The change in you. I don't know why I never noticed it before. I guess I didn't believe that you would ever be able to change, so I stopped looking. There is more light in your eyes. Perhaps, you are beginning to reawaken. You're becoming something more."

"I don't understand. What do you mean? What change?" I was confused. I thought he would only see my current weak state. The way I felt when I wasn't around her was worse in many ways than the way I had been before. At least it felt that way to me.

"I have never told you much about the change because I believed for so many years that you were incapable of accepting it. Those that you have been hanging out with certainly are." His voice was soft and full of emotion as he went back to his desk to sit across from me. "Haven't you ever questioned why your sister and I are so different from the rest?"

"Yes, but I guess I just assumed that it was because you fought your urges."

"That is partly true. Just because you are an immortal being, doesn't mean that you need to be a monster. You see, you must remember that we suffer from a disease. You aren't dead, but you aren't alive either. Your body is in a sort of hibernation. That's why we are so cold. The blood flows at a much slower rate. It makes us cold-blooded in a sense. Our temperature is controlled by our surroundings. But of course, you know this. Our hearts beat, but at a much slower rate, and our senses become more acute, which is why our hearing and sight are so good. Even our sense of touch is heightened." He breathed in deeply, settling himself further back into his chair. His hand lightly toyed with the miniature portrait of my mother that I knew was on his desk. I followed his arm up to his face and could see that he was staring intently at her, forcing me to quickly look away, feeling like I was intruding on a private moment. When he spoke again, his voice was softer.

"It is our emotions that undergo a much bigger change. While our bodies hibernate, our souls become dormant as well. Our emotions begin to leave us, unless we can hold onto them by feeling them. Inevitably, anger becomes an often-used emotion and begins to take over, causing the soul to disappear. Eyes become glazed over, and there is no happiness or love left as the light leaves us. That is also why we thrive on despair. The longer someone has been immortal, the more of a monster he or she can become. The more we will focus on darkness, and the more hopeless we will become. It's something that our kind must fight against. We must maintain some sort of hold on our humanity. If we do, this life isn't so bad." He paused again and leaned toward me, his hand sliding off of the portrait. "This has been my biggest fear for you. I was afraid that the hate you carried was beginning to consume you. I could see the light disappear from your eyes more and more every time I would see you. I kept asking you to come home, hoping that I would see a change. I stupidly assumed that this time was no different. My biggest fear was that someday soon, I would lose you to yourself forever."

His words sunk in, and I began to really understand him for the first time in this life. I stood up and went to the window this time, gazing out over the calming presence of the lake. This explained so much to me. I knew our history. I knew how it worked, I just never knew that it was possible to fight it in this way. I always felt the anger and darkness closing in around me. My father had held on to the memory of my mother's love for all these years and my sister had too. Or maybe for her, it was the hope of finding that kind of love someday. I never thought I had a choice. Honestly, I had never cared, until I met Julia. She made me see the goodness, even though it had been her despair that drew me to her. She made me want to be something more.

Behind me, my father rose from his desk and came to stand behind me.

"I loved your mother very much." He held the tiny portrait of her in front of me on the windowsill. "And she loved us very much. There are circumstances that have prevented her from being with us, but we can't keep being angry over losing her. After all, she is in a better place, and I wouldn't have wanted her to live this life with us. Still, we all have to find something to hold on to."

My father gave me a few minutes to mull things over before speaking again. I stared at the portrait, taking in my mother's features. She had been so beautiful. Just looking at her made me feel her loss. It had been so long since I had looked at her, I barely remembered her. I had forgotten how much Celia looked like her. Perhaps that's why it was so easy for my father. It was like looking at my mother every time he looked at her.

"Tell me about her, this girl who has brought you back to us. Tell me what has made you change."

At the mention of Julia, images of her flashed through my mind. Julia playing the piano, Julia laughing, driving home with her, and watching her silhouette laugh in the dark. I smiled.

"She's hauntingly beautiful and wonderful. No, she's more than that. She is amazing." My words began to come out in a rush. "I have to admit, at first I was attracted to her because there was something dark and hopeless, but there is also much happiness and life in her. I saw her switch back and forth and it intrigued me. I wanted... no, I *needed* to know more. The more time I spend with her, the more I begin to focus on her happiness." My father was smiling back at me, so I continued. "I haven't indulged since I came here and I don't even feel like it when I'm with her. But, tonight has been difficult. I haven't seen her all day, and I won't be with her until Monday. I'm finding that it's always hardest when I'm not with her. " My face contorted with pain and longing, although I could feel the ache lift a little just by talking about her. "She plays the piano, and when she plays, she's happiest. Her songs have awakened something in me that I can't explain. When I'm with her, I can almost convince myself I'm human again. She makes me want to change... to be a better person." I nearly collapsed against the window, exhausted with the thought of her.

I felt an arm around my shoulders as laughter sprang from my father's lips.

"That, my son, is your soul, *reawakening*. Love can do that. *Passion* can do that." I smiled at the word love. I suppose I did love her. I hadn't thought that was what it was, but certainly, in this last week she had become such a deep part of me that I didn't think I could go on without her. I was reminded of my visions, of my connection to her and remembered the real reason that I came to talk.

"There is something else though, the reason that Celia thought that I should talk to you about things. I know how Julia feels when I'm not with her." I explained what had been happening. "I don't know what that means. It's like she's a part of me."

The look on my father's face told me that this was not good, and it scared me a little. Maybe it was a bad thing, something that could be done to others to draw victims in before being killed by them. His silence continued and was stifling.

"Are you okay? What does it mean?" I asked.

"It is very rare but not bad." He must have been able to read the pained look on my face. "I have only heard of this a few times. It's something that transcends even us. It's the sign of a true soul mate. It could happen to anyone, immortal or human but rarely between the two. Your mother and I had it, and I have only known of a few others who have felt the same way. It means that your souls are truly connected. This is something I had hoped for you my whole life." He looked at me in disbelief.

"Connected?" I didn't understand. "But that's impossible! How could we ever be together? She's mortal! Our life expectancies alone, would keep us apart. It's not possible." This was certainly not what I had expected to hear. This was a joke. A cruel joke played by fate. My fists balled at my sides and dark anger welled up. The air around me swirled in darkness and I could feel myself begin to break.

"You shouldn't fight fate, which is what has brought you together. You can't fight what was meant to be, and apparently, you were meant to be with her even if it's only for part of your lifetime. The power that binds you is more powerful than any of us. It transcends time." My father's firm grip still on my shoulder, grounded me and brought me back from the dark place. His gaze was set firmly on me.

"But how..." Suddenly I felt a sharp pain in my chest. Like a knife was being driven in. I saw a flash in front of my eyes, and I could feel Julia's pain. I didn't know what to do, I just knew that I needed to find her.

"It's her, isn't it," my father quietly asked me. "I can see it on your face. You must go to her." I didn't wait to hear if my father said anything else. I was already out the door. Whatever trouble she was in, she was calling to me, and I had to find her.

IT DIDN'T TAKE LONG, EVEN in my father's car, to follow my senses to where I found her curled up in the cemetery. I wasn't sure why she was here sitting in front of a gravestone near the old maple. Her face and hair were soaked with tears. I went to her cautiously so as not to alarm her. She was shaking as she silently cried.

"Julia?" I called out softly.

"What are you doing here?" she whispered sitting up slowly. Her voice was hoarse, and her eyes red with tears.

"I'm taking you home."

I was prepared for a struggle as I put my arms around her frail body, but she was too weak to fight back. Instead, she grabbed the front of my shirt and buried her head against my cold chest. I walked quickly to the car, setting her carefully in the front seat. I felt the solitary beat in my chest as I leaned over her to fasten the seatbelt. She looked so small and sad curled up on the seat. The despair radiating off of her caused the monster to rumble, but my concern and newly found love for her slowly overpowered it. She was shaking uncontrollably, and I wrapped the blanket I found in the trunk around her. Within minutes, we arrived at her house. She had stopped crying but was still limp in the seat next to me. I picked her up and carried her onto the porch. It was unseasonably warm for October, and since I didn't want to intrude in her house, I gently set her down on the swing and took the seat opposite her. My body, now warm from holding her, suddenly felt very empty without her there. She pulled herself up onto her elbows her eyes studying me.

"How did you find me? What were you doing there?" She repeated her earlier question.

"I was driving by, and I saw you," I lied. "It's not really important. What is important is that you are back here. Safe." I emphasized the last word and leaned forward resting my elbows on my knees. I looked back at her. I didn't want to explain how I knew where she was, so I turned the questioning back to her. "Are you okay? What were you doing there so late at night?"

"That's really none of your business," she snapped unexpectedly and pulled the blanket tightly around her.

"Okay, fine, be cryptic. I was only trying to help." I stood up, tempted to leave. The sadness was locked within her eyes. She clearly wasn't ready to talk about it, but I wasn't ready to leave either.

"Wait. Don't go," her voice was barely above a whisper. "I'm sorry. I just don't like to talk about it. In fact, I never talk about it with anyone." She paused for a minute and twisted her hands. When she looked back up, her green eyes glowed with intensity. "I go there to talk to my brother. He died a few years ago." Her lips were pursed and I could see that this confession took a great deal of effort. She looked at me anxiously, as if waiting for me to say something.

"You really shouldn't go in there alone at night," I pointed out tersely.

"I didn't go at night. It was light when I arrived, just after school. I guess I just lost track of time. Sometimes that happens..." she pointed out, matter-of-factly. "Besides, why should it matter to you," she tried to sound harsh, but it came out too softly.

It mattered a lot to me. I knew that now. Julia's disclosure made me cognizant of my own secrets. I needed to tell her something, but now just wasn't the time to tell her the whole truth. I guess I could at least tell her how I was feeling. I swallowed hard, almost choking on the lump that now resided there, as I prepared to tell her how I felt.

"I don't know if I can explain it, but I feel like I need to watch after you. I know you can take care of yourself, but I worry about you. I think about you and just want you to be safe." It was the best explanation that I was ready to give.

She absentmindedly slid her foot down to the floor and began to rock the swing gently.

"Oh." Her voice was barely above a whisper.

"I'm not a stalker. I swear," I said, my hands out in mock surrender. "I know it sounds weird, but it's the truth. I guess I've gotten so used to making sure you got home safe after practice that I get concerned about you easily. There is still a lot about me that you don't know." Even as I said it, my reasoning just sounded stupid.

She looked puzzled for a moment and bit her lip. I wondered if I had just scared her off. I prepared myself for her to start yelling and screaming at me to leave and never come around again, but after a minute when that didn't happen, I began to relax a little. Finally a small smile pulled at the corner of her mouth and pink spread over the cheeks.

"So you think you need to keep me safe?" She stood up and rubbed her hands across her thighs as if she was drying them off. "That sounds so weird. I mean, I hardly know you, but you seem to be in the right place at the right time. You always seem to know how to help me when I need it."

I didn't know what else to say. She just stared at me. Her auburn hair cascaded over her shoulders, and her green eyes were still smoldering brightly. She was flushed, as if she had just gone for a run, and I was absolutely positive that there could be no one in the world I adored more. My cold heart ached just looking at her. What I wouldn't do for just one human day with her. A pained sigh escaped my lips, and at last she looked away.

"Well, I guess that's settled." She smiled widely and relaxed even more.

"What's settled?" I chuckled, not aware that we had anything that needed to be settled.

"If you're going to keep being in the right place at the right time, then I might as well accept it and get to know you better. All this time we have spent together this week and you have barely talked about yourself, other than to answer the few questions I asked you on our first day. So start talking. I need something to take my mind off of my own problems." She plopped back down and crossed her arms in front of her chest, daring me to defy her.

My eyes widened with surprise. I wasn't sure that getting

to know me would be a great idea. I didn't think I could bear for her to learn who I really was. Not only that, it would be dangerous.

"What do you want to know? I already told you the basics," I asked hesitantly.

"Tell me more about your family. I want to know more about them."

"Well, you know it's just my dad, my sister, and me." I hesitated. "My mom died a long time ago."

"Do you miss her?" her voice was soft, and I could hear the longing in it.

"Yes." I locked my jaw in apprehension. I didn't want to lie to her, but I didn't want to give away too much.

"My parents are gone, too." She looked away and was suddenly in a far off place. "Sometimes I miss them so much." She gestured toward the house. "This is the house I grew up in, you know. At times, it's hard to live here alone. There are just too many memories. I keep expecting them to walk through that door any minute." She looked up at me, and I could see all of the sadness in her face. I could see it run deep, right down into her soul. This is where it came from, the deep darkness I had wanted to know. I could feel the hurt radiating up through her, and I wanted so badly to take it away. I wanted her eyes to sparkle with happiness again. It surprised me to want that for once.

"I'm sorry. I didn't know that you lost your parents, too." There wasn't much more to say, so I waited for her to say more.

"I don't talk about it a lot. Everyone in town knows, and

they tend to keep their distance. They just wait for me to snap. Sometimes I do." Julia moved back toward the swing and plopped down. "No one wants to be around someone who is so... broken."

"Broken? Is that what you think you are? Losing someone doesn't make you broken. Death is a part of life." I got up and slowly made my way next to her and sat down. "We all lose something or someone, eventually."

"Now, I know you are new to town," she said. "Clearly, you haven't heard what people say about 'poor Julia.' They just seem to take pity on me. Honestly, I'm pretty sure that's why I actually got the job at the school." Her brow creased in a frown, and my fingers ached to reach out and smooth it out.

"You mean because you're a great teacher and an incredibly talented musician? That's why you got the job, right?" Surely people in this town saw her for what she was.

She let a laugh escape and brought a slender hand up to stifle it.

"You must have been talking to Kara, my one and only friend. She is my biggest and only supporter. She knew me before and went through it all with me."

Her mystery was only beginning to unravel, and I was hungry for more.

"Tell me." I spoke quietly reaching out and daring to grab her hand only to feel a surge of something run through me. "I want to know what made you think this way."

She startled, and I knew she felt it too. She looked back at me but didn't let go and instead laced her fingers through mine.

"I suppose I should start at the beginning. I already mentioned my brother, Aaron. I often go to his grave to visit him. He committed suicide when he was in high school. We were really close. My parents fought a lot after that. Eventually, they split and my father remarried. We never really spoke again. He died in a car accident a few years later. My mom died of breast cancer not long after that. When Aaron died, though, that was the start of everything. Things had been fine up until then. After he died, things just fell apart. My family fell apart and now, here I am, alone. I'm the only one left. I'm the one who has to pick up the pieces. I'm the one who has to move on from a terrible loss, and because of that, people feel sorry for me. It's like no one recognizes me as a whole person anymore. I am nothing more than the tragic girl who lost it all, and everyone else just expects me to freak out or something. I'm the sad girl with the horrible past."

Her soft voice became angry as she stood and walked a few feet away from me, as if to emphasize the point. Her eyes seemed to glow, and her tear-stained cheeks reddened again. My hand felt colder without hers in it, and I glanced down at it as if it were a foreign object. I wanted her so much right now. To touch her, to take her pain away. The dull thud in my chest quickened slightly as I stood up and went to her. We were standing inches apart. Her warm breath warmed my skin, yet the cold thud continued. I've never noticed it so strong before. My hand raised up and swept a stray hair from her face. And then, I couldn't help myself; I bent and kissed her lightly on the lips, feeling a hunger awaken in me. She melted to my touch, but then suddenly, she pulled away.

"Will, I... " She hadn't moved from my embrace and was grasping handfuls of my shirt while she breathed deeply.

I feared that I had crossed the line. She was staring at my chest as I slid my hand down from her face and rested it on her shoulder. My breath was just as labored, as I struggled to figure out what to say. I didn't want to scare her off by kissing her again, but I needed her to know I cared.

My eyes searched hers to let her know that I didn't feel the same as the others. I did not pity her, and I would be here for her for as long as she needed me. She had to know the effect she had on me. I felt anchored when I was near her, but I had to wonder if maybe this was too much, too soon. It was time for me to let her go for the night, before anything else happened. Both thoughts terrified me. I pulled her close to me once more.

"You are not broken," I whispered softly against her cheek, as I kissed her gently one more time and then took off into the night.

Chapter 9
Celia

MATH. I ABSOLUTELY HATED AND despised math homework. I was sure that no amount of studying throughout my immortality would convince me to like it. No matter how many times I took it, I would never like all the busywork. I guess you could say that math was the one thing that made me restless and anxious.

It was late on a Friday evening, but I was bored. No one to go out with, nothing to do. I tapped my pencil absentmindedly on the notepad in front of me, when I heard a sound outside. Well, not a sound, but a series of crashing followed by some choice words. It was coming from the garden below. The noise escalated with the sound of glass breaking. I looked out the window and saw Will, standing in the middle of the garden path, a broken pot at his feet and plants strewn across the walkway.

I rushed down the stairs and out into the night, nearly running into my brother.

"What the hell are you doing? Father is going to kill you! Well if he could kill you, he would," I screamed, pointing to the carnage behind him. "He has been working on those roses for weeks!"

"Oh God, I really messed up today, Cee. I can't believe it. I was so stupid. Reckless!" Will turned around and walked back toward the garden, a wild look in his eyes, hands shoved in his pockets. I'm not sure which looked worse, the mess or Will.

I followed behind him, then sat on a bench when he began to nervously pace back and forth in front of me, the sound of gravel crunching under his feet. I waited for him to say something, but he kept on stomping past.

"What happened, Will?" I finally asked, not willing to wait for him to talk.

"I kissed her, Celia! I couldn't help myself. She was just so... I mean, she told me things. She made me feel, and I kissed her and it was everything, but then she pulled away like it was wrong and... I just... " his words faded, leaving me with more questions than answers. The anguish in his voice was incredible, and I reached out my hand to grab his.

"Will. Stop." He turned to face me, and he was trembling. "Why do you think this is so bad? I mean, I think it's great! So, you kissed her. You didn't hurt her. And you *felt* something." I didn't understand why Will was so upset. I thought this was what he wanted. He sat next to me on the cold, stone bench, anxiously running his hands through his hair and leaned forward, his elbows on his knees.

"It's no good. I still... I just don't think it was a good idea. What if it was too much, too soon? She pulled away, what if she didn't want to? What if she doesn't think of me like that?" He was still stumbling in his frustrated state. His eyes were blazing when he gazed up at me, but what I saw underneath wasn't anger, it was fear. He was as afraid as I had never seen him before.

"You're afraid, Will. Why are you afraid?" I squeezed his hand in mine. "Look at me, Will. This is a good thing."

"I'm not afraid." He yanked his hand from mine and went to the gazebo's edge, looking off at the lake in the distance. The silhouette of the pier and the lighthouse reached out from the beach like a slender finger. The rhythmic light blinked on and off, letting the ships know where the channel began. The evening was calm, and I could barely hear the sound of the waves crashing on the shore. Clouds blanketed the sky, leaving only a few stars to shine through. I joined him and looked up at the sky. He sighed loudly, and I couldn't help but think about him as a lost little boy.

"Will, you are good and you deserve this, whether or not you believe it. I've always thought that you deserved it. Why do you think I have had faith in you all these years? I mean, I know I've had my moments of doubt, but I really do believe in you." I bumped him with my arm, teasing him in a sisterly sort of way. "Come on. It's nice out, let's walk. It will relax you."

I grabbed his arm and dragged him out into the night and we began to meander through the maze of the garden, working our way down to the beach. The hoot of an owl broke the silence and it startled me a bit. Will was silent, so I left him to his thoughts, knowing that when he wanted to talk more, he would. Eventually, I could sense the tension begin to leave him, and finally, he spoke.

"You're right. I am afraid. I'm afraid that I assumed too much. That I pushed myself on her in that way. I'm afraid that I might have driven her off." He stopped and turned to look at me. "She told me about her family. Her brother's suicide, her parent's deaths. She thinks this makes her broken. She said that everyone in this damn town treats her with pity. They don't see *her*; they just see someone who has issues. I wanted so bad to fix her, just like she is fixing me, so I did the only thing I thought I could do. I kissed her. I wanted her to know that someone in this place cares about her more than anything."

"What makes you think that you scared her off? Did she push you away? She didn't run, did she? "

"I didn't give her a chance. I left before she could. In fact, I left before she could even say anything."

"Will, you did not scare her off, I'm sure of it. I've seen the two of you together. I've seen how she looks at you when you don't realize it. She definitely feels something for you, too." I smiled at him.

"Celia," his voice scolding, "have you been spying on me?"

I giggled cryptically.

"Not exactly spying. I just wanted to make sure that things were going okay. I care about you, and I want you to be happy. It isn't hard to hang around school during practice sometimes. You two are so preoccupied with each other that you don't even know that I'm there. But don't worry; I'll stop, if you want me to." I honestly didn't need to see to believe anymore. My brother had changed. He was feeling. There was no denying that now.

"So what do I do, Cee?" He stopped to face me, no sign of humor on his face.

My eyes were drawn to the lights of a solitary barge on the horizon, and I sighed loudly.

"I think you did what you were supposed to do, and you need to see her again. And you shouldn't wait until Monday. You don't want to seem like you're ignoring her after something like that happens. Talk to her about it if you're so worried. Personally, I think your concern is all in your head. You love her and she loves you. I know it," I said, placing my hand on his shoulder. "Just go to her. Tell her how you really feel. Have your happy ending, Will. You deserve it." I was happy for him, but I was also thankful for the darkness that hid my face. As happy as I was, I would be lying if I said it wasn't difficult to watch him find true happiness with someone after all this time. Living with what I had was okay, but finding someone to spend my life with would be even better. In truth, I was a little jealous that after all these years of screwing around like he had, he seemed able to find it so easily.

"Thanks, Cee," he said, wrapping his arm around my shoulder. "You're right, there isn't a need to panic yet. I guess I'll just go back in and try to get some rest. Maybe I can go see her in the morning. Thanks for helping me keep it in perspective."

He gave me a quick squeeze and then walked back toward

the house. There was a lightness in his step as he turned, and I watched him disappear in the dark. I stayed where I was, letting the cool breeze off the lake envelope me, refusing to let my own sadness take over. I thought back on my life and on my father, which is what I always did to feel better. It was the only way to keep my own humanity strong. My life could be worse. I would never give in to the dark urges. I did know how to control that. Even if I ended up alone, I would never let myself feel so low that I became like the others in Chicago.

The barge that had been in the distance was now close to the pier. I watched it move quietly up the channel until it was obscured by the dune, and I could no longer see the lights. My eyes pinched closed, and I shook my head, erasing any dark thoughts. I went back toward the house, stopping to smell the late blooming roses on the way.

Chapter 10
Julia

STUNNED, I WATCHED WILL SHOVE his hands into his pockets and hunch his shoulders in the chill, until the darkness swallowed him and he was gone. My hand involuntarily moved to my lips, which still tingled from his lingering kiss. A kiss that was ice cold, yet left my body on fire. It had scared me so much, I turned away. I tried to talk, tried to call out after him, but no sound came out, and I was left standing there in silence.

There were so many questions about tonight and his kiss only confused me more. I still didn't know how he had known where I was. Driving around the cemetery just didn't seem like a logical answer. I didn't think he had followed me, although one minute I was alone and the next, he was there. I think I would have been able to feel his presence if he had followed me. And sitting here, he was just so easy to talk to. I never talk about my family. This town knew enough of my secrets, yet I had just confessed more to him than I ever had to any stranger before. And then, when I thought I had surely driven him away after finally showing him how messed up I was, he kissed me. I couldn't figure him out. I didn't want to figure him out. No, I wanted to know everything. The thump in my chest told me one thing, though; I was falling for Will Bradley. There wasn't much about my past that hadn't been revealed. He now knew how people in this town treated me because of how much I had lost, and he didn't run. I mean not really. He listened. Then he kissed me and told me I wasn't broken.

My legs were shaky as I walked back inside and caught a view of the piano out of the corner of my eye. I sat down to play, just to try to calm myself down, the nerve endings on overdrive all the way down to the tips of my fingers. I found a quick melody, but my mind wasn't there and I kept messing it up, my hands fumbling around on the keys. I shook them out a little and began again, but my head was still swimming. It's not like I had been in real trouble when I was at the cemetery. Yet somehow, he had known I was there and he seemed to know that I was hurting. Maybe I had been lost. It was becoming clear that I had been wandering around, lost in my own mind until I met him. I mean, going to the cemetery to talk to my dead brother for an unknown amount of time was not necessarily unusual for someone who has suffered a loss, yet it definitely wasn't the behavior of a rational person. Who knows how long I would have stayed tonight if he hadn't come. I was thankful that he had been there. It seemed that he had been there for me a lot lately. And I felt so much better when he was around, that I looked forward to the time I would spend with him. My dark cloud was definitely lifting, and I felt more centered. There was something about him that made me start to *feel* again. His presence energized me and his touch made my body want to explode.

My fingers continued to fumble over the keys, creating a melody that resembled my shattered state of mind. It was no use. Even the piano wouldn't soothe me tonight. Eventually, I gave up and stopped, frustrated with myself for not being able to keep it together. The clock told me it was after midnight, and the sheer magnitude of my day suddenly made it impossible to keep my eyes open. The bed called to me, and I crawled in, still wearing my clothes as I pulled the comforter over my body. It didn't take long to fall into a deep and dreamless sleep.

SATURDAY MORNING WAS A BLESSING. I didn't have to be anywhere or do anything. I felt better after getting a great night's sleep. I rolled over and stretched and saw how late I had slept in. Suddenly, I remembered the events of last night, and my hand involuntarily moved to my lips again. Will had kissed me. He had held me and made me feel so much. I felt a longing inside of me that I had never felt and found myself wanting to see him today. Would it be weird if I just stopped over? What would Celia think? Maybe I could come up with some excuse to work together today. I'm sure there was something related to the play that we could deal with. What if his father was there? I laughed out loud at myself. There was no way I could go over there without looking like some crazy stalker. Besides, how would I handle that kiss? It didn't seem like I could just ignore it. Instead, it seemed as if we had crossed some important threshold, and there would be no turning back. Maybe he would bring it up first. Regardless, I couldn't deal with it today. *Calm yourself down*, I coaxed internally. I didn't want to sound desperate, did I? My crazy adolescent girl crush would just have to wait until Monday to see him. I would have to find other ways to occupy my time.

Book in hand, I went down to the kitchen to scrounge around for some breakfast and tea. I would simply spend the day lost in a good book. I added some water to the teapot and turned on the stove, only to be interrupted by a soft knock on the door. The perfect silhouette of Will Bradley was standing in my doorway. My heart paused briefly, and I waited for it to jumpstart before I answered the door.

"What are you doing here?" I hadn't intended it to come out so harsh. I was just surprised to see him so early. It had been late when he left my house. "I mean, hi," I recovered.

"Hi, uh... I need to talk to you. Do you have time? Are you busy right now?" He seemed a little on edge. Nervous. His hair had flopped onto his forehead, and I wanted to reach out and put it back in its place.

"Do you want to come in?" I offered, but becoming embarrassingly aware of my pajamas, I wrapped my robe tighter around my body and slid further behind the door leaving only my head looking out. I must look like a mess! I hadn't even showered yet!

He looked up at me nervously.

"Actually, maybe we could just talk out here."

"Um, sure. Can you give me just a minute?"

I shut the door before he could answer and turned to run down the hall to grab a coat or something that I could cover up a little more. The cami and shorts I had changed into sometime during the night was a bit too revealing. I walked calmly back to the door, avoiding the mirror. I didn't need the mirror to remind me of how disheveled I probably looked this morning. It was possible my hair was sticking up in crazy angles, considering the nature in which I went to sleep.

The door clicked behind me as I walked over to the swing and took a seat. Will was standing with his back to me, hands on the railing. I could see his muscles straining through his jacket.

"Okay, shoot." Nonchalant, that's how I would play it.

"About last night. Um, I was thinking," he started, pacing across the floor. "It's just that..." He broke off and dragged his fingers through his hair. Whatever he wanted to say to me, he was having a hard time saying it. I waited patiently.

"We've been spending a lot of time together and then there was last night." I looked down at my hands and blushed at the thought of the kiss. Suddenly he was in front of me, grabbing my hands. "I know that we just met, and this is so soon, but I think I have feelings for you, Julia."

My breath caught in my throat at his words. I tried to hide the redness of my cheeks and the accelerated beating of my heart. Could this really be happening?

"What do you mean feelings?"

He smiled at me, his silver grey eyes boring into my soul. If he hadn't been smiling, I would have been scared at his intensity. It captured me and as usual, I couldn't look away.

"I... I don't know. I'm sorry." He dropped my hands and stood up. "I guess this... I can just talk to you Monday." He started to leave, but I didn't want him to because, to be honest, I had feelings for him, too. I needed to say something this time. I needed to tell him how I felt, too.

"Wait," I called out standing up. "It's okay, you don't have to go." He turned back to me, his eyes still intense. I looked down blushing again. "Please stay." I looked up at him again and spoke with more confidence. "I don't want you to go."

Will walked back onto the porch and stood in front of me, leaving only a small space between us, waiting for me to speak again. The air was so electric, it made me stumble back a step. I reached for his hand to steady myself, and the current ran up my arm, making it even harder to concentrate. My other hand found his solid chest and he wrapped his hand around it. I looked at his lips, wanting him to kiss me again. My eyes wandered up his face until I was looking into his eyes again. He was waiting. Waiting for me to give him permission, not wanting to overstep some invisible boundary. Suddenly, I remembered my appearance and felt the urge to go clean myself up a bit. I stepped away for a minute and walked toward the door to collect my thoughts.

"I want you here. And we do need to talk, but can you give me a few minutes to get myself together and then maybe we could go somewhere?" I was still caught in his eyes.

"Sure, I would like that." There was that grin again, and he began to relax. The tea kettle began to whistle inside, pulling me out of my stupor. "I'll be right back. Just give me ten minutes. Don't leave," I warned as I scampered inside.

I ran inside, turned off the stove and quickly tried to put myself together. I didn't know where we should go, so I threw on jeans, a t-shirt, and a light jacket. My hopeless reflection stared back at me from the bathroom mirror. If only I had time for a shower, or at least a chance to put some make-up on. Throwing my hair in a quick ponytail, I ran back downstairs expecting to see Will still waiting for me on the porch, only to find it was empty. I caught a movement on the driveway out of the corner of my eye. Will was sitting on a sleek motorcycle. He patted the seat lightly behind him.

"Wanna ride?" His smile was dangerous *and* seductive.

"Isn't this a little dangerous?" I asked.

"You've never lived life a little dangerously? I thought I would show you how I normally travel."

"Well, I guess I could use a little danger in my life." I laughed nervously. This was very risky behavior for me. I was normally so practical and cautious, but the magnetic pull guiding me toward Will and his machine was too strong to resist.

I sidled up next to him near the bike.

"So where do you want to go?" He still hadn't kissed me yet, and it was all I could think about.

His eyes held a mischievous look, as he grinned from ear

to ear.

"Let's just get out of here. It's a nice day." He could sense my hesitation. "It's okay. I have a good driving record." He flashed the boyish grin I was growing to love and helped me climb on behind him. He grabbed my arms and pulled them around his waist. I didn't fight, liking the feel of holding him.

"Hold on. I won't let anything happen to you." I gripped my arms tighter around his waist and hugged my body to his. He was cold but his body was rock solid and any fear I had melted away.

We raced down the street in a rush. I leaned into him, gripping tightly and breathing in his scent deeply. He gave no indication of where we were going and at this moment, I didn't care. Right now, I just wanted to be with him, loving the feel of my arms around his body.

The wind tore through my hair, and I clasped my hands tighter in front of him, as he sped his way down the winding road. He turned down Lakeshore Drive, and I instantly recognized that we were heading toward the lake. Our pace slowed as the road twisted through the sand dunes. It had not taken us long, and I was a little saddened to see that the ride was over as we pulled into a small parking lot. Will reached around, lifting me off of the bike and steadied me on my feet. My knees felt like gelatin from the ride. Or maybe it was from being with him.

"I hope this is okay. I thought it might be nice out here. We could just sit or we could walk." He smiled and I became dizzy until he looked away.

The beach was deserted. A light breeze was blowing, and I listened to the waves crashing on the shore as we walked toward the lake. The steady rumble of the waves had mesmerized me since childhood. The rhythm of the water was its own sort of music that I found comforting. This place had become a refuge for me after Aaron died. It was almost as if Will knew I loved coming here.

"It's perfect. I love this place." Will reached for my hand, and we began to walk in the sand, his thumb caressing small circles on the back of my hand. Dark, thick clouds warned of a building storm.

Over the last week, Will and I had been alone many times, but never like this. There was always something there to occupy us, like the students at rehearsal or the console of the car between us. This felt awkward. We were completely alone. There were no interruptions, no distractions. And there was more electricity in the air. I wasn't sure if it was from being with him or because of the imminent storm.

"So," he stopped and looked at me. Did he want me to talk first? I bit my lip nervously, and Will withdrew his hand and put it in his pocket before clearing his throat.

"I want to apologize for last night. I'm not sure what you think of me, but that was very out of character for me. I don't just go around kissing people I hardly know. " He looked away again at the waves. "Then again, I'd do it again if I had the chance."

A nervous laugh escaped my lips.

"It's okay," I assured. "Actually, as long as we are being honest, I'm sorry I pulled away. I just wasn't sure I was ready for all of this." I looked up and smiled shyly at him. His face was soft as he looked back at me. "It's not every day that a girl like me is kissed by a guy like you." I thought I saw his face falter a moment, but his smile was back making me wonder if I had imagined it.

Now we both watched the waves lap the shoreline. The sound was spellbinding. My foot began to make little circles in the sand, and I anticipated what would happen next.

"Do you want to sit a minute?"

"Sure." If I didn't sit soon, I was afraid my legs would collapse. The sand cushioned us as we positioned ourselves side by side, gazing out over the water. We both looked out at the lake. I hugged my knees to my body. A storm was definitely approaching. The air that had been warm, now contained a chill.

"Julia, I have to say something to you." I angled my face toward him, resting it on my knee as he continued. "I came by last night to tell you this, and I know I already said something earlier, but it didn't come out right. I don't think I can explain it well, but I like being with you. I mean, I enjoy working with you and all the time we've spent together this week." His brow crinkled for a minute and he groaned in frustration. "No, that's not what I mean. Enjoy is not the right word. That makes this sound so frivolous."

I looked at him and waited patiently, a little thrill going through me as he said my name.

"I adore every moment I spend with you. I look forward to

it. I count down the minutes until I will see you again. I love it." Will's face twisted, pained for a moment. He reached out and grabbed my hand, cradling it between his own. It was ice cold, probably from nerves, yet I could feel the tingling start again. "It's so soon, and we hardly know each other, but I feel like you know me better than anyone and I... " He hesitated again, and I simply gave him the room and the time to speak. "I think I'm falling in love with you."

I hoped that there was no shock registering across my face. *Falling in love? With me?* This was all a dream. Just a fantasy. Who would love me? Yet as I looked into his grey eyes, I felt all of my own emotions come to the surface. Everything that I hadn't felt in years, all came to a head, and despite all of my reservations, I knew at that moment that I loved him back.

"I think... I think I'm falling in love with you, too," I stammered back. His whole face lit up as he turned his body toward me, placing his face just inches from mine.

"You do?" Will's voice came out as barely a whisper. His eyes were magnetic, pulling me in. I leaned forward toward him, and put my hand on his shoulder, wanting so much to touch his face. I waited for him to kiss me, but he didn't. Instead, a pained looked crossed his face.

He looked away, stood up abruptly and brushed the sand off his jeans.

"Oh God, Jules," he said, and I savored the sound of my nickname. "There are things you don't know about me. Things that might make you want to stay away. You aren't the only one with secrets."

I didn't know if he was waiting for a reaction from me or not, so I just waited for him to say more.

"I haven't always been a nice guy. I've done things that I'm not proud of. I have a dark past." He shoved his hands in his pockets and looked away. I watched him for a moment. He clenched his jaw and stared out intently at the lake. There was a darkness cascading off him that I hadn't seen before, and he seemed to be struggling to push it back in. I had my own darkness and secrets, so I could only imagine what he could be hiding.

Moving to stand in front of him, I stood on my tiptoes so that I could be as close to eye level with him as I could. I tried to stare into him to unravel the mystery, but all I could see was sadness and worry in his eyes. I needed to convince him that I would be here for him. He hadn't run from me, and I would not run from him. This I could promise.

"We all have our secrets, Will. It's part of who we are. Nobody is perfect. Love makes people want to stay. We can figure things out. Together. We can help each other fight our demons. Lord knows you're already helping me get past mine." He wouldn't meet my eyes. Instead, he was looking just past my shoulder.

I touched my hand to his cheek and pulled his face closer to mine, urging him to look at me. "Will, look at me."

I traced his jaw bone with my fingertips, feeling the roughness of his stubble and then ran my finger over his mouth. His lips parted slightly inviting me in for a kiss and for a moment, there was only the two of us in the world. I leaned in, our foreheads touching, and closed my eyes until our mouths met, just as the first raindrop fell. The sensation was unbelievable. Last night, his kiss had been tentative and questioning. Today there was a want, a primal hunger coursing through his lips. His hand reached up to my face, sending an electric charge through my skin, as if I was being burned. I ran my hands over his back and through his hair, wanting to stay this way forever. Our tongues and lips tangled and became one.

Finally, Will pulled away tentatively and looked up as the rain began to come down in big drops. When he turned back to me, there was a fire flashing in his eyes, and I knew that the only thing that made him pull away was the weather. A flash of lightening over the lake and thunder that followed emphasized that point, and since we came on the motorcycle and not the car, it was going to be a wet ride home.

"I think I'd better take you home." His voice was a raspy whisper, and he was breathing hard. Hell, we both were.

All I could do was nod, as any words stayed stuck in my throat.

We ran to the bike, and within a few minutes, we were on our way. The rain was assaulting, and I buried my face into his back, my hands gripping him tightly. I closed my eyes and my house loomed ahead soon enough. We ran up to the front porch, my hand in his, and he pulled me into an embrace once we were out of the rain, his face snuggling into my neck.

"We need to get you inside, you are soaking wet!" he cried

out with laughter.

"I'm okay," I started, but my teeth were chattering. I didn't want to leave his arms.

"No, you're not. Now go inside and put some dry clothes on!"

"What about you, you're just as wet!" I didn't want him to leave, but I didn't want him to be cold either.

"I'll be okay. I'm not as wet since you were blocking most of the rain from hitting me," he said smiling. "Just bring me out a few towels and I'll be fine."

The initial chill brought in with the rain was gone and the air had warmed a bit with the now steady rainfall.

Reluctantly, I went in the house to change. Once inside, I ran upstairs, struggling to get out of my wet clothes and into clean, dry sweats. I toweled my hair a little, grabbed another towel and a couple of blankets, and rushed back to the door.

I opened the door slowly to try to make it look like I wasn't hurrying when in reality, I couldn't wait to be with him again.

"Here," I said, crossing the porch to hand him the towel and a blanket. He was standing and waiting for me, leaning against the porch railing. I started to wrap a towel around his shoulders but Will grabbed my wrists and pulled me in for a kiss.

"You need to dry off. You're going to get me all wet again," I joked, pulling away smiling. His hair was wet and the rain was dripping off of his chiseled features. He had taken his wet jacket off, and the black t-shirt he wore clung to his muscled chest. My breath caught in the back of my throat. He was irresistible. Insecurity rose in me again as he toweled off his hair. I turned to sit on the swing, drawing my legs up under me, and wrapping the blanket around me. Will wrapped the other blanket around himself.

"Can I sit with you?" His boyish grin always took my breath away.

"Sure." He sat closer than I had expected. The space between us again became electric.

"Are you okay? Are you warm enough?" I must have had a shocked look on my face. I had to admit that I was still in awe of him.

"Oh, I'm fine." I shivered a little, but not because I was cold.

"Come here." Again his voice was dark and seductive. He opened his arms and pulled me in, throwing my legs over his own so that I was practically sitting on his lap. I laid my head on his chest, and as usual, felt a sense of calm come over me.

"So where do we go from here? What are we now?" I had been afraid to ask the question for fear that I wouldn't like the answer. He pulled away a little and I could feel him stiffen.

"I was serious when I said there are things you don't know about me, Julia. I'm not sure if you'll feel the same way. I never want to hurt you." He caught me off guard and I could feel my defenses rise again.

"I told you I loved you, too. Doesn't that mean anything? Whatever happened in the past doesn't matter to me. I'd like to forget about my own past and start over."

"Well, I didn't know what you would think." I could feel the warmth spreading through my cheeks again. I looked up at him longingly.

"We do have lots of time to get to know each other." I could see him thinking. Or was he deciding.

"True." He tipped my chin up toward his face and kissed me lightly on the cheek, the nose, and finally my lips. My skin felt cool where his lips had been. I don't know if I would ever get used to that feeling. It was delicious, and I could feel it all the way into my toes.

We sat in silence, rocking back and forth on the swing, my head on his chest, his hand running along my back. A phone vibrated and Will tensed. He looked at the caller ID and frowned. I could feel his mood change instantly.

"I think I had better go. I didn't mean to monopolize your entire day. You may have other plans and I didn't even check."

I could sense his hesitation. Hesitation to leave or hesitation to stay?

"Are you sure? You don't have to go. Maybe we could get some dinner later?" I questioned.

"No." His voice sounded resolute. "I mean, I want nothing more than to take you to dinner or something, but I do have to go. I have some things to take care of."

He swung my legs down and hopped off the swing. I immediately felt his absence.

"I'll call you later, I promise," he said, as he loped off in the rain and back to his bike. Just when I felt I had started to unravel the mystery of Will Bradley, he would elude me again.

I shrugged it off, went back inside to warm up, and decided I needed to call Kara. I had left my cell phone here, and by the looks of it, she had been trying to reach me for quite a while. Besides, this is not something I could keep from my best friend or I would never hear the end of it!

The phone rang loudly before I even had a chance to dial her number.

"Hello?"

"Where have you been all morning?" she accused on the other end.

"I've been out. Am I not allowed to go out?" I teased. I wasn't sure how much I wanted to tell her now that I was hearing her voice. I felt that this was too new for me to just broadcast it to the world. I could tell her that I kissed him, maybe, but not that he said he loved me. "I forgot my phone. Sorry. Did you need something?" I said.

"Well, I just wanted to see if you wanted to catch a movie today or something, but now I really want to know what you were up to. Were you alone or was a certain stranger with you?" Kara wasn't asking, she already knew.

"What does it matter?" I didn't want to lie to her, but I couldn't hide the smile in my voice.

"I knew it. You have to tell me everything!" The excitement in her voice was infectious, and I couldn't help but feel like a school girl dishing out gossip.

"Well, he came over this morning and we took a drive out to the lake to go for a walk. But then the storm came, so we came back. No big thing. I think we are going to get dinner tonight or something." I tried to sound nonchalant, but didn't think she was buying my blasé attitude. She was silent on the other end for a moment. I could almost hear the gears working as she tried to figure out my new secret.

"Well, I don't believe that's all that happened. I think there is way more to this story that you're not telling me." I stayed silent on my end, wanting to make her sweat a bit.

"Fine, be that way," she said suddenly. "I *will* find out one way or another what really happened. But for now, I've got to run. I'm hoping to bump into that cute guy on the bike path again. This conversation isn't over, though." Of course, her own boy problems would be the *only* reason why she would stop pestering me about mine.

"Okay, I'll see you later," I said innocently.

"You know I will get it out of you. You won't be able to hide it for too long. Bye."

The phone clicked and she was gone. I smiled to myself at Kara's silliness. I shouldn't be so hard on her; she was just being my friend, as she always had. And we hadn't had a reason to gossip about *my* love life in years. I'm sure she was simply excited for something that might finally improve my social life. She did know me better than anyone.

My book was still sitting on the counter next to the now-cold tea pot on the stove. Right where I had abandoned them both when Will had come over. Feeling good, I started the tea pot again, and prepared to settle down with my book until Will called.

He was still such an enigma to me. One minute he was baring his soul, and the next minute he was warning me of his past. Maybe I was just scared and reading too much into it. No one had ever paid any attention to me like this and the feeling was so new. Still, I couldn't believe that he wanted to be with me. It felt like I was waiting for him to just disappear; waiting for him to ride off into the sunset on his two wheeled horse, after he realizes that he rescued the wrong princess. But a few hours later, Will showed up on my doorstep with flowers, ready to take me to dinner.

Chapter 11
Will

I DISAPPEARED INTO THE DARKNESS again, but this time my heart was lighter. I never knew that life could be like this. We had gone out to dinner and spent hours just talking, wanting to know everything about each other; favorite color, favorite food, favorite song. Afterward, we stood on the porch and I kissed her tenderly, leaving before she could say anything, giving only a quick glance and a little wave as I reached the sidewalk. I was afraid of staying and screwing up again, and she was so wonderful. I needed to leave.

Once I was out of her line of sight, I jogged back home. This was getting to be very difficult. I was torn between my need to be with her and the need to still keep her safe from my other self... from what I really was. The weight in my chest was returning again, as I put distance between us. It was so easy to forget who I was when we were together. She just made me feel so... human. Maybe it wasn't that I forgot, maybe I really didn't know anymore. It was, perhaps, the most dangerous, reckless thing I had ever done. In truth, I was a little scared of what I was doing. What kind of danger had I put her in? Would she be suspicious of my cool lips? Closing my eyes, I pictured her innocent face and her green eyes. I took in her image until my vision fogged, and the ache became all consuming.

I crept silently into the house, hoping I wouldn't run into Celia again. Fortunately, the house was empty, allowing me to make it to my room uninterrupted.

My cell phone was flashing. I was sure it was Chris. He had been calling me for days now, but I didn't want to talk to him. It only complicated things. Suddenly, I was very tired, the events of the entire day having drained me.

This morning, I had risen early, while the house was still shrouded in darkness. Sleep had been elusive as I tossed and turned most of the night. I remembered kissing Julia and felt the ache again, I had needed to see her. I had needed to gage her reaction and waited as long as I could before knocking on her door. She was everything I had remembered as she stood in her pajamas at the door and within minutes, she was tucked in tight behind me on my motorcycle, as we drove to the beach.

My thoughts were a whirlwind, as I again tried to tell her about me and about what I really was, but I just wasn't ready. I hadn't wanted to leave her after returning from the beach, but I was afraid. I was afraid of these new human emotions that were awakening in me. They were strong, and I didn't want to scare her. There was still something so fragile and vulnerable about

Julia. I knew that she didn't fully trust me yet, and honestly, she shouldn't. There were things I hadn't told her about myself. I didn't know how she would react when I *did* tell her. I wanted her to not be afraid, to say that what or who I was didn't really matter.

And now, here I was trying to figure out what to do with these new pieces of my life. I peered around the curtain toward her house. I could barely see the light of her porch glowing faintly through the trees; a beacon for my heart.

"HOW WAS YOUR DATE WITH Julia?" The early morning light seeped through my window as Celia barged into my room with her questions. So much for sleeping in.

"Fine," I mumbled, rolling over and burying my face in the pillow. I didn't really want to talk to her right now. I wanted to be alone with my thoughts.

"Did you tell her? How did it go?"

"Mmm," I replied.

"Come on, Will. Spill."

I sighed loudly, turning back to her. She wasn't going to let me sleep. This much was evident.

"Celia, I just couldn't do it. Okay? I don't want to scare her off. It's just too soon." It was hard to hide my ire. Being woken up early and pestered about my love life made me agitated. I tried to calm myself before continuing. "I'm sorry, Celia, I don't really want to talk right now. I'm feeling kind of off. Please understand. We can talk later."

I tried to make my tone sound as normal as possible, but

it was a struggle. Her eyes glared into mine, trying to find answers. I couldn't hold her stare for long before I turned my attention back in the direction of the light I had seen in the distance last night. Fortunately, this seemed to be the sign she needed to understand that I was serious about wanting space.

"Oh alright, I guess I will just leave you alone." She turned to walk out the door, but stopped to look over her shoulder briefly. "For now."

The door clicked softly behind her, and my thoughts began to wander to Julia again. I didn't think I was going to be able to see her today because she had some things to do. I didn't want to come across as too overbearing. Instead, I had to wander around and occupy my time.

It was still warm late in the afternoon, so I found myself driving back to the beach. It was strangely calm on the lake, and I was easily able to walk out to the end of the pier. Once I was surrounded by water on three sides, I could feel the tension leave. This wasn't going to be as hard as I thought. I was doing it. I had fallen in love and was changing, and while these new emotion were new and confusing, I knew this is what I wanted. My father and sister had been right. Julia was all that I needed now.

I would need to take one more trip to Chicago, to get my things. I would need to tell Chris I was moving back here. Back home. Break all ties. I could get a real job and maybe even go to college. I could be with Julia. I wouldn't allow myself to think beyond that, but it was enough hope to get me through.

The sun began to fall from the cloudless sky. It met the

lake in a flash of brilliant color and soon it was growing dark. Content for the first time in what felt like years, I turned to go, happy with my decision, happy with the new direction my life was taking.

The house was quiet again when I returned. My sister and father both off doing their own thing. I found it odd at first, but then realized that maybe they both were giving me the space I wanted. I paced back and forth in the living room, anxious once more. I took in the pictures and artifacts scattered throughout the room and actually found them comforting. I grabbed a glass paperweight from the table and rolled it around in my hand. The petals of a brilliant purple zinnia were preserved inside. Paperweights had been a favorite of my mother. She collected them for their beauty and simplicity. I set the zinnia down and picked up another one. The glass was cold and smooth. I rolled it over in my hand just like I had the other one and felt closer to my mother than I had in many years.

No matter how I tried to distract myself, my eyes continued to settle out the window in the direction of the farmhouse down the street. Again, there was a light on, signaling that Julia would be home. Should I casually stop by to see her? My heart leapt at the thought, when the grandfather clock chimed the hour, reminding me just how late it was. It didn't matter. I needed to see her. I felt that right now, it was essential to my existence. With one last glance toward the light, I made my decision and rushed out the door.

The streetlamps hummed and flickered, leaving gray

shadows on the street. I slowed as I neared her house because I could hear her music. I stayed hidden behind the tree, peering carefully through the window; I saw her sitting as she played a song. Suddenly, she stopped, and a look of pain shot across her face. Then, just as quickly, it was gone, and a new melody was coming from her slender fingers. At this moment, I needed her more than anything in the world. Even more than the blood I needed to survive. I couldn't take my eyes away from the scene before me, completely pulled into the melody coming from the instrument beneath her. It was haunting. Her body swayed with the tune, waves of auburn hair swirling about her shoulders. Her music seemed to find its way into me, filling the holes. I wanted nothing more than to make my presence known, to sweep her up and carry her away.

I knocked lightly on the door and listened, as her footsteps treaded toward me.

"Hey." Julia smiled brightly. "Is everything okay?"

"Not really. I'm sorry, I should have called. I just wanted to see you." I hesitated.

"That's okay, please come in," I stepped into her house, and she stepped into my arms.

"I heard you playing and... I missed you today," I whispered into her ear as I buried my face into her hair. "Will you play for me?"

She turned her face toward mine, her lips parted and then we were kissing. She tasted so good and I melted into her. We both pulled away, a bit breathless.

"Of course," she said against my lips. I kissed the tip of her nose and smiled. "Come on."

Julia smiled back and grabbed my hand, leading me over to the piano; her eyes never leaving mine. She slide down onto the bench gracefully and began to play. I stood behind her, my hands resting on her shoulders, and the music she played became a part of my soul, making me feel whole.

DAYTIME WAS BECOMING HARDER AND harder, since I couldn't be with her. She was at school all day and it wasn't exactly somewhere I could be with her discreetly. I tried reading but couldn't concentrate. Walking down to the beach was a daily distraction and was becoming increasingly boring. I even tried my hand gardening with my father, but nothing could leave me feeling truly content, other than being with her. Finally, I could wait no longer, so I decided to head over to the school early.

She was still in her classroom sitting at her desk. There were very few students left in the building; it was easy to show up unnoticed. I stood at her doorway watching the way she gripped the pen she was holding in one hand, while biting the cap. Her other hand was running though her hair, twisting it in concentration.

"Knock, knock." I tapped the door lightly, trying not to startle her, but she still jumped as she looked up. "I wish my English teacher had looked that hot while grading papers," I joked.

"Oh, hi." Her face broke into a smile. "I didn't expect you

for another hour."

"I couldn't stay away any longer." I bent over slightly and kissed the top of her head. She looked anxiously at the door and I realized that I may have been a little too forward. "I'm sorry, I guess I shouldn't do that at school."

"No, it's okay but maybe we should keep this kind of quiet here."

"I guess you're right." I moved away from her and sat on the edge of the desk so that I could look at her.

"I just have to finish correcting this paper and then we can head to the auditorium if you want." She tapped her red pen against the paper in front of her.

"Take your time." I nodded and looked around her room giving her time to work. I glanced through the titles on her shelves. Mostly weathered, dog-eared classics like *Frankenstein*, *Great Expectations*, and *Pride and Prejudice*. I sat in a desk near the back of the room and pretended to thumb through a book so I could watch her. She had an intense look of concentration and was still biting her pen cap. Her body was entirely still while she read. And again, I thought she was absolutely beautiful. How could it be that she wanted to be with me? Her melody began to play in my head, and I began to think about all that has happened to me in the last month. The monster from Chicago seemed so far away. A month ago, I never would have guessed that I would be able to sit so near someone like this, with thoughts other than those of death. She had completely changed me.

"Ready?" she had finished sometime during my daydream

and was standing up ready to go.

"Ready when you are."

I grabbed her bag from her so that I could keep my hands occupied, and we began to walk toward the auditorium.

"How was your day?" I casually asked. My free hand was itching to grab hers, but I wanted to be respectful of her wishes. I switched her bag to my other shoulder and jammed my other hand into my pocket.

"It was long. The kids had an essay due in Senior English and most of them didn't turn it in. I get to hear all of their excuses, while they beg me to accept it late. It makes for a tiring day. I mean, I really don't understand why they can't just do it!" Her outrage flushed her cheeks and her eyes flashed momentarily with anger. It made me want to laugh and protect her all at once.

"I'm sorry. Hopefully, rehearsal will go well tonight."

She smiled back at me, the corners of her mouth slightly upturned.

"Yeah, maybe."

"YOU KNOW WHAT? LET'S TAKE a 20 minute break."

Rehearsal was not going well. Julia and I had been working with Rosalind and Orlando for over half an hour on a pivotal scene, and they just weren't getting it. The kids slowly began to file out of the auditorium, grumbling under their breath.

"Why is this so hard today?" Julia questioned rhetorically, sinking her face into her hands. I placed my hand on her back in an effort to calm her, happy for the chance to touch her.

"I don't know." I didn't have a lot of experience with this sort of thing. I didn't know how to answer her. We sat in silence, not knowing what to say. Finally, Julia jumped up and took a seat at the piano. She started to play and then stopped suddenly and turned to me, her cheeks flushed.

"I'm sorry," she apologized, "I just need to play for a minute. It centers me and then I feel like I can think straight." Of course, I already knew this about her and would never turn down the chance to hear her play.

She began again, and I sat back and let her music consume me. It was a melancholy tune, perhaps Chopin. I joined her at the piano and leaned on it, remembering the first time we were in this same auditorium and she caught me listening to her play. How odd it was that she had become comfortable with me so quickly.

I knew the music conveyed how she was feeling, which made me want to help so badly. What could I do to turn this rehearsal around? The students didn't seem like they were really capturing the love between Rosalind and Orlando.

"Maybe I could talk to them." I started, as she began to fade out. "Show them some lines. Perhaps we could act out the scene together to give them a better idea."

Her hands paused above the keys, and she cocked her head to the side in thought.

"I suppose we could try. I'm not sure any of them has actually seen it being performed before, so I guess it might help." There was hesitation in her voice, but I wasn't sure if it was because she didn't want to act out a scene, or that she didn't want to act out a scene with *me*.

"Yes, I think we should show them how. Let's run through it first, just to make sure we have it down before they come back."

She stood up and came to the middle of the stage.

"Ready?" I asked.

She nodded and took a place across from me.

"*Fair youth, I would I could make thee believe I love.*" I began, delivering the lines of this poignant scene between Orlando and Rosalind in disguise.

"*Me believe it?*" Her voice rang against the walls. "*You may as soon make her that you love believe it; which, I warrant, she is apter to do than to confess she does. That is one of the points in which women still give the lie to their consciences. But, in good sooth, are you he that hangs the verses on the trees wherein Rosalind is so admired?*" Julia delivered the lines perfectly, as if she really were Rosalind.

"*I swear to thee, youth, by the white hand of Rosalind, I am that he, that unfortunate he.*"

"*But are you so much in love as your rhymes speak?*" Her voice was barely above a whisper, and she had moved close to me. I could feel the heat radiating from her body.

"*Neither rhyme nor reason can express how much.*" I answered softly. I reached out and tucked a loose strand of hair behind her ear. It wasn't Orlando speaking those words, it was me. I did love her. More than anything. I knew that I had to tell her who I was. A love like this could hold no secrets. She needed to know what I was if she was ever to love me back, like this. It pained me because I knew that she would run. She wouldn't want to be with someone like me. Someone who had killed for the sport, someone who, up until recently, barely cared if they were alive or dead. She didn't want to love someone like me. She deserved someone much stronger than me. I couldn't give her what she needed. Yet the selfish part of me was not willing to let someone else have her. I wanted to be the person who could give her what she needs.

The sound of the students returning to the auditorium broke the mood. They slowed and eyed us cautiously when they saw us standing so close together on the stage . Perhaps they could sense the tension, the love, the fear.

Julia snapped out of it first.

"Okay, we had an idea that I think will help you. Will and I are going to act out this scene, to give you an idea of what it looks like. Remember, this is just an interpretation. I just think that you should show more emotion. Orlando is saying these things to Ganymede as if she's Rosalind. And Rosalind, in disguise, is more freely able to express herself." She turned to me. "Ready?"

Yes, in disguise, you could express yourself more freely. Wasn't that what I was doing? Hiding behind the guise of a normal human man when really, there was a dark past stalking me? Julia's nudge pulled me out of my inner nightmare and reminded me that we had a task.

I could only see the students out of the corner of my eye

as we went through this scene, only looking at our scripts when necessary. We flowed together, and again, I could feel the love.

After that, practice went by much quicker. We sat in relative silence next to each other, but I could feel the tension between our bodies. At one point, I touched my finger to the back of her hand, lightly caressing it only to have her jump from the sensation. From then on, I kept my hands to myself.

Finally, we were alone, walking out together. I grabbed her hand, and she let my fingers curl around it. My awareness of her touch was unlike anything I could remember and no matter how many times I did it, it always felt like the first time. Tiny volts of electricity ran up and down my arm and warmth slowly moved through my body. As much as I had been waiting my whole life for this, I couldn't help but feel how foreign and strange this all was. My fledgling feelings were so intense.

The car ride home was quiet. I never felt like I had to fill the silence when I was with her. I was just content to be. She started humming a tune, and I pictured her playing it.

"Julia?" I began, feeling the need to confess as the darkness swirled around me.

"Hmmm," she replied lightly, a smile playing across her lips as she continued to hum. Shadows played across her face, while the streetlights gave her a sort of glow. It was like she had an aura around her. And she looked happy. Happier than I had seen her since I had met her. The smile had finally reached her eyes, and they were sparkling. I couldn't do this to her now. Not here in this dark car. I couldn't admit my secrets in a place where she would be terrified. I wanted her to see me in the light, where I hoped she wouldn't run in fear. Not to mention the fact that I was selfish. I was thrilled that I seemed to be the reason for this happiness, and I wanted to surround myself with it.

"I think rehearsal turned out ok," I replied back, my confidence fading. No, I would not tell her like this. Maybe I could hint to her and she would figure it out for herself. No, that was cowardly. It needed to come from me.

We pulled into her driveway, and I walked her to the door. She wrapped her arms around me and I could feel her warmth invade my body again. Her lips found mine and I responded back. I could hold her like this forever.

"You're always so cold; you really should wear a coat." Her observation alarmed me. Maybe she already had her suspicions.

"I'm okay. I don't like to wear coats." I chuckled into her hair trying to keep the mood light. "I suppose I should get home."

"You could stay for a while tonight if you want to. I'm not ready to let you go," she looked at me sheepishly. The hole in my chest ached for her.

"Ok. But, not too long. I don't want to have to explain things to my father and Celia." I laughed a little to lighten the mood.

I followed her in the door and stood awkwardly, as she hung up her coat and walked into the kitchen to check her answering machine. Such everyday mundane things, yet I could see the anxiety growing in her. Neither one of us knew what the next step would be when we were alone like this.

"Um, do you want to watch a movie or something?" She bit her lip in such an adorable way, I had to grasp the countertop to physically restrain myself from sweeping her in my arms, kissing her, and carrying her off to bed.

"Sure." I turned away and pretended to straighten a stack of papers on the kitchen counter.

"Anything in particular you feel like?"

"It doesn't matter to me." As long as I'm with you, I thought.

"I hope you don't mind, but my only DVD player is in my bedroom."

I couldn't help but laugh.

"Are you worried I'll take advantage of you if we're in there?"

"No, of course not," she tried to cover. "It's more like I thought you would be thinking that I was coming on to you." She laughed nervously, too, but it was enough to help break the awkward tension between us.

"Lead the way, I promise I'll behave," I said, reaching for her hand.

We walked in silence but with hands still locked. Her warmth began to radiate through me.

Her bedroom was not what I had pictured. Instead of taking the largest bedroom, it looked like she was still in the bedroom she had as a child. I looked at the closed doors hiding the memories behind them and decided not to ask. Her room was sage green with a modest desk in one corner and a TV on the dresser. There were a few pictures, in which she looked rather young. A few band posters were scattered on the walls. Between them were shelves housing trophies and ribbons from various music competitions. Bedside tables flanked the mission style oak bed in the center of the room. A ragged quilt that looked to be homemade was thrown messily on. The room was a mix of old and new, almost as if she couldn't decide what she wanted to remember and what she wanted to forget. A representation of her life before everything changed and what her life was like now.

She quickly straightened out the quilt and threw some pillows toward the headboard before settling on the bed, remotes in hand.

"If you don't really have an opinion on what you want to watch, I was in the middle of watching something and was thinking that we could just finish it." She looked at me anxiously and sat on the edge of the bed.

"Sure." I kicked my shoes off and climbed on the bed to sit next to her. She settled into the crook of my arm and pulled a blanket over us. The movie began to play but I barely paid attention. It was some period film, but I was so distracted by her being in my arms, I didn't care. I began to stroke her silky hair and instantly felt my ache subside. I kissed the top of her head, and she turned in my arms, her green eyes piercing into mine. She tilted her head toward me closing her eyes. Our lips met, ever so softly, and a flash of emotion followed. God, I loved this girl. I loved this girl so much, my life would never be the same.

She sighed as we separated and laid her head back on my

chest. I could feel her warmth and her heartbeat, which brought me back into the present, where I remembered how different we really were. I couldn't help but wonder if she noticed my lack of a regular heartbeat. By now, my body was warm from having her in my arms, and I reveled in the warmth.

We sat like this until the movie ended. I waited for her to get up and turn the player off, but she only snuggled further on my chest. The even sound of her breathing told me that she was asleep. Maybe I could just stay here all night, holding her. No, I knew that my father would worry if I didn't show up at home.

I slowly moved out from under her, careful not to wake her, and slid her under the covers. My hand moved to caress her cheek and I kissed her lightly.

"I love you." I whispered quietly and then slipped out into the night.

A FEW NIGHTS LATER, CELIA was waiting on the porch when I came home. She had a glass of blood waiting for me. Funny, I hadn't been thirsty until I saw it in her hand. I counted backward in my mind and realized that it had been over a week since I had anything. I hardly noticed anymore. I didn't want blood with Julia next to me. Our pattern rarely altered, and basically involved being with each other as much as we could. I frequently came to school early, just to be with her. We ran rehearsal and went back to her house afterward. Sometimes she played for me. Sometimes we talked. Sometimes, I just held her, running my hands through her soft hair. I wanted more. I wanted to know all of her. To caress her bare skin. To make her feel as beautiful and she was. She wasn't the kind of girl to jump into bed with someone right away, so I knew I had to be patient. For now, I would have to be content holding her and kissing her madly.

"Here," Celia said as she handed me the drink. "You've been a little pale, and I thought you could use it. You can't forget that you still need this to survive." She followed me like a shadow, waiting for something.

"Yeah, thanks." Thanks for reminding me what I was.

"You didn't tell her yet, did you?"

"No. But I almost told her tonight."

"You say that every night," she reminded.

"Well, this time it's true," I replied, pushing my way past her and into the house.

"What's stopping you?" she asked, following me inside. "I mean, you have changed. I can see it. Your eyes are brighter every day. And we talked about this. She deserves to know. Will, you know that I love the new you and that I support you completely, but I don't think the change will be complete until you open up about who you are."

I stopped when I reached the kitchen and stood there with my back to her. She was right. I felt different every day. It was easier to forget who I was. But holding this glass in my hand was a stark reminder. Its sweet, metallic smell wafted through my nostrils and stung my throat. The desire for more was always there. In fact, I needed it to survive. My frozen body could only go so long without it before I would wither away, and I would become a shell. Neither dead nor alive. Immortality had its price.

"I don't want to hurt her," I quietly replied. "I don't want to scare her."

"You love her, don't you?"

"Yes," I answered without hesitation setting the half empty glass down and pushing it away.

"Then you have to tell her. It's not fair." She hesitated. "Just tell her what you are and leave out the Chicago part. You don't have to tell her how things used to be."

"Of course I do! I can't hide who I was from her. What if I'm still that same person? What if I slip back? I just want more time to process all of this." I paused a minute to let my anger subside slightly. "I'm different now and she must know. She must know what she has done to me."

"Then what are you waiting for, Will? What are you afraid of?" Celia lifted her hand to touch my arm.

My hands grasped the corner of the countertop, my fingers digging into the wood underneath.

"I don't want her to see through me. I don't want her to run." My eyes pinched closed and I shook my head. "You know what, Cee? I can't do this right now." I grabbed my keys from the table and ran out the door before Celia could stop me. Within seconds I was on my bike, racing through the sleeping town as fast as I dared.

I was angry with the world. I was angry with Celia for reminding me of this disease, but most of all, I was angry with myself, for being this way to begin with.

I didn't know where I was heading, but I drove around all night. I was well aware that I was running from everything, but I also needed to be alone. Finally, I found myself driving up the winding road in the sand dunes. I skid to a halt at one of the lookouts, letting the gravel and dust settle around me. By now, the sun was rising, splashing brilliant pinks and oranges across the sky. I peered off in the other direction at the waves of the lake. I knew what I had to do, but it was going to be difficult. I had to tell her and the sooner the better. Maybe she wouldn't run, but maybe she would. I didn't want to think about that or the pain that it would cause. I'd come too far to crawl into that hole again. Yet, I couldn't guarantee that wouldn't happen. Watching how peaceful the waves were lapping on the shore, I could almost believe that things would work out and that she wouldn't run from me; that she would actually understand.

I knew my sister was right, but I hadn't wanted to admit it. I needed to do this soon, before we became anymore invested. Before *she* became more invested. Before watching her go would break me into pieces.

I jumped back on my bike and headed back to her house, anxious to get it over with. I had to find her and do this now, before I lost my nerve. Her driveway loomed ahead, but I could tell immediately that she wasn't there. I could drive around for hours looking for her but I already knew where she would be this early in the morning. The tires ate up the road in front of me, as I headed to the place beneath the red maple in the cemetery, the place I had found her before.

Chapter 12
Julia

THE AIR WAS CRISP WITH a slight chill, although the sky was beginning to wake up to the east. I breathed deeply and started on my morning jog. My thoughts were swirling already with visions of Will. I had fallen hopelessly in love with him. Of this I was positive. I hadn't felt like this ever, and I couldn't believe it. I felt lighter for the first time in years. I wasn't sure when he slipped out last night, but while I do know that my bed felt empty waking up without him in it every morning, falling asleep in his arms was a delicious feeling I would never tire of.

Despite my euphoria today, there was still a small part in the back of my brain that didn't feel right. Perhaps it was my own mind not allowing myself to be truly happy. I desperately missed my brother at times like this and maybe this was a form of sabotage.

I tried my best to push it out of my head and concentrate

on the pounding of my feet on the pavement. My hand found the volume and turned my iPod up louder, needing to drown out my thoughts. There were very few leaves left on the trees and it was clear that winter would be here soon. I passed house after house, eating up the ground beneath me until it was clear where I was going. So much for an easy jog.

The huge gates of the cemetery loomed ahead, and I pushed myself faster to reach them. They creaked under my touch as I opened them and slipped in. I crept quietly so as not to disturb the silence of the morning.

I meandered through the paths to the corner where my brother lay. I could see someone through the dawn already near there. How strange to encounter someone else here so early in the morning. The person was standing a little ways off from Aaron's grave. I slowed, not wanting to intrude on someone else's private time and watched as the person bent down and looked as if they were brushing off a stone. He stood abruptly and shoved his hands in his pockets, shoulders hunching over either in the morning chill or in sadness. As I walked closer, the silhouette became familiar to me. The way the broad shoulders filled out the leather jacket and short, dark hair hung just past eyes that I knew were a shade of gray. It was someone I knew well. Will. I smiled and began to walk faster again. He must have known that I would be here this morning and thought he would meet me.

"Hi," I greeted warmly, as I grabbed his hand and kissed his cheek. He wrapped his arms loosely around me, making me shiver beneath his touch. I quickly attributed it to the coolness in the morning air and not to the coolness of his touch. "What are you doing here? I mean, not that I'm not happy to see you, but it's really early and it *is* a cemetery."

The sun rose higher, sending rays of light through the trees, like fingers reaching and stretching toward me. Somewhere in the distance, a bird called out softly.

He shifted away from me and slid his hands down my arms to grasp my hands lightly. Glancing sideways, he began to lead me away but stopped underneath the naked maple tree that was near.

"Jules, I need to talk to you." His face was somber and full of longing. His eyes were dark and stormy today. I didn't understand. Whatever was bothering him, was something all encompassing.

"I'm listening." I walked over to Aaron's grave, staring down at the letters carved in the granite, trying to hide the uneasy look that I knew was on my face.

"There's something I need to tell you." His voice faltered as he hesitated and his silence swallowed me whole, waiting for him to continue. "I'm not who you think I am."

I bent down to trace the cold letters of my brother's name and breathed a small sigh of relief. No one is who they think they are. Was this the big secret he had been keeping from me? I thought we had already been over this. I mean, it's not like I didn't have my own secrets.

"Will, none of us are who we think we are. It's what other people see that's important." I tried to keep my tone even, to hide the hint of amusement in my voice.

"Yes, but…" he hesitated. "I'm not like you."

I stood up and took a step toward him, but the look on his face stopped me from going any further. He stared at me intently, his gaze no longer somber but hard and steadfast, eyes turning a dark charcoal. Then he didn't seem to be looking at me so much as through me, as though this whole conversation was one giant inconvenience. I looked away, hurt by this sudden change. The cynical part of me that had been warning me all along was now celebrating. I looked away toward the trees so that I could respond without looking at him.

"Of course you aren't, we are all different but that's okay. What is this about anyway? " I swallowed hard, my confidence beginning to slide like sand in a sieve. Slow but deliberate. I knew where this was going now and like the sand, it would only be a matter of time before I was empty.

"That's not what I mean." His eyes changed again, swimming with confusion as he looked back at me.

"What *do* you mean then?" I hugged my arms around me, careful not to look at him again.

He began to pace quietly near the graves he had been by before and then stopped suddenly. He kept glancing toward the ground nervously, as if the words he was trying to find were lost in the grass.

"I've done some things in my life that I'm not proud of," he offered tentatively. "I have hurt people."

I sucked in my breath quickly and held it until my lungs

burned, trying to put my mind around what Will had just admitted. Part of me didn't believe it or didn't want to believe it, but the apprehensive side knew that all along. Finally, I exhaled loudly and placed my hands on my hips cautiously.

"You've... hurt... people? I don't understand." I stepped back from him, not sure what to do anymore. The part of me that had felt undecided was now screaming at me. A stick crackled beneath my foot, and I jumped slightly at the unexpected sound.

"I guess... well... I hung out with some people in Chicago that kind of got into some trouble." His eyes wandered to a spot just over my shoulder, and I couldn't help but look to see if someone was over there. There was nothing but the trees and a few leaves blowing around.

"But it's not who I am anymore," he continued. "I didn't know how to control... I mean, I didn't know what I was doing. You have to believe that I am not that same person. You have made me a better person." His voice was pleading with me now, as he turned his gaze to me, the intensity in his eyes pulled me toward him and made me want to turn away, all at the same time.

I didn't know how to respond, so I just stood there listening to the leaves rustling and the quiet sounds of the small creatures in the trees around me. I felt paralyzed as I tried to put it all together in my mind. Chicago. There had been some problems in Chicago lately. No, not problems. There had been *killings* in Chicago lately. He couldn't be. There was no way that he was involved, yet he said that he had hurt people.

"Chicago," I heard my lips whisper. "Those killings... " My

voice trailed off, hoping to God that I was wrong. I couldn't get the rest out but the look on his face told me my suspicions were right.

He put his hands in his pockets and glanced nervously toward the spot over my shoulder that he kept staring at.

"I had to. Or at least I thought I had to. I thought it was part of what I am." His voice was barely audible, but there was a hardness to it. Something dark and distant that didn't feel right. "I'm not *human*." He said it forcefully and then looked straight at me, his eyes now flaring. "I'm immortal."

The world was suddenly still. As if time itself had stopped. The cool breeze that had been blowing through the trees seemed to stop at once, and the chatter of the woods ceased.

"Immortal. What do you mean? Like a vampire?" My mind stumbled over the fantastical word, spitting out images of comic book-like characters, creatures of the night, bats, blood, and things not real. "I don't... vampires don't exist." Or at least I didn't think they did.

"I'm not a vampire, although I do need blood to survive. I'm an immortal. My family... there was an accident... it's an illness... a curse."

The way he said it sent chills down my spine, causing me to look around nervously.

"This is crazy. I don't believe you." But even as I said it, I knew that it was true. Slowly backing up from him, I saw what he had been staring at over my shoulder and his dark eyes filled with pain. Sometime in the stillness, he had moved back toward it. He followed my glance down to the words on the grave at his feet. He began to slowly walk toward me reaching his hand out.

"Julia... love... please. I love you. I want to be a better person. You make me want to... live. I'm not that *thing* anymore, but I needed you to know the truth. I just want to love you. Please, let me love you," he pleaded.

The wind picked up again as if on cue and swirled around me. The sound of leaves on stone turned my attention back to the ones near our feet that Will had kept looking at. With fists clenched at my side, I began to walk slowly toward them. Within a few feet, I was able to clearly read the closest aged stone. Surrounded by green moss were the words, *William Edmund Bradley* 1889-1910. I didn't need to read the others. I already knew they would contain the names of his father, mother, and Celia. The accident, the rumors, they were true. And they were about him.

"No... no," I mumbled, shaking my head. This couldn't be happening. He reached a hand out and started toward me.

"Jules?"

"Don't... just stay away!" I was practically shouting at him, but he continued to walk slowly toward me. I opened my mouth to scream but nothing came out. What he said was true. He wasn't human, He was something else. I didn't stop to think. There was only one thing left to do. Run.

"Jules... please... wait. It's not like that... please let me explain! "

His voice was fading behind me. I never looked back, I

just kept on running. I must be dreaming. This is not happening to me. I knew he was too good to be true. Maybe that is why he wanted me. He didn't love me, he was just waiting for the time to come when he would kill me. He said he had killed before, and I would just be another casualty.

And so I ran. I ran away from the cemetery, away from the man who said he loved me, away from my brother, dead and rotting in the ground. When I burst into the house, I shut and locked the door behind me. Finally, my knees gave out and I slid to the floor in tears.

CHAPTER 13
WILL

I WATCHED HER RUN AWAY, frightened of me, and I suddenly felt very cold. I looked down at the gravestone at my feet and cursed silently. I thought she would understand. I had hoped she would stay, because I thought she was different. Hell, I thought *I* was different. A deep anger and hatred began to course through me until finally, a sadness like I had never known settled in. The void in my chest was back and the empty ache that it brought. I wished Celia were here. She would be able to tell me what to do next. Should I go after her? Try to explain? Or would it just make it worse? If only I knew what to do, which direction to turn.

I don't know how long I stood there staring in the direction she had gone before I finally retreated. The trees were a blur as I raced home, and I knew what I would do. There was only one place to go now, and I would be gone before they even knew it. I had tried and failed, therefore I wasn't going to live their stupid life any longer. Anger swelled beneath my skin again, as I thought back over the events of the last few weeks. I was happier than I even knew was possible and yet, when trying to tell the truth, I ended up alone. Despite everything that I had done and everything that Celia had told me, I was alone. Celia and my father were wrong. I was a monster. Nothing would change that now. The hunger began to course through my veins as the bloodlust I had been able to ignore began to scream at me. It was clear that no one or nothing could save me.

On my way out the door, I made one last call.

The house was empty when I got there, and it didn't take me long to grab my things. I hadn't brought much with me and there was little that I cared to keep. At the last minute, I stopped only long enough to leave a short note to Celia, telling her I was leaving and not to come after me. I didn't give her any details; I didn't want to face her after what had just happened. I was sure this would be the last time I would come here. It would be too painful.

On my way out the door, I made one last call.

"Chris," I said when he picked up. "I'm on my way back, finally leaving this shithole. I'll be home in a few short hours. Just let me know where to meet you. I need to go out."

Within minutes, I was racing on my bike out of town, back to Chicago. Back to the place where I knew I belonged.

CHAPTER 14
JULIA

THE TRAIL NARROWED AS I ran over the hardened surface. I leapt over stones and pushed the brush out of my way. Suddenly, I felt as if I wasn't alone. I ran faster. I could see the end but it never seemed to get any closer. I could feel the chill as someone came up on my heels. Darkness started to surround me and pull me down. My legs and arms were heavy as I tried to crawl my way forward.

The alarm sounded beeping loudly and I sat up, shaking. It had only been a dream. I thought my heart would pound right through my chest. My feet shuffled across the floor as I went into the bathroom. The chill of water splashing on my face was enough to bring me back.

I stared at the face in the mirror. The girl staring back at me had dark circles under her eyes. She looked so sad. But I wasn't sad, I argued back at myself. There was nothing to be sad about. I was scared, or at least I *should* be scared. I should be terrified. And I should feel lucky to be alive. Kara had tried to cheer me up, but I rationalized that I didn't need cheering up. I wasn't sad. It's not like I could talk about it with anyone. All I told her was that things hadn't been working with Will and he had to go back to wherever it was he came from. It was never serious anyway, and I knew he would leave eventually, I had lied. There was no real way to come right out and tell my best friend that my boyfriend and I really broke up because he was some dark, immortal creature. A creature that lusted for blood and killed for sport. A vampire as far as I was concerned. And, oh yeah, so is his sister. It was up to me to figure this one out.

I tried to research immortality but only found the old vampire folklore, which I didn't believe. Will didn't fit any of this. So I was left with nothing but emptiness and the feeling that I had jumped to conclusions too soon. If only I could find something that proved him wrong or made me understand.

It had been almost a full week since Will told me what he was. As much as I wanted to forget, he scared me. Or maybe the truth scared me because I couldn't fully shake the feelings I had for him. Did I love him? I said I did, but did the truth change that? If I really loved him, should the truth matter? Yes, if you were trying to hide what you were. And no, because you were still you when you were with the person you loved.

He said that I changed him. That I made him want to be a better man. He said he wasn't the same person he used to be. Wasn't I the same? Hadn't he changed me? I just didn't know what to think anymore.

After calling in sick to work for three days, I finally decided that I should go to school. Truth be told, I was also afraid of seeing Celia. Yes, I did know what she was, but I also didn't want to talk to her about Will. Now, she seemed just as terrifying. When I finally went back to class, she didn't show up. In fact, she hadn't been there all week either. I had to cancel play practice and with Will disappearing, it wasn't hard to convince my boss that we needed to take a week off.

Fortunately, today was Saturday and I could just avoid school all together, but I couldn't avoid the jumbled thoughts going through my head. Cup of tea in hand, I found myself staring out the window toward the old Victorian at the end of the road. Snow was beginning to fall lightly, its fluff just beginning to stick to the trees and grass. It looked so peaceful. Suddenly, despite my earlier run, I was itching to run again. I could always think better when I was running. Within minutes, I changed into my running clothes and took off.

The pavement pounded under my feet, creating a rhythm to match my heartbeat. A light snow lay on the sidewalk but wasn't enough to be slippery. I ran hard, trying to get him out of my head. The harder I ran, the more thoughts of him entered into my mind. His ash colored eyes looked at me. His arms embraced me. His lips kissed me. I could feel him. I could taste him and my heart ached.

I ran until I could run no more. There was nowhere else I could go to escape. He was all around me. He was even haunting my runs now! Tears streamed down my face, blurring my vision and I ran harder. The air pumped through my lungs and my feet found their own way. Before I knew it, I was standing in front of Aaron's grave. I could barely see his name engraved as the tears clouded my vision. I sank to my knees, ignoring the wet snow seeping through my running pants, my entire body throbbing. I thought I would feel relief breaking it off with Will, but right now I felt the opposite. I should be more scared, I had been telling myself all week. Yet all I felt was cold and alone. Empty. Numb.

"Oh, Aaron, what should I do?" I spoke to the gravestone through my tears. "If I am doing the right thing, why do I feel so dead inside? I just don't think I should be in love with someone like Will. I *shouldn't* love him." The tears were flowing freely now. "I wish you were here," I whispered. Time was irrelevant when I was sitting at his grave. I could stay for minutes or hours and never know how long it had been. *Get up*, a voice said. *It will be okay. You will be okay.* I anxiously looked around, but saw nobody. *Get up and go. It will be okay*, the voice repeated. A voice that sounded strangely like my brother, and I realized that it was coming from inside of me. A wave of peace, comfort, and understanding overcame me, and I suddenly felt better. My head was still clouded but slowly clearing. My feet seemed to listen, and I got up and began to walk home, puzzled.

The snow was still falling in a soundless cascade. It was wet and thick and left branches weighted down. My feet shuffled through the thickening blanket as I tried to rationalize with myself the entire way home. I never really did give Will a chance to explain. If he had been given the chance to talk, there could have been some sort of explanation. Maybe I had jumped to conclusions. Maybe I was the one who was wrong. Could I forgive him? Was I really considering this possibility? Reconciling the monster I thought he was with the person I knew, was the hardest part. By the time I got home, I had almost convinced myself that he wasn't different from me at all.

I found myself standing on my porch in a daze watching the snow fall harder now. So much snow had accumulated that the tips of the grass were no longer visible. The entire yard was being covered in a white blanket. I needed to get inside. But I couldn't move. My body was rooted in place. This porch now reminded me of him. I remembered the way his touch felt as we sat out here. Closing my eyes, it was almost as if he was here. And, there was the way he kissed me. A lump began to rise in my throat and tears began to well up again. No, No, No! I must get that image out of my head. I tapped my temples with my fingertips. Get out of my head! This had to stop. With reservation and regret, I forced myself to go inside. I needed to do something to get my mind off of him. The tears stopped and the awful knot in my throat began to subside. The pictures hanging in the empty halls reminded me that I had been through worse. Losing my family had made me strong. My resolve was strong and I vowed to not let it get to me.

There were lots of things to keep me occupied, but as night crept in, my mood began to change again, as the dark feelings of loss began to consume. I wasn't okay. In fact, the reprieve from my emotions that I had felt earlier was all too brief.

As usual, the piano beckoned. I didn't want to play tonight. There hadn't been any music in me all week. Just a sadness within. Still, the pull was magnetic and there was no denying it tonight. Lightly, I placed my fingers on the keys and let the song find me. It started slow and built to fast and angry. When I finished that song, I started another. I couldn't stop. The music just kept on flowing through my soul. All of the emotions I felt kept surfacing on the keys of the piano. Scenes of Will and me together flashed through my mind. I saw what used to be, I saw what could be, and I saw what I would become if I wasn't with him. When I finally did stop, my face was soaked with tears, I was out of breath, and I could feel the light sheen of sweat on the back of my neck. I stood up, shaking. The images scared me. *He* should have frightened me, but he didn't. The truth was when I was with him, I wasn't frightened at all. What terrified me more than anything, was the thought of never being with him again. Of never finding that kind of love again and living alone. He had changed me too. He had made me feel things I hadn't known were possible and my decision finally became crystal clear. I knew what I needed to do. Pushing him out of my mind wasn't working. And neither was spending my life talking to a headstone. I needed to talk to someone who knew. Someone who could help me. I needed to find and talk to Celia.

I HAD NEVER BEEN TO Will's house, but I knew the way to the old Victorian at the end of the drive. I ran until the house was in view and then when I slowed my stride so as not to appear too anxious. I hoped she was home. The stairs of the porch creaked when I walked up to the door. My hand was poised to knock when the door suddenly opened. Celia was standing in the doorway a somber look on her face.

"Hello, Jul~, Miss Cavallo," her voice was cool and controlled. Her sharp features were beautiful. How had I never noticed how different she looked from the others? How had I never noticed that there was something distinct about her, as well?

"H-h-hello, Celia," I stammered. "Can I talk with you?"

"Sure, won't you come in?" She stepped aside, warmly opening the door wider for me.

My hesitation was brief, but I had made my choice. If I wanted to be with Will, I needed to accept what he and his family were. I stepped inside and looked around. The foyer opened up into a large great room which was full of what looked like impeccable antiques. Celia took me to an exquisite leather sofa and motioned for me to sit. She sat calmly across from me, her eyes still cautious, and I could tell she was waiting for me to speak.

"You haven't been at school," I started.

"No. I thought it was best to stay away. To give you some space." She shrugged and looked at her hands.

"I understand. I mean, I know what you and Will are. He told me everything." I stood up and began pacing around nervously. I couldn't look at her when I talked about this and not because of who she was but because she reminded me of him at times. Her face softened a bit when she saw that I wasn't going to run off screaming. Not this time. I was facing this head on, and so I continued. "You see, the thing is, Celia, I freaked out when he told me. I was scared and I panicked. I ran. I didn't want to listen to him explain. I didn't want to hear the truth. But, I can't stop thinking about him, and I realized that it doesn't matter to me. I don't care what he is or thinks he is, because I believe in him. I believe in the person he has become. The person I fell in love with. He makes me happy, and for the first time in years, I can *feel* again." I turned to look at her, my heart bleeding and exposed.

I was embarrassed to be rambling to her like this. After all, she was still my student and here I was pouring my heart out to her about her brother. A bubble of air caught in my throat and I could feel the tears stinging my eyes as I fought to control them from rolling down my face. My hands clenched together in my lap, and I could no longer meet her eyes.

"He left," she said softly. "He didn't tell us where he was going, he just took off and left. He hasn't called and he won't answer his cell phone. He left me this note."

She handed me a folded up piece of paper from her pocket. The words *I'm sorry. I guess I am not as good as you thought. Don't come find me,* were scrawled messily across it. I flipped the note over to see if there was anything else.

"He didn't say where he was going," she repeated. "I can only guess that he went back to Chicago... to those he has been living with for years."

"You mean he has family somewhere else?"

"Yes and no. I mean, there are a few others like us that he

lives with in Chicago. They live very differently from the way we do here. You see there was a little bit of trouble with them. That's why Will came back here for a while. He needed to distance himself from the trouble, and my father hoped that he would choose to stay this time. I can only guess back to Chicago is where he went."

"Trouble. He did mention something about that. I didn't believe him at first but... " I was unable to finish my sentence. My head ached with confusion. I know that he had told me about it, but part of me still didn't want to believe it.

"He killed someone," Celia said, standing up and walking toward me. "Well, maybe many 'someones' over the years, in the stupid quest for more blood. I don't really know all the details. That group is responsible for the strange deaths in Chicago. I don't agree with what they do. And I don't think most of it is Will. I have always gotten the impression that he just follows along. "

I sucked in my breath. Will had hinted at that, but it was different actually hearing Celia say it. I rubbed my brow trying to make sense of this affirmation from her. The tick-tock of the grandfather clock in the corner acted as a metronome for my mind, slowly counting the seconds as they passed by.

"I'm sorry," Celia said quietly. "I'm sorry that he got mixed up with you. I think it's partly my fault. I thought he had changed... or was changing. I thought that he was discovering what was really important. Things like family and love." She slumped next to me on the sofa and suddenly looked much older.

I suppose she was. An old soul stuck inside a 16 year old body. I suddenly felt the need to comfort her, as she looked to be hurting as much as I was.

"Well, I didn't know him before," I said, tenderly putting my arm around her shoulders in a sisterly fashion, "but I knew how he was with me and I thought he was happy. He was kind and understanding. He was there when I really needed him. And, I *love* him." I choked a little on the last few words. I hadn't admitted that yet. Not even to myself. That despite everything, I still loved him. But, it was true. Just saying it out loud felt right.

Celia's eyes opened wide, and I could hear her breath catch. She turned to me and smiled.

"You do? Even knowing what you know, you still . . . *love* him?"

I stopped for a moment and thought. Did I still love him? I knew that I did. I knew that he had helped kill someone or maybe many. Was he really a killer or just someone trying to survive? I felt that there had to be more to the story. There was still so much that I didn't know, so many questions that I needed answered. Perhaps Celia was just the person to answer them.

"I do. So much that it hurts, but I have so many questions, so much that I don't understand. I mean, you are so different from... me." I breathed the air deeply and closed my eyes. When I opened them, she was looking at me quizzically. "Maybe you should tell me everything."

CHAPTER 15
CELIA

"SO, HE TOLD YOU WHAT we are, but he didn't tell you about his life or about the disease and how we got it?"

"I don't think I gave him a chance. Once he said what he was, I mean, what you all are, I jumped to my own conclusions and ran. I never let him explain. I just kept picturing images of Stoker's *Dracula* and the blood and everything. It's taken me a few days to make sense of it all. I guess I just had to process things..." Her voice trailed off and she was nervously wringing her hands, a habit I had begun to notice. Her gaze took her out the window, her thoughts turning somewhere else.

"We aren't all like that, you know. Monsters, I mean. Some of us choose not to give in. That whole Dracula myth is a fallacy. And we aren't vampires, by the way. Just strangely immortal." She eyed me wearily and bit her lip. "I suppose I should start at the beginning. You have to know who we were and how we became what we are. Is that okay?"

Julia hesitated only slightly before nodding her head.

"Yes. I think, no, I *know* I need to know it all." She sat up straighter now, and I knew she was preparing. Bracing herself to hear the whole truth.

"Well, let's see," I continued. "It all started in 1905. We were living here in this very same house. My mother, father, brother, and I. We owned the fox farm that this neighborhood was built on. Business was good. The farm thrived, selling fox pelts. My family was happy and comfortable. We had more than enough money to live off of. Our family, especially my father, was highly respected in town. Things were going well until one fateful evening. My family and I were traveling by train from Chicago after spending the weekend there. The train was attacked. Not by robbers. But by the diseased. They took no gold or jewelry; instead they bit and drank the blood of several of us. It was a massacre, but they made it look like a horrid train accident. Some of the bodies were taken from the train, and were never found, their identities erased from ever being on the train. The passenger log tampered with. Others were burned when they set the train on fire to hide the evidence. My family was presumed dead.

"Those of us that survived woke up feeling slightly under the weather. It was damp and we were in some dark place. At least at first. Within days, our symptoms progressed to sweating, fever, and finally, coughing up blood.

"Coughing up blood? Do you mean like Tuberculosis?" Julia interjected.

"Well, yes and no. Tuberculosis... or Consumption, is what it was commonly called to explain the deaths. No one really realizes that some survive and become a frozen shell of themselves. There is no blood left in our system, so we need to ingest blood to survive. Without the blood, we can't regulate our body temperature and our organs don't function. Everything has hardened except our heart, which beats very slow. We are basically immortal, unable to be harmed by injury or disease. That is not something easily explained by the medical field. I guess they just started calling it 'consumption' because it consumes the whole body."

"But, isn't TB an airborne illness?"

"That is what they want you to think. True, many people in closed in areas would get sick. That's how attacks occur. The entire group will attack, leaving several people dead or sick. The ones who become sick either die or become like their attacker. It depends on how their body reacts."

"So there is no cure." Julia's voice was barely a whisper.

"No. There is no medical cure. At least not yet. My father has been trying to find a cure for years but to no avail. He's convinced that since there is a chemical reaction within the body, there must be a way to reverse it," I answered. I could see the hope drain from her face and all that was left was the sadness. I hadn't noticed it before, but she had also changed since meeting Will. And now, I could see her face return to the same sadness that existed just a few short weeks ago. I felt the compassion in me rise and wanted to give her a hug, to comfort her, but I didn't think she was ready.

"Oh." Her brow furrowed in thought. "Is there more? I mean more about Will?"

"Yes. My entire family became sick. Days later, my mother died. Her body didn't survive the change."

"Your mother was affected, too?" she interrupted. "I thought she died alone of cancer or something after losing her entire family. Or is that simply the rumor that has been floating around for years?"

"No, she didn't survive the exposure, and I'm sure that after all these years, people have speculated about what happened," I answered and then continued with my story. "After a week, the fever broke and my father, brother, and I regained consciousness. We had survived the change, but it wasn't long before we realized that we weren't fine. We faked our deaths so as not to draw attention to ourselves. People were suspicious... we disappeared for a while, and then came back to bury my mother. There were questions that we didn't want to answer.

"There used to be a barn on the property. We burned it and made it look like all three of us were caught inside. No one questioned the fact that our bodies were never found in the mess. We disappeared and the farm was passed on to a 'relative.' The taxes were still paid and that was all the city cared about. My mother is buried in the cemetery right next to three empty graves."

"I know. I saw."

I looked at her in surprise.

"You saw them? But you didn't know?" I was puzzled that she hadn't said this before. I figured that would have been a giveaway for someone as observant as she was.

"That's how I figured it out. Will started to tell me, and I looked down. He was standing near a headstone. A headstone that bore his name; all of your names. It was then that I realized he was telling me the truth. That's when I ran." She looked exhausted, leaning back against the sofa and sighing deeply. "You happen to be buried near my brother."

"Are you okay? Are you hungry or thirsty? I think I should stop and let you rest a minute." I hadn't noticed the dark circles that had settled under her eyes. It was almost as if my explanation was beginning to take its toll on her. This was a lot for one person to take in at one time.

"No, I'm fine. Just please tell me more."

Her eyes pleaded with me and her desperation came through. I had no choice but to continue.

"We had to move away for several years. Too many people knew who we were in this town. We've been able to come back only once before this but in disguise, so to speak. This is the first time I've been able to actually enroll in school and try to be normal. My ever-cautious father finally thought it would be safe for us here." I got up and walked to the window. My confessions to her were dredging up all sorts of memories of my own past. Some of them I didn't mind, but some of them I would rather forget. Suddenly, I felt very old.

"And what about Will? What did he do? I mean, did he

come back here with you?" Julia's questions brought me out of my memories.

I paused and folded my arms in front of me. This was one of the memories that I didn't necessarily like to recall. Thinking about our early years was painful.

"Will stayed with us for a few years. It was a struggle, learning how to adjust to our new life. My father, always the intellect, locked himself away in his study, trying to find a cure once he realized that we had been diseased. My brother and I were left fending for ourselves. I fought the urges and found that I was content with stolen blood from the blood bank. Will, on the other hand, was not. He would disappear for days at a time. He discovered the thrill of live human blood. And, he was always restless, edgy, like he had to be doing something constantly. It wasn't long before I noticed that he was different. There was something missing. Eventually, my father and I discovered that by not totally giving in to our urges, we were able to hold onto some part of our humanity. Our souls weren't lost. I found hope in that discovery, but Will found nothing. Perhaps he was already too far gone.

"Finally, my father figured out what he had been doing. They had a huge argument, and my father threw him out. He had been trying so hard to keep us together and Will had done nothing but make a mockery of it. He had become a monster. Someone who took pleasure in other people's pain and torment."

"Do you have to... drink it?" she asked. "Does it have to be fresh?"

"Yes unfortunately. It absorbs into our organs better. The veins are too hardened for it to actually flow through, so giving ourselves a blood transfusion doesn't really work. As for it being fresh, just like with food, fresh is always better, but we can survive just the same on blood bank donations. And we don't have to take all of their blood and kill them. That's where the group in Chicago has got it wrong."

She seemed to think about this for a minute, perhaps reconciling her previous ideas with what I was telling her. I gave her the time and space she needed, choosing not to speak again until she asked for more.

"So how did he happen to find the others in Chicago? How long has he been living there? Is your father still mad at him?" Julia questions came quick and resolute. It was an indication that she really did care... something that made me smile.

"Sorry," she continued, realizing how much she had asked. "I suppose I should let you answer one at a time."

"Well, the big fight between Will and my father was about 70 years ago. I begged and pleaded for Will to stay, but he wouldn't listen. I had already been feeling him slip away and I feared that if he left, I would lose him for good, and I had already lost so much. It was selfish, really. I cared more about being alone than I did for my brother's soul.

"He disappeared one night and I didn't hear from him for a long time. Finally, one day I received a letter addressed only to me. There was no return address, but it was postmarked Chicago.

It was from Will. He told me all about a group he had found there, and how they had taken him in. They weren't like my father and me, and instead preferred to kill others, feasting on fresh blood, taking advantage of the desperate and downtrodden. He begged me to come join him, telling me that this lifestyle was who we really were. He said he would come find me soon and then I could come. But, I didn't want to. As lonely as I was, I had come to terms with who I was and knew what I had to do for myself to survive. I had found my little niche with my father, even if we were moving around often. And I still held onto what little hope my father had given me for a cure."

"Did he ever come back for you?" Julia asked.

"Yes, about a month later, he came to find me. He snuck in to avoid my father. I told him that as much as I didn't want him to leave again, I didn't want to go, either. We argued for a bit, and then my father walked in. I expected my father to throw him out again, but he was hoping that Will had changed his mind. His reasons for coming were soon evident, and I could see how disappointed it made my father, especially since Will seemed to care even less about life than before. Finally he ordered Will out for good. I knew that I would never see Will again, so I begged and pleaded with my father to please let him come back once in a while. He and my father came to an understanding. Will could live in Chicago and do what he wanted, but he could still come home to visit occasionally. He just had to live by my father's rules when here. If enough time passed, my father would ask him to come home for a few days, saying that he just wanted to visit with us, or some other excuse. Really, it was to make sure that he hadn't totally lost his soul. I'm sure now that he did it for me."

Julia seemed to consider all that I had said, although I hadn't really told her about all of the bad stuff that Will had done, at least not in any detail. I figured she needed to know as much about this disease first, in order to understand why Will chose the life he chose.

It was starting to grow dark outside, the evening light creating shadows, and I squinted to try to see the lake in the distance. Julia stood up and paced back and forth quietly before walking over to the grand piano in the corner.

"Do you play?" she asked quietly, running her hands lightly over the keys.

"Not really. I took some lessons as a girl but I'm not very good. It was my mother who played for us. My father keeps it around more for sentimental reasons."

"Do you mind if I play?" she asked. "Music helps me process things."

I nodded. The ancient bench sighed with age as she sat. She placed her fingers over the keys and closed her eyes. A melody emerged, something I recognized. "Moonlight Sonata?" I couldn't quite remember. She nodded an affirmation. I could hear the pain and emotion in her playing, and I knew instantly why my brother was drawn to her. I didn't know how anyone couldn't be drawn to her.

"So this group in Chicago isn't exactly good, are they?"

Her voice rang above the quiet sounds of her playing.

"No, they aren't. They hurt people. They take too much. They are reckless in their actions. Sometimes, they *kill* people." I tried to gage her reaction but I could only make out the concentration etched in her brow as she continued to play. "Will isn't as bad as everyone else. There is still a shred of his humanity left, right?"

I nodded and she stopped playing. I could tell by the confusion on her face that she didn't completely understand how it worked. I told her about my father's theory regarding our souls and how I believed that Will hadn't totally lost his. I told her about the light in his eyes and that I believed it was because of her.

"I thought I was broken when I met Will," she continued to play. The notes sang beneath her fingertips, almost as a sort of soundtrack to my story. "I thought that no one could love me because... because of... I don't know. I just didn't think it was possible. Everyone in this town thinks they know me, but they don't. Still, I just can't bring myself to leave. This is my home. I have felt so empty inside for years. Except when I play. It was the only way I felt alive. Until I met Will."

"You know he loves you, don't you? He fell in love with you because of who you are. He told me once that when you played, it was angelic. It made him feel for the first time in many years. I think it's what brought him back to life... brought him back to me... to us. It was you who saved him. Or, maybe you saved each other." I stood next to the piano and placed my hands on top, feeling the vibration through my fingertips.

"And now, I've turned him away." Her voice was a whisper and her hands slid off the piano keys. "I didn't know and he tried to tell me. I didn't know. I thought he was something... someone else." I watched as a tear slid down her cheek and landed on the ivory and I was torn apart all over again.

"I think I should find him." Julia looked up suddenly and said. "I need to apologize and tell him how I feel."

Relief flooded through me. She was right. She needed to find him. And I wanted my brother back.

"I am fairly certain I know where he is. We can leave for Chicago in the morning. I don't think he will run off. Besides, you need to rest." She looked relieved and exhausted at the same time. Like a weight had been lifted from her.

I grabbed her arm and pulled her to her feet and into the kitchen. There wasn't much more than blood in the refrigerator so I gave her some water and ordered a pizza.

After I got some food into her, I coaxed her to go upstairs to lie down and get some sleep. I needed to make our travel arrangements. I quickly steered her away from Will's room, fearing that it would be emotionally too much for her to be in his room. Instead, I took her to a spare room where there would be no reminders.

"Thank you, Celia. You are wise beyond your years, you know that?" she said, a smile crossing her tired face.

"Well, I *am* almost 100 years old."

She giggled a little, as she laid her head on the pillow. Her expression changed back to reveal the sadness that had been there before.

"Celia, do you think we'll find him, so I can tell him how sorry I am?" I could see the tears welling in her eyes again as she blinked them rapidly away.

"Yes, I do. But we can talk about it more in the morning. Get some rest right now."

I sat in the room until I was sure that she was asleep. Once her breathing evened out, I went to find my father. He needed to know what had happened. As usual, I found him in his study.

"Father, I need to speak with you."

"Ah, Celia," he turned to look at me, and his eyes suddenly became alarmed. "What has happened? Are you okay?"

"I know why Will left." I hesitated, unsure how to continue. "She knows. Julia knows. Will told her at the cemetery. She saw the graves and was afraid. She ran from him. She found out and didn't think she could handle it, and Will ran. He was so close. I mean, he had been doing so well. I thought we were finally going to get the old Will back, and we did, for a few weeks. He didn't leave because he couldn't handle this," I said gesturing around. "He left because he thought that he had lost her."

His eyes sank and he let this new information absorb. Finally, relief washed over his face as he realized what this meant.

"Julia came over tonight. She wanted to know everything. We've been talking and now she's asleep upstairs. I convinced her to get some rest so that I could figure things out. She wants to go to Chicago, to find him. She wants to get him back."

"She's *here?* But I thought she said that she was scared of him . . . of us."

"She was, at first, but then she had a few days to think about things. I guess she realized that she still loved him. She wants to find him to tell him."

"Well, that could be difficult. You know how his friends in Chicago operate," my father could not hide the venom in his voice when talking about them. "It would be extremely dangerous for her to be anywhere near them." He shifted in his chair and ran his hand along the side of his face.

"Yes, but I don't think that I can get him to come back here to talk to us about this. I'm not even sure we could get him to talk to her. He hasn't answered a single one of my phone calls. And I'm not so sure that he would believe me anyway, if I told him that she wanted to talk to him."

We talked for most of the night, trying to decide the best course of action. Eventually, we decided to explain the risks, and if Julia still wanted to find him, we would support her.

"Well, I guess we'll leave things up to her. This should be her decision," he said. "We must tell her of the dangers in the city and let her decide."

As if on cue, I heard her stir outside the door. Julia walked in, looking slightly better than before, but her eyes were still sad.

"Ah, Julia," my father crooned. "It is delightful to meet you. I am Will and Celia's father, Samuel."

He clasped his hands around hers.

"Hi. It's wonderful to meet you too." She let a small smile slide out between the corners of her mouth.

"My father and I were just talking. We know where Will lives." Her eyes lit up. "But, I think you had better sit down so I can tell you the rest."

An hour later, we had briefed Julia on the Chicago coven and the dangers that we would face there. It was decided that only Julia and I would go. There was no love lost between the leader, Chris, and my father. It would be much more dangerous for him to go. We would take the train in order to rest and conserve our strength. With any luck, we could find Will alone, but we needed to be prepared if we ran into Chris. I wasn't sure that this plan would work, but Julia seemed to believe that if she could just talk to Will, things would work out.

"Julia, you're sure that this is what you want? You could always walk away and I wouldn't think less of you," my father asked quietly. I could hear the pain behind those words as I knew that he longed for Will's happiness.

"Yes," she answered resolutely. "I made a terrible mistake." I could see tears springing to her sad eyes. "I know I shouldn't, but I love him. Despite everything, I love him no matter what he is. He makes me feel."

If I could cry, I would be crying right along with her. She loved him. I could really see that now. She had forgiven him... but would he forgive her? My only hope was to find Will in Chicago and let Julia explain. Hopefully, it wouldn't be too late.

CHAPTER 16
WILL

"WHAT THE HELL IS YOUR problem?" Chris spat in my face. "You have been like the walking dead since you returned." He grabbed my shirt and pulled me up roughly, trying to get a reaction or at least my attention.

"Nothing," I said. My voice sounded normal, but I was afraid that my eyes would betray all of my secrets. I shoved him off of me and straightened my shirt, feigning anger. "Let's just go. I'm ready. I need to get out of here." I added the last part for good measure. In all reality, I could care less what I did.

I had only been back in Chicago for a week and had tried to get back into the swing of things, going out at night, satisfying the blood lust with the occasional human, but it wasn't enough. There was a distinct void that was now permanently housed in my chest. The ache that had been controlled before with blood never left, only now it had a name. The ache had been there for decades, but I had never known what it meant. Now I knew, and it made me want to die. I thought I had been miserable before, but now I knew immortality was nothing but a silent hell for me. My life would never be the same. Julia had awakened human emotions in me that I could never forget. The love I felt for her would never change, and I would have to live with this knowledge for eternity.

Still, I would always be haunted by the look on her face when I admitted to her what I really was. The terror that took residence in her eyes was harrowing, and I regretted ever making her feel that way. I regretted making her feel anything for me. And, I missed her. I missed the smell of her hair, her eyes that swallowed me whole, and the softness of her hands. Ah, her hands. The way her hands flowed across the ivory keys of the piano entranced me. I could never forget that.

"Yo, Will, let's go!" Chris was standing holding the door open shouting at me, waking me from my stupor. The others were already outside waiting.

Another night out. More people in this town to terrorize. What used to thrill me, only sickened me now, but still, I went along with it. There was nowhere else for me to go. There was no one else who would accept me. Reluctantly, I mustered up a smile and sauntered out the door trying to convey that I had no care in the world. I would pretend that everything was just fine; that I enjoyed living like this.

My phone buzzed in my pocket, and I checked it as I walked. Celia. She had been calling me all week but had been rather insistent tonight. No doubt to convince me to come back. I couldn't talk to her. I didn't want to talk to her, at least not yet. I hit ignore on my phone as the sadness settled in my chest. I just needed blood. It would all be better after that, I tried to reason. I would feel stronger, yet my stomach churned at the very thought of the unknowing and unwilling victims of the evening, who would pay the price for my unhappiness.

The others were slightly ahead, leaving me to walk alone. I watched them all surround Chris. Why had I never noticed? They followed him blindly, like a god. Granted, he was known for taking others in, but I had realized since coming back how little anyone questioned him. He made it sound like everyone in the group would all be equal but really, we were all there for him. Things between the two of us had been strained ever since I came back. Chris was constantly berating me with questions about my few weeks with my family. I answered them nonchalantly, trying my best to act as if it meant nothing and was merely a trip to get my father off of my back. But he was so perceptive and never seemed to be happy with my answers. The last few days were making me realize that perhaps I needed to find a way out of this life, even if I couldn't go back home.

"Hey, Will," Kyle had fallen back and into step with me. "So what's new?" It sounded just like small talk, but I had a feeling there was an ulterior motive.

"Not much. Just aching to get out there." I flashed my teeth in a sinister grin hoping to give him the hint.

"Well, I just wondered if you were okay. You haven't

seemed the same since coming back. Did your crazy old man finally get to you?" He threw the question out there casually, a hint of mock concern.

And there it was, the reason he had been sent to come "talk."

"No my crazy old man didn't get to me. He doesn't keep fresh blood around so I don't have as much fun as I'm used to. It just makes me feel weak for a little while after. I'll be fine once I feed a few more times." The lie tasted bitter on my lips.

"Good. I don't suppose you've been successful in getting your cute little sister to join us down here, have you? I'd be happy to show her a good time." Kyle tried to grab my shoulder in fun, but I swept it away not wanting to be touched.

"Leave my sister out of this!" I snarled and he instantly backed away. He held his hands up in mock defeat.

"Kidding! I was just kidding," he said but quickly jogged up next to Chris, no doubt to fill him in on what I had said.

Christ, it was going to be a long night.

CHAPTER 17
JULIA

"HE IS STILL NOT ANSWERING," Celia slammed her phone shut and crammed it into her pocket. "What's the point of a cell phone if you're never going to answer it?"

I smiled to myself. I was notorious for never answering my phone. Not because I didn't want to, but because no matter how high I put the volume, I didn't seem to hear it. That, and the fact that not too many people were calling me. Maybe too many years of pounding on the piano had affected my hearing. Or maybe I just didn't want to be so easily found.

We were on the train to Chicago after deciding that it would be easier than driving. Celia had never bothered to get a license, and I wasn't sure I could keep my emotions in check on the long drive around the lake.

Traveling with Celia was relaxing. I knew she was being kind by making small talk to get my mind off of things. Even still,

Will was always in my head distracting me. She told me stories about her and Will as children. She told me about their mother and about learning to live after the change. She told me all about the life she and her father had been living. Inevitably, our conversation turned to Will and the life that he had chosen.

"It breaks my father's heart to see him living like this. He truly believes that we don't have to live like the others. Sure, there are people in this world who romanticize the idea of being immortal. There are even those who let us take blood from them willingly, even though we don't need to. I guess people have long glamorized the idea of immortals being vampires. Will, however, has taken this lifestyle to the extreme." I looked down at my hands tangled in my lap, trying not to think about Will in this way. Celia, ever aware, could sense me pulling back. "I'm sorry, I probably shouldn't tell you this," she added placing her cool hand on mine.

"No it's okay, I think I need to know the whole truth. I'm not sure anything could change my mind at this point, anyway. I guess I just don't see him that way. At least he wasn't when he was with me..." I let my voice trail off.

"No, he was never that way when he was with you," Celia interrupted. "He has changed in the last few weeks. I know he struggled at first. He was so drawn to you. I could sense it within the first week. His humanity, no, his soul, was reawakening. I mean he was being bombarded with all of these new feelings. He didn't believe it at first. Or didn't want to believe it. We can't deny what we are, but we can make the best of what we have and not give in to the urge. Will never understood that. He has always thought that he just had to completely give in. He never understood he had a choice. At least, not until he met you."

"And then I threw that in his face when I ran. God, how could I be so stupid! If I had just given him a chance to explain, this could all be different." I looked ahead at the empty seats across from me, feeling the train humming rhythmically on the track.

"It's not your fault, Julia. This is Will's way of dealing with things. He tends to run from them. If he could have been patient for a few days, to give you a chance to calm down, I could have helped him, too, you know." Of course I knew that she was right. I couldn't completely blame myself for Will's actions.

I looked out the window, trying to hold back the tears that threatened to erupt in my eyes. It was my fault. I knew that things would be different if I hadn't left. If I hadn't gotten scared. If I had only given him a chance to talk to me, to explain. Instead, I was the one who had run first, which then drove him away.

"I know. I tend to be the one running away too," I said quietly.

I leaned back and closed my eyes. The train was nearly empty. A few passengers dotted the car, but there was no one within earshot which allowed us to talk candidly.

"You know there is no cure for us. No hope of becoming human again." Her tone was soft and sad.

"I know. At least I assumed that, or you and your father wouldn't still be infected." I paused as I sorted my thoughts out and sighed loudly. "Celia, I have had a lot of loss in my life and if there is one thing I have learned, it's that sometimes you need to think about the now. I can't dwell in the past and I can't think about the future. I need to do what makes me happy right now. Life is too short." Celia chortled a little, which puzzled me, and then I remembered why. She was immortal. Life wasn't short... which made me smile a little. "That probably doesn't seem like much to you, I realize."

"Actually, human life is short. I do know what you mean. I think you're brave for feeling that way. Most people are too focused on the past and the future to enjoy what is around them right now. I guess that is a luxury I have. Someone like me can spend an eternity dwelling on what happened and why, or they can learn to enjoy the here and now as well. That is the difference between my family and others. We have learned that by enjoying the now, we are able to maintain our humanity. I don't spend a lot of time thinking about what I am. Instead, I just live. I don't want to give up and give in. Besides, if I spent all of my time thinking about the past and the future, I would go crazy!"

She was right, her family was very different. I mean they didn't fit in with the mythology I knew, but they also seemed happy. They didn't have to hide. Not much, anyway. This is the Will that I knew. Someone who lived in the now. Someone who loved deeply and thought about others first, not the monster that Celia described before. I began to wonder if I would be disappointed once we got to Chicago. Would he still be the same person I had fallen in love with? Or would he have resorted back to the person who had lost hope.

We sat in silence again. I checked my watch. We had at least another hour. Absentmindedly, I began thumbing through the pages of the magazine next to me. There was nothing of interest in it, although, I suppose not much would have held my attention. Finally, I asked Celia a question that had been nagging at the back of my mind.

"Celia," I said tentatively setting the magazine back down and sitting up to face squarely toward her. "Have *you* ever been in love?" She looked up, and I saw a momentary flash of sadness in her eyes.

"Yes. A very long time ago. Before I became... before I was infected." I looked at her hoping that she would finish but not wanting to pry, but she was silent, and I couldn't control the question that came out.

"What happened?" I leaned forward, and my body swayed with the motion of the train slithering along the track. In a way it was relaxing.

"I was engaged to be married. His name was Jonathan. He was smart, handsome, and perfect." Her eyes were soft as she began to remember the past. "We were so in love, but then I got sick. At least that's what he thought happened. I didn't want to just abandon him or let him think that I didn't love him anymore. He was devastated when I died and there was no way that I could tell him what I had become. I was too much of a coward back then. At the time, we didn't know it was even possible to live out in the open like this. And if I hid it from him, it wouldn't have worked anyway. He would have figured it out when I stopped aging. I'm not sure he would have been as brave as you are. I think he would have run out screaming instead."

I laughed at her willingness to forget my shortcomings.

"You're forgetting that I did do that. I'm not as forgiving as you give me credit for."

"But you did come back, don't you see? And it was only a few days later. You must really love him because you came back. And then, when you found out the actual truth, you still stayed. A love like that shouldn't be held back. If there is one thing I have learned in the last century, it's that."

I couldn't imagine living through everything she had lived through. How hard to not feel alone and yet, she was happy in this life.

"Do you still love him, Jonathan, I mean?"

She smiled sadly, not letting it reach her eyes.

"Yes, I always will. He's gone now. He died several years ago. I went to his funeral in disguise. He was the last connection to my old life. The last connection to what I could have been, and I needed to say goodbye."

"Oh. I'm so sorry, Celia. It's never easy to lose someone you love." She smiled at me and leaned over as she squeezed my hand.

"You won't have to go through that. I will help you make things right with Will. It's the one thing I can do to help. I don't want him to have regrets like I do."

"How do you do it? How do you stay so positive after

suffering a loss and not let yourself succumb to the sadness?" I asked.

"You mean, how did I not become like Will," she stated.

I looked away, embarrassed.

"It's okay," she said, "I know what you mean. Basically, no matter how sad I became, I tried to remember the good times. I reminded myself that I was still alive, and there was still goodness and happiness left in this life. You have to find happiness in the little things. I guess I've tried to do that and not give in to any darkness that may try to break through."

She made it sound easy, but I knew thinking in that way could not have been. Especially when your whole life changes so suddenly. And then watching your brother implode because he can't get past it. I shuddered just thinking about it, because I knew exactly how she felt. Exactly how she did it... because I did the same thing.

We sat in silence during the last part of the trip, both of us thinking of the past and perhaps, how it intersects with the present and the future. The train crept through the suburbs of Chicago, inching us ever closer to the city until finally it pulled into Grand Central Station downtown. Groggily, I gathered my things, and we stepped out onto the platform. Despite sitting for so long, I was still exhausted.

"Well, now what?" I looked at Celia expectantly.

"Are you sure you don't want to rest first? Do you want to check into a hotel or something?" she asked.

"No, I think I need to do this right away. I will feel so

much better after I talk to him. But where do we start? Do you know where to find him?"

"Yes and no. I have my suspicions of where he will be right now. I have his address, although I've never been to his place. We can check there first."

She hailed us a cab, and I found myself gazing up at the tall skyscrapers that bordered the lake. The city looked magical and harmless at night and I was finding it hard to believe that even now, there were monsters lurking in the city.

After what seemed like an eternity, we pulled up to a gothic looking building. An apartment or a brownstone. Glancing down the street, I noticed it was one in a line of many. Each side of the street looking identical. Tentatively, I got out and followed Celia up to the door. It was starting to rain lightly and I pulled my jacket tightly around me.

"You might want to hang back a little bit. Like I told you, the others that Will lives with don't really like me and my father very much. If Will isn't around, I don't want them to take too much notice of you. It doesn't look good to bring a mortal around unless I'm... well, you know what they do."

"Oh. You're probably right." I tried to hide the horror on my face. The thought of what they may or may not do to a mortal sent shivers down my spine. Part of me refused to believe that Will would have anything to do with this. "I'll just stay back a little and let you do all of the talking."

"It will be okay. I'm not trying to scare you, I just want to warn you about things. These guys can be pretty barbaric."

"I understand. I'm not scared." Okay maybe just a little bit.

Celia pushed the call button on the brownstone. No answer. She pushed it again, more fervently. After a minute, a groggy voice answered.

"What?" the voice demanded.

"Hi, it's Celia, Will's sister. Is he around?"

"Oh yes, Celia, the little blond, right? Hold on," his voice snidely replied.

Less than a minute later, a tall, lanky guy with ink black hair and dark, beady eyes opened the door.

"Well, well. Will's little sister. What are you doing here? Change your mind about us?"

"Listen..."

"Mark," he interrupted, providing her the name I'm sure she could care less about. Both of us could read right through his mock show of civility.

"Listen, Mark. Is my brother here or not?" the twinkling of her tone was gone. Instead, the edginess gave a sharp contrast, like fingernails on a chalkboard.

"Easy now, I was just trying to be friendly. He's not here right now." Mark leaned against the door in a way he clearly thought was seductive, and I had to fight to keep from rolling my eyes.

"Well do you know where he is?" I could tell her patience was wearing thin.

"He's out with the others. They went to a club or

something. You know, the usual. I didn't really pay attention. I had my own plans tonight." I could hear the smile in his voice. Whatever he meant, I didn't want to know.

"Could you just tell him that Celia is in town and to please call me? We'll be at the usual hotel. He'll know where." Mark peered around Celia and his gaze caught mine. He sniffed the air and flashed a grin.

"I didn't know you were keeping in the company of humans like that, Celia. Or maybe you were bringing a present to Will? To try to get him to come home?" he hissed.

"I don't know who you think you are, but knock it off," Celia was standing in front of him in the blink of an eye, her hand to his throat. Her tone was like ice. "You have no idea what you're talking about. Just tell him I'm in town." She shoved him aside and turned abruptly. I felt a sting as she grabbed my arm and led me out to the street. I fought the urge to look back, but I could feel his black eyes peering into my back. We didn't speak until we were around the corner and well out of eyesight.

"What was that all about?" I asked, rubbing the sore spot on my arm.

"I'm sorry, I didn't mean to grab you like that. He's just one of the idiots that Will lives with. You can't pay attention to any of them or they'll take advantage of you. I find it best to stay indignant and assert some authority." She raised her hand to hail another cab.

"I figured that. I mean what was his deal about seeing me?"

She bit her lip and scowled. "You caught that? He thought you were with me. That you let me drink from you. Some immortals keep specific humans around them in order to get blood whenever they want. Most of them still aren't willing to drink donated blood in a glass. They prefer it straight from the source. Like I said, barbarians. Although, the fact that he saw you could work in our favor. He'll probably tell Will that I didn't visit alone. Hopefully, he will put two and two together, realize that you are here in town with me, and actually call me back."

A cab pulled up to the curb, and we both jumped in. It was raining harder now and despite the fact that the inside of the cab smelled like moldy bread and cigarettes, I was happy to be in from the cold, damp street.

"The Knickerbocker Hotel, please." The cabbie only briefly glanced into his rearview mirror at the source of the voice before tapping to start the meter and jumping on the accelerator.

"What's at the Knickerbocker?" I asked quietly.

"A bed, a shower, and food. We need to rest. There isn't really anything we can do until Will arrives home. So, we sit and wait for his call... or at least give him a chance to call. If we don't hear from him after a while, I can try to find him again, but my suspicions are that as soon as word gets to him, he will find me. He knows I'm serious if I show up in the city because it doesn't happen very often."

"Oh. Okay." I sat back against the seat and felt the rain from my hair trickle down my back. I watched the raindrops collect and drop down the window. My life had sure changed in the last few weeks. And despite my current state, I felt truly alive for the first time since losing Aaron. I wanted to see Will more than anything. I wanted to apologize and tell him how much I loved him. I wanted him to hold me. There was, of course, a very real part of me that realized that this may never happen. He may truly want nothing to do with me and I would have to accept that as well.

"There is nothing else we can do now, so don't try to be a hero. I can see it in your eyes, you are exhausted!" Even as she said it, I knew she was right. It had been a long few days with little sleep and my emotions running on overdrive.

A few minutes later, we pulled up to an old looking hotel, complete with a doorman outside its gold revolving doors and bright lights. I was sure that if I could see the top of the building, there would be gargoyles perched on the rooftop, watching the city. Celia paid the cab fare and we slid out.

"This hotel is sympathetic to our kind," she whispered. She must have read the concern on my face.

We walked into the lobby and Celia made her way up to the desk with authority. I figured she knew what she was doing, so I hung back and just watched. Within minutes, Celia had a key and we were opening the door to a room with two double beds in it. After a hot shower, I crawled into the crisp sheets.

"Aren't you going to sleep, Celia?" I questioned. She turned and smiled warmly at me. The way she had been taking care of me over the last two days made it hard to believe that she was currently "playing" a high school senior.

"Eventually. I'm just going to sit here and wait for a bit to see if Will calls. I may try to call him again, too. You should rest. I can go a lot longer without sleep than you."

"Okay. Just wake me up if he calls or you talk to him." I closed my eyes and could feel myself drifting off, no longer able to stay awake.

I don't know how long I slept before a nightmare woke me. Something about eyes, watching me in the dark jolted me awake. The room was dark and it took me a few minutes before I realized where I was. Celia was sleeping soundlessly in the other bed, her body still. It seemed strange, surreal, to be here in Chicago, sleeping in the same room as her. Not only that, but to be here with someone who, until a week ago, had just been a student to me. My life had taken such a strange turn.

I lay awake staring at the ceiling and listening to the sounds of the city trying to slow my heart and wondering if there was any way that this could all work out. The artificial light of the city was streaming in through the windows. I got up and pulled the curtain back, looking out at the cityscape. He was out there somewhere and it excited me to be in the same city as him again. It made me feel closer. We could make this work. I knew that we could be together.

A sigh escaped my lips. I only hoped that it wasn't too late and that I could fix everything that I had broken.

CHAPTER 18
WILL

A PETITE BLOND SIDLED UP to me, her syrupy voice purring in my ear.

"Hey there, stranger. Where have you been? I haven't seen you in a few weeks, and I missed you."

I glanced down and vaguely recognized the person speaking to me. "Nowhere important," I said coolly to her.

"So do you want to go in the back?" She ran her hand lightly up the inside of my thigh, leaning closer to me. The touch repulsed me, and I began to pull away. Molly. Now I remembered her. Six weeks ago, she wouldn't have had to ask me twice. She had been one of my "regulars." Someone who let me take from them often. Blood, sex, whatever I wanted. She had been nothing more than a prop to me. Someone to use and then throw away. It never dawned on me until now, how much I used to do that. I wrapped my hands around Molly's thin wrists and pushed her to the side.

"No, I'm okay right here. Thanks." I tried my best to dissuade her with my tone. I just wasn't in the mood. "I think you should leave. Go find someone else to be around. "

She stared at me, and I glared back until finally, she walked away in a huff. I sighed deeply and ran a hand through my hair. What was with me? I had been trying to get back into the way my life had been but to no avail. Every time I looked into the eyes of someone else, all I could think about was Julia. I was confused by the dull, thumping, irregular heart, beating with a thud in my chest. While a random heart beat always existed within us, mine had been more noticeable in the last week. I hadn't told anyone about it. Especially not Chris. It was faint, but definitely there. And the dreams! Or rather nightmares, were all consuming. I was finding that no matter how hard I tried, I couldn't shake pictures from my mind of the girl with auburn hair, sitting at the piano. I could still feel her presence, her feelings, but only faintly. There had been a lot of anger and fear at first. Now, it was just sadness. I knew that I would never truly be able to forget her.

The music thumped around me, pounding into my brain and for the rest of the night, I watched from a dark corner as Chris took one girl after another into the back room to do what we did. What I used to do. He had so many, I couldn't keep track. The girls came out groggy and unaware. Usually he drugged them first so that they wouldn't remember. It was sickening and something that I definitely didn't want to be a part of anymore. I couldn't do this. I couldn't pretend that this was me. I stood up quickly, hoping to sneak out before Chris came back looking for his next conquest. I had to get out of there. I had to escape this life.

The cool air on the streets welcomed me, even though I could barely feel it. It felt less claustrophobic than the confines of the bar, and I liked its numbing effect. And without all of the voices and the loud music, I could think without distraction. Who was I kidding? I was always distracted with thoughts of Julia, but out here in the night air, I could allow them to take over. I could let go. My body ached from wanting her, and I let myself remember visions of her in my arms, visions of her biting the end of a pen, visions of her at the piano, playing while I sat next to her, her long fingers hovering over the keys while she let the music flow through. In my dreams, she even turned to look at me with a smile. I turned down the closest alley and slid against the rough brick wall, unable to go on. My eyes pinched closed, and I felt as if my chest would explode from pain. I could feel her sadness and worry. It was strong tonight. Almost as if she was near. As if she had come to Chicago. I couldn't let myself hope, but it pushed and shoved against me like a competing force.

One thing was sure, I still loved her. I felt that I would always love her. I was not the same person and Chicago was not the right place for me. I no longer had a life here. I couldn't go back home, though. It was too close to her and after her reaction, I was sure that she wanted nothing to do with me. The problem was that now, I knew what I was capable of. I knew what life could be. My father and sister had been right. There was no going back to the way I had lived before.

I sat hidden in that alley, wallowing in my own self-pity, until a light rain began to fall. The brownstone was only a few short blocks. I didn't even bother trying to stay dry, letting the dampness slip into my pores and drench my clothes. Frankly, I just didn't care.

The sidewalk was nearly empty as I rounded the corner of the brownstone-lined street, most people dodging in an out of the rain quickly. The two dark figures getting into a cab near my building alarmed me for some reason, and I quickly leapt into the shadows to avoid being seen. I'm not sure why, but the figures looked familiar. Suddenly, I knew as I recognized my sister's jacket and her long stride. The other person was smaller and graceful with auburn hair falling all around her, and I could feel her all around me. Julia. What in the world could they possibly be doing here? I felt a thud in my chest again as my heart gave out one solitary beat. Within seconds, the taxi was roaring down the street, and I was able to step out of the shadows. I took the stairs of the brownstone two at a time and slipped inside. The house was quiet, but I paused feeling that there was someone here.

"Well hello," Mark's voice rang out from the shadows. He was sitting in the living room with a girl passed out next to him.

"Mark," I greeted him curtly. I disliked Mark intensely. Of all of the other immortals, he was the oddest. He rarely went out with the others, but rather preferred to prowl the streets looking for prostitutes and loners to bring back to our house. It was creepy, and he very often went too far, resulting in the death of more than one innocent girl.

"Early night tonight? That's three in a row. Rather strange for someone who used to stay out until morning wreaking havoc on the city," he smirked.

"I've had my fill," I lied and motioned toward the girl. "I'll leave you alone with your... uh... guest. I'm going to crash." I began to walk away to my room when he interrupted.

"Your sister came by," he spit out. "And some delicious looking human was with her, I might add. I didn't know your sister was hanging out with mortals now. Or perhaps she brought her as a gift to try to convince you to return back to them." I stiffened at the mention of Julia. The tone of his voice implied exactly what he thought about both of them. My defenses were up and the thought of Mark thinking of my sister and Julia that way made me snap. I lunged at him from across the room, catching his throat in my hand.

"Don't talk about my sister that way. In fact, don't even think about either one of them. Ever. Got it?" I let my grasp around his neck loosen, figuring that I had gotten my point across. He gasped for a minute, his hand moving up to his neck. He wasn't strong enough to beat me and never would be. Picking a fight with me would be his demise and he knew it.

"You don't need to be such an ass. Chris is right, there is something wrong with you. You haven't been the same since you came back. Besides, I was simply going to tell you that she said she was in town and to call her. Something about her usual place. " I was already walking away as he spoke, but I heard what I needed to. I brought my hand up to my aching chest. They were here and Celia wanted me to call her. I wasn't surprised. Celia had been calling me all week, but Julia was with her. I could scarcely hope that she had changed her mind. Maybe she was here because Celia brought her against her will. Or to tell me once and for all that she never wanted to see me again. That could be the only answer. I mean, she had run screaming from me. From the monster that she saw. I couldn't deal with rejection again. Thinking about it only made the ache gnaw at my chest even more. I couldn't deal with this right now. I would call her in the morning. Maybe. For now, I just wanted to put tonight out of my mind. But hope had already begun to poke through, and I couldn't stop thinking about the fact that Julia was actually here.

After a while, a fitful sleep came. I started to have the same dream again, but there was something different this time. I could see more. Julia was there again. She was at the piano, playing. At least I assumed it was her. I still couldn't really see. Her hair was cascading around her shoulders in long waves. Her fingers glided across the keys. She turned and smiled slowly at me. The smile that lit up her eyes and for a brief moment, I could really see her. And then everything went blank again, and I awoke with her scream in my head.

It was daylight and there was a single ray shining into my room, landing at the foot of my bed. I could feel the heat as my body absorbed the rogue beam. If only the dream could be decoded. In fact, I wish I could figure out why I was even dreaming. Why could I see some things better than others? Why was she so out of focus until she smiled? I rolled over and rubbed my eyes to glance at the clock. It was almost noon.

The house would be quiet for several hours. Most of the guys stayed out so late that they slept all day. Just like them to play the big, bad immortal. Sleep wouldn't come to me anymore. Julia was here. I could feel her constantly, knowing now that my mind was not playing tricks on me. In a way, it brought me a bit of peace. I should call Celia and at least let her know that I was okay. No, I needed to call Celia to see what she wanted. Who was I kidding? I needed to call Celia to see why Julia was with her.

Reluctantly, I let my fingers dial Celia's number.

The phone rang a few times before a sleepy voice on the other end picked up.

"Hello?"

"Celia?"

"Oh my god, Will! Is this really you? I have been worried sick about you! Why didn't you answer my calls? Are you okay?"

"Celia, calm down. I'm fine. What are you doing in town?"

"I brought someone who wants to see you, but not at your house. We don't want to be around those disgusting creatures you live with. I think it should be somewhere else." Of course. Julia was still scared and didn't want to be seen with me. Celia must have told her everything about my life.

I couldn't say no to her. I was intrigued, and a solitary heartbeat confirmed the hope pulsing through my veins. I mean, Julia had come to Chicago with my sister. Maybe she wasn't scared of who I was anymore. I don't know what would be worse, Julia being terrified of what I am or just being terrified of what I was capable of.

"Where do you want to meet?" I calmly asked.

"Maybe we could meet at The Bookshelf? The one right next to the Oriental Theater. How about in the coffee shop upstairs? Does 6 o'clock work for you?"

"Sure," I answered. It would give me time to figure out what I would say to her. "Celia? Is... is Julia okay?" My voice came out pained, catching in my throat slightly.

"She's fine, but I'll let her talk to you later. She's still asleep. She's had a couple of long days. It was a lot to take in. Don't worry, just meet us there. She wants to talk to you. Are you okay?" I sighed audibly, letting the relief flow through my body.

"Better," I answered after hesitating for a few moments. "I'm sorry I didn't call you Cee. I just wasn't ready to talk to anyone.

"You can't keep running away, Will," her voice whispered into the receiver.

"I know. I just panicked; I didn't know what to do. I was in so much pain, and I wanted to numb it. I thought that things would be better if I came back here, but I can see now that they aren't. I don't want to live like this anymore." I looked around nervously to make sure no one had overheard. That was the first time I had admitted it out loud. It was a feeling that had been awakening and festering in me for quite a while. Julia made me realize that there was so much more. She reminded me that I could still be human. I only hoped that it wasn't too late to tell her that. I longed to ask Celia if she thought it was too late, but I didn't want to hear the answer. I was still absorbing everything.

"Things will all work out, Will. And then maybe you can come home. We'll see you at six. Take care."

I held the phone to my ear, listening to the silence at the other end after she hung up. I could hear it echo in my head. And then the quiet sound of a singular heartbeat. It reverberated in my chest and reminded me of so much. Everything that I longed for and everything that I had to get back.

I opened the blinds over my window and let the sunlight stream in, feeling more human than I had in a while. Things would change now. I would leave this place. I may not be able to go live back home, but I certainly could find somewhere else to go. Or maybe Julia would forgive me and I *could* go back home. I tried not to focus on this hope. My skin warmed and tingled from the sunlight still shining upon it. I would need to tell Chris and the rest of the guys that I was leaving for good. They will not be happy. They felt betrayed if anyone left. In fact I wasn't sure that I could remember anyone leaving in the 50 or so years I had been with them. I knew that Chris, especially, would be upset. He felt that humans were toys to be dominated by the immortal and all powerful. I certainly couldn't tell him why I was leaving. If he found out about Julia, or about my newfound feelings, he would never forgive me. Chris was not someone you should make angry.

I crept out into the hallway to see if anyone was awake. It was quiet, except for the heartbeat I could feel rhythmically beating a few times a minute. I couldn't believe the feeling it was bringing to me. I couldn't wait until tonight. I couldn't wait to see her again. I couldn't wait to begin again.

CHAPTER 19
CELIA

I LISTENED TO THE SOUNDS of Julia's rhythmic breathing and I knew she was still asleep, despite the fact that it was late morning. I had heard her pacing around for quite some time last night. Everything was going well, almost too well, making me wonder if something wasn't right. I had been calling Will all week long with no hint of an answer. Then, we show up at his doorstep and he calls a few hours later? I made a split second decision and raced down the stairs, faster than humanly possible. I wanted to go talk to Will in person. I needed to see how he really was. I had grown to like Julia as more than just a teacher, and I wasn't ready to throw her into a bad situation.

Within minutes, I was in a cab to his apartment, unable to breathe until I finally pulled up in front of the brownstone. His horrid roommates may be awake or they may be sleeping. It would be so much easier if they were sleeping, because I didn't want to have this conversation with them around.

Chris answered the door almost immediately after my soft knock. Damn, the last person I wanted to see.

"Oh hi, Celia. I heard you were in town. What can I do for you?" he purred. "Have you come to hang out with us tonight?"

"I need to talk to Will," I stated calmly, trying my hardest to push aside my disgust. "Is he around?"

"Yeah, I'm sure he's around here somewhere. Won't you please come in?" His voice dripped with sarcasm, and I couldn't help but wonder exactly what he was up to. His mere presence was unnerving, even to me.

The entryway was dark and I followed him into the living room. He turned and gestured to the sofa, urging me to sit down. He leaned against the doorway, arms crossed in front of him and just stared. I cleared my throat to remind him of what I wanted.

"Will. Your sister's here," Chris called out never taking his eyes off of me. I ignored him the best I could and sat down.

"Why don't you come out with us tonight, Cee?" I grimaced as he used my brother's nickname for me. "You could even bring that human you have in town. We could have a lot of fun." I caught the gleam in his eye and wanted nothing to do with the sort of fun he was proposing. But if there is one thing I had learned about Chris, it was to not piss him off.

"Thank you, but *we* have plans already but maybe next time." I emphasized the "we" in case he was planning on trying to get to Julia. Flashing my brightest smile at him, I hoped that he would buy into my fake sincerity.

"Your loss. The clubs around here are fantastic. You can find anything you like." I thought I saw his tongue dart out briefly, like a snake. How fitting for someone as slimy as he. At that moment, Will came into the room.

"Celia. What are you doing here? I thought we weren't meeting until later on." He stiffened and looked around nervously.

"We are. I just wanted to talk to you first. Would you please excuse us, Chris?"

"Sure." Chris skulked out of the room and disappeared around the corner. I waited until I thought he was gone before continuing quietly. Will glanced around nervously, and I instantly knew what he needed to know.

"She's not here. She's back at the hotel room. I wouldn't bring her here," I whispered. Immediately, Will's posture relaxed. "You will talk to her, won't you?"

"Yes." He hesitated. "I just don't want her to see this." He gestured largely around the room, but I knew it wasn't the bachelor pad he didn't want her to see but his life here.

"It doesn't have to be this way, you know. You could come back home to live."

"I want to, but it's not that easy. These guys don't understand. They have never been in this situation. I'm not sure what they would do if I left for good. I made a mistake by coming here and now I'm not sure I can ever leave." He looked so lost, not the overconfident person I had grown accustomed to over the last several decades. This was my brother. My real brother. The one who cared. The one who loved.

"How did you get away last time?"

"I told them that father wanted me around, which was partially true. I have always been able to leave for a while because I think Chris knew I would always come back. He knew I hated it, and I was always back within a few days, but this time, my father certainly hadn't been the one to make me stay. I made my own decision and stayed far longer than I usually do, because of Julia. I didn't tell you, but for the last few weeks, Chris had been calling me to check up, insisting that I come back."

"I know. Whatever your reasons for staying, I'm happy that you did. I'm only sorry that things happened the way they did. And I only wish you had let me help you before just taking off and leaving."

"When I was back in Michigan, I changed. I woke up inside, and I realized that I couldn't hide anymore. I didn't want to. And then when everything happened with Julia, I thought I could just leave and I would go back to the way things had been before. I felt as if I was empty again." Will got up and paced around the room glancing around the corner, only to come sit back down. "I think Chris knows something is up. I just haven't been my usual self around him and I think that it's making him suspicious. I haven't been able to go back to living the way I did before and it doesn't go unnoticed. I tried, lord knows, I've tried to not care, but I just can't. This isn't working anymore, but I don't think I could leave without a scene."

We sat in silence for a moment, neither one of us knowing how to proceed. There was so much that I wanted to say to my brother, so much unspoken between us after all of these years, but I held on to my silence.

"I think he's watching me," he finally continued. "They all are. If I leave, I'm sure he will follow. No one gets out this easily."

The air in the brownstone was filled with unease, and I began to look around nervously as well. Maybe I had underestimated Chris. It would never be that easy for Will to leave. He was simply a pawn. A toy for Chris to play with and manipulate. I thought about the mindless drones that followed him, and I had to get my brother away from all of this.

"She loves you, you know," my voice came out barely a whisper. "And she is sorry." I should let Julia tell him this, but I was fearful that he would still be too afraid to meet. That the fear of Chris would keep him here, instead of in her arms, which is where he should be. I didn't want to lose this new Will. The Will that actually cared about something real.

I placed my hand on his arm as a comfort and Will sighed beside me.

"I love her, too. I haven't been able to stop thinking about her since I came back. I only wish I had done things differently. If I had just been upfront with her from the beginning, we may not be here right now." He ran a nervous hand through his hair and clenched his jaw.

"So you will still come tonight, to the café?" My tone conveyed hope.

"Of course. I need to make things right. And then, I guess, we will go from there."

I stood up and gave him a brief hug.

"This will work. You two can still fix things. I'll drop her off and let you two have some time together to talk. This will all work out, Will. I believe in you." I glanced back with a smile and slipped quietly out the door, never noticing the sulking shadow that had been listening to our every word.

CHAPTER 20
JULIA

T HE SMELL OF FOOD AWOKE me the next day. I opened my eyes and sat up sleepily to see Celia waiting with a big table full of food.

"I didn't know what you would want to eat, so I ordered a little bit of everything," she smiled cheerily.

I pushed the blankets aside, sat up, and made my way over to the food, my stomach grumbling loudly.

"You're in a good mood today," I commented. I glanced at the clock which read 1:30 pm. I must have been really tired to sleep that long. Waking up every few hours didn't help. "I can't believe I slept this long." I grabbed a piece of bacon off of a plate.

"I heard from Will," she stated rather matter-of-factly. "Actually, I saw him. I'm sorry that I didn't wake you, I guess I just needed to check in on my brother first."

My heart skipped a beat briefly as I took her words in. She had talked to him. He knew I was here. *Don't get ahead of yourself,*

Jules, I told myself. *Just because she talked to him, does not mean he's willing to talk to you.*

"Is he... okay?" My voice betrayed me, my attempt to be nonchalant ruined. The lump in my throat prevented any other words from coming out.

"Yes. He's okay. He said that he will meet with us later." She picked absently at a piece of toast.

"Really?" Relief flooded through my body, and I could feel tears beginning to prick at my eyes.

"We have to meet him near the Oriental Theater at 6 o'clock tonight. I wasn't sure how long you would rest. I thought it was better that we meet in a public place. Just in case."

My euphoric mood was dashed slightly with her last comment. Why would we need to be in public? Was he afraid that I would make a scene? Did he not trust himself around me? Maybe he was just afraid that I would freak out and he didn't want to be somewhere private.

"Okay. Whatever he wants." I tried to calm my nerves as Celia stared at me silently, trying to read my thoughts. "If you don't mind, I think I'll just go take a bath or something. I would like to think."

"Sure, no problem. I've actually been wanting to go to the Coach store down the street, so I'll be back in a while. Might as well get a bit of shopping done while we're here," she giggled.

The door shut quickly behind her and I was alone. The tears I had been holding back now streamed down my cheeks. I couldn't believe that I was here and that in a matter of hours, I would be able to talk with Will again. To try to explain. To try to apologize. To try to get him to forgive me for how awfully I treated him. I had learned so much about him, and I knew now that I was ready to deal with it... with us.

Within minutes, I had drawn a bath and was stepping in. The steam rose all around me, wrapping around my skin like velvet as I slipped into the hot water. I had replayed our last conversation in my mind hundreds of times. I thought of all the different ways it could have gone. How different life would be if I had reacted another way. Instead, all I could picture was the pain on his face as I turned and ran from him. I should have known that if he really wanted to kill me, he could have done it there in the cemetery, or a million times before that. How many times had we been alone? In the school, at my house. Hell, I had fallen asleep in his arms on more than one occasion. I should have trusted him. My eyes closed as I leaned against the back of the claw foot bathtub, trying now to picture what our next conversation might be like.

I stayed in the bath until my fingers were shriveled. Dressing slowly, I started to hum a song, letting the melody relax my soul. Suddenly, I really needed to play. I remembered there was a piano in the lobby of the hotel. Without thinking, I threw on the rest of my clothes, my wet hair dripping down my back. The door clicked behind me as I left, and I hurried down to the front desk.

"Excuse me," I said. The concierge looked up, and I was suddenly aware of my wet hair and lack of make-up. "The piano over there. Can I play it?"

"Sorry, we usually only let professionals play it at night. It's not for guests." He looked me up and down scrutinizing my disheveled look and turned back to his work.

"Please," I pleaded. "I do play. And it is really important." He glanced up in time to see a single tear escape before I could hastily wipe it away. A frown played upon his mouth, and I could see him contemplating it in his mind. He glanced around the lobby, taking note of anyone I might disturb.

"Well, I suppose I could allow it this once. But if you start banging away, playing something like 'Chopsticks,' I will have security haul you out."

"Oh thank you!" I hollered over my shoulder as I was already on my way to the sleek instrument.

The lobby was nearly empty, which suited me. I didn't really care for an audience at this moment. I played a few chords and reveled in its perfect pitch. Not a single key was off; its tone rich and resonant. My eyes closed and my fingers slid over the keys to find their rhythm. Rachmaninoff. Something I hadn't played in a long time, but that expressed all of the emotions I needed to let out. I hardly noticed my fingers flying across the keys. All I could focus on was the way I felt.

The song ended several minutes later and the sound of applause filled the room. There were now 20 or 30 people standing in the once vacant area, listening to my mini concert. A warmth spread through my cheeks and I stood up tentatively and walked straight into Celia.

"That... I have never... Wow."

"I just needed to play. It's the way I've learned to release my emotions. Sorry, I probably should have just stayed in the room." We headed toward the elevators and back up to the room.

"Will told me you were amazing, but I never knew you were *that* good. I mean, I'd heard you play before we left, but that was unbelievable."

The elevators closed behind us, and we had somehow managed to leave the crowd behind.

"Thanks. I haven't played like that in a while. Well, not in front of a crowd. I played like that around Will." I pushed the button for the 5th floor and waited for it to lurch.

A smile crept upon Celia's lips.

"Your playing is what helped bring him back, did you know that? It's the music that made him feel. Just a theory of ours."

I had never thought about that. I never realized my music could be used to fix someone other than me.

"No, I didn't know that, but I'd like to think it's true. I know that it always brings me happiness."

Celia clicked our hotel room door open and piled her shopping bags down on the floor before flopping down on the bed, her blond curls bouncing. She grabbed the TV remote and soon settled on a romantic comedy. Unable to concentrate on the show, I stared out the window. The city was below me; cars zipped by, men in suits hurried past, and families lingered at store windows. It was all so normal, and watching made me begin to believe that everything would be okay. I wrapped my arms around myself and thought about how much I missed him. We only had a few hours left before we would meet. Playing had made me feel better, but now I was more anxious than before to tell him how I felt. I could almost feel his arms around me and his breath on my neck, as if he were whispering something into my ear.

I LOOKED IN THE MIRROR and touched my hair for the tenth time before Celia stopped me.

"You look fine! Stop fussing. We need to go." She grabbed my hand and squeezed. It was hard to believe that a few short days ago, I had thought of this girl as just a student. Now that I knew the truth about her, she was becoming a friend.

"Okay. I'm ready. Let's go." I glanced sideways one more time as she pulled me away.

The door swung shut behind us and we made our way through the lobby and out onto the sidewalk, where we were assaulted with honking horns and people rushing by. I stood rooted near the building while Celia hailed a cab. Despite the busy day, it took less than a minute.

It only took 10 minutes to get to the theater but it felt like ten hours. Dusk was beginning to settle over the city, painting the sky in brilliant hues and leaving colorful reflections on the windows of the skyscrapers. People passed by the window of the cab, never really taking shape. It was rush hour and we spent a fair amount of time meandering through the stopped cars. My mind was too preoccupied and it prevented my eyes from truly focusing on anything.

We pulled up near the ornate theater and Celia quickly paid the driver. I stepped out and looked up at the marquee flashing brightly. I was still staring when Celia grabbed my hand and walked me to the book shop right next door. With a show starting at the theater, the store was nearly empty, a fact that made me glad.

"I think I'll wait down here for a few minutes. To give you some space," Celia said pushing me toward the stairs. "He's upstairs, in the café waiting."

I made my way upstairs to the café, and I was sure that every face I looked at was Will. The café was nearly empty, and I scanned the few remaining people anxiously, until I saw him. He was leaning up against the wall with a book, trying to look relaxed, but I recognized the tension in his body. He glanced up, looking through the hair that had fallen into his eyes and smiled timidly. My eyes fixated on his hands as he shut the book and set it on a table somewhere between us.

"Will?" My voice was barely above a whisper as it caught in my throat. I began to walk slowly toward Will, fighting my urge to run into his arms.

"Julia?" My name was a whisper on his lips. "How are you?" He was near enough to touch, but I was too afraid. I could feel the energy in the air and I didn't want to break it.

"I'm fine. How have you been?" We were both still too nervous to move past the formalities. It was my turn to speak. I opened and closed my mouth a few times the words never truly taking shape. I had so much to say but just didn't know where to start.

"I..."

"Julia..." We both started at the same time.

I laughed nervously and looked down at my hands. He shifted across from me and when I looked back into his eyes, which were the color of the lake in winter today, I became lost. They were dark and stormy, and I could read the pain in them. Pain that I had caused. Tentatively, he reached out and put a stray hair behind my ear, brushing the skin of my cheek softly.

"It's okay. You first."

His lingering touch gave me the courage to go on and tell him what I needed to say.

"Will, I need to tell you that I'm sorry. I was a fool. I never should have run. I should have listened to you. I should have heard you out." The words came out in a jumbled mess. Once they started, I just couldn't stop them. "I was an idiot, and I was scared. I guess I just needed some time to figure things out. I needed to understand..." I stopped to swallow the lump that was rising. My shoulders sagged, my lungs and pride deflated.

"It's not your fault, Julia. I should have told you before. I never should have kept this secret from you. I never should have hid who I was. What I am. I guess I was afraid that you would leave."

"But I did. And I'm embarrassed by that. I ran because of what I thought you were and not what I knew you to be. I had these horrible images of creatures from books and legends. I never took the time to take things into consideration." I wanted him to forgive me so much it hurt. I wanted him to take me into his arms and tell me that we would figure everything out somehow. I reached for his hand and took it between mine for a moment before I placed it on top of my heart, needing to show him that I wasn't afraid. A single tear escaped. "Can you ever forgive me?"

He smiled my favorite smile and then took my hand and placed in over his heart.

"Don't cry, Jules." He brushed the tear away with his thumb. "I forgive you."

With that he swept me into his arms, and I could feel myself melt into him. It was like I had never left. His lips brushed the top of my head and he sighed. This would all work out, I could feel it.

We pulled apart and he tipped my chin up with his free hand, his other hand wrapped tightly around my waist. I looked into his eyes, saw the softness and knew that I was forgiven. Our lips sought each other and when his tongue parted my lips, hungry for more, something in me exploded as I felt any trace of sadness leave. His hands were in my hair, then touching my back, my arm, my face, touching me anyway he could, both of us needing each other. He was with me now. He was mine, and I was his and there was nothing left to do but think of the future.

A sardonic laugh and the sound of clapping broke us apart, but Will still held me tightly.

"Well, isn't this a nice little scene. You really have played the part well, haven't you Will. Aren't you going to introduce me to your girlfriend?" the voice called out. I couldn't help but notice that the café was strangely empty.

The look on Will's face instantly changed as his smile faded and his eyes hardened. He pushed me protectively behind him, and I grabbed the back of his jacket tightly not wanting to ever let go.

"What do you want, Chris?" Will's voice was like acid and I peered around his arm to take in the scene.

"Oh, I just wanted to see how my protégé had been spending his time. I have to say, I didn't quite buy the story that your daddy wanted you home for so long! I know you too well. You have never been able to stand your family for more than a few days. Even your little tart of a sister." Chris walked around us slowly.

"You don't really know me anymore, Chris. I don't want your life anymore. Why can't you just let this alone?"

"Because you have exposed us to their world!" He spat angrily and pointed at me. "You have been living with us for too long. This cannot be," he added, reaching around to try to grab my arm. Will spun me in an instant keeping me out of Chris's reach.

"What does it matter to you if I leave! You still have the others. Why can't you just let me leave! I won't say anything and neither will Julia!"

"Oh, so she does have a name!" Chris gasped mockingly. Faster than I could process, he was next to me holding his hand under my chin.

"Leave her alone. She has nothing to do with this!" Will tried to shove his hand away, but Chris twisted until he was between us.

"I'm not so sure. I mean, she does know our little secret, and I don't know that she can be trusted." Chris held one of my arms behind my back with one hand and ran his fingers down my free arm with the other one. My body tensed, and I stifled a scream. I wanted nothing more than to run, but Chris held my arm too tightly. I stared intently at him, pleading with my eyes for him to not do anything. He held my gaze for a moment, his eyes intense.

"Why don't we take this somewhere else, shall we?" His tone told us that we didn't have a choice in the matter. We began to walk and Will went to my other side. I didn't realize that I was shaking until he grabbed my arm to hold me up.

"Try to run or scream and I will kill you and Will right here," Chris whispered in my ear. He dragged us out the door and began walking next door to the theater. The show had just gotten out, spewing forth a mob of people. I smiled to show that I understood as we filed past and into the theater.

As quickly as possible, Chris led us to the back of the lobby, never once relieving the pressure on my arm. When we reached a peculiar spot in the panel, he opened a hidden door and pushed us both through. It was damp and dark inside and I didn't dare move. Will never let go of my arm and I suddenly felt myself being pulled along a dark corridor. We walked for several minutes, winding around dimly lit corridors that all looked the same. The only light was coming from bare bulbs randomly hanging down the center. If he was trying to get me to lose my bearings, it was working. Finally, we reached another door which opened to a flight of stairs heading down.

I cautiously followed him down the stairwell, relieved that at least Will was still behind me holding on. The walls opened up to a large cavern. I wasn't sure where we were anymore. Underneath the theater? In the sewers? I couldn't be sure. Stone walls rose around us and torches hung from the walls, giving the space an eerie old world feel.

"This is a better place to talk, don't you think?" Chris asked. He threw me down on the floor and Will crouched instantly next to me.

"Are you okay?" he whispered.

"Yes, I'm fine."

A whimper from the corner alerted me that we weren't alone down here.

"Celia!" Will gasped. My eyes adjusted, and I could see her small figure crouched in the corner. Celia was tied up in the corner. A chain or rope of some sort threaded around her wrists and ankles leaving her immobile. They must have grabbed her while Will and I were talking upstairs.

Will stood beside me, torn between staying with me and going to his sister. Chris made that decision for him by stepping in between Celia and Will.

"Now, we have some things to discuss if your sister and your human friend here are going to survive." He sneered as he continued. "You have betrayed us, Will. You have betrayed our kind. You and your whole family disgust me! Thinking you could live with them." He pointed in my direction as he spoke.

"I always accepted them because of you. You were loyal to us and they didn't seem to attract too much attention. But then you left and didn't come back right away. And now I find out why! A girl! You betrayed us over a human girl! You know what the consequences are. She must die."

"That's not true, Chris. She doesn't have anything to do with your feelings about me or humanity. Just let her go and I will come with you."

"No!" I cried out and tried to pull away from Chris's approaching grasp. I couldn't let Will go, now that I had found him again.

"Loyal little human, isn't she! You have always had a gift with mortals, haven't you? You have always gotten them to do what you want. Does she know all about that?" Chris remarked. He ripped my arm from Will's protective hold and I gasped in pain.

"It's not like that. Will hasn't made me do anything." Anger at both his accusations and the pain I was in was making my courage come back. "He's not the same. And, I choose to be with him. He isn't forcing me to do anything. He isn't like you," I added.

"That's all fine and well, but we still haven't addressed the fact that our code has been broken and that you must die!"

"There is no stupid code, Chris, and you know it. This is

all just some bullshit that you have been telling others for years, to get them to follow you. To get them to feel safe, when really, you're the one they need protection from!" Celia, finding strength, called from the corner. "Besides, maybe it's about time that humans knew that we existed. Then maybe we could find a cure." Her eyes narrowed and she glared directly at him. "There is nothing about this disease that says we have to kill others to survive! We don't all want to be bloodthirsty like you. You are the monster, not this disease."

Her comment only stung for a moment before he was on her, teeth snarling, his fist reaching her gut, causing her to double over in pain.

"Don't argue with me, you little bitch! If you weren't around, Will would never have left to begin with! We are bloodthirsty monsters! That's what this disease does. Don't you get it? You're the one who is trying to deny what you are! In fact, I think that you should die as well."

"Chris," Will interrupted, "this is between you and me. Let Julia and Celia go. I will come back with you and do whatever you want." He stood up and took another step toward him, his eyes pleading. "Just let them go."

"Oh, I think it's too late for that, Will. I can't trust you anymore. How do I know that you won't just run back to both of them at the first chance?" His laugh was like sandpaper crackling in my ears. "No, I think that we should end this right now."

Chris shoved me to the floor in the corner and pulled a dagger out of his pocket. He lunged at Will, and I ducked out of the way. Will grabbed a torch from the wall, its metal handle the only available weapon, its flame casting a glow over his face. I could see the glow in his eyes as he prepared to fight.

"Will, stop!" Celia cried out from the corner. I realized that she was still bound and needed my help. Carefully, I crept along the wall toward her stopping only when Chris got too close to me. Will saw what I was doing and did his best to keep the fight away. As much as I wanted it to be Will that I was crawling toward, I knew that I needed to save Celia. When I reached her, I gingerly removed the tight bindings, trying not to hurt her too much.

"Thank you," she breathed rubbing her hands across the angry flesh. "Quick, over here!" she moved us away from the fight that was taking place. I tried not to gasp, as Will dodged one swing after another from Chris, trying to stay out of harm's way. At times, he managed to land a blow. Their bodies were a blur as they quickly moved in a sort of dance around each other. I could hear the sound of fists pounding and flesh ripping as they each tried to best each other. At last, a hard blow sent Will sprawling on the floor on the other side of the cavern.

"Will!" I screamed, my hands flying to my mouth. His eyes met mine in alarm and then softened.

"Julia," he whispered back.

Chris took advantage of his distraction and jumped on him. Will tried to move to the side, but Chris was too fast. He raised the dagger over his head and drove it through Will's chest. He instantly went limp his eyes rolling back in his head. My vision tunneled as I screamed, running to Will's side.

"No! Will, please!" I pleaded, tears streaming down my face as I watched his labored breathing. I grabbed the hilt and tried to pull it from his lifeless form.

Chris saw me and began to advance. I didn't care. If Will was dead, I wanted to be dead too. I closed my eyes and crouched over Will's dying body and prepared for the impending blow. When it didn't happen, I opened my eyes and saw a surprised look on Chris's face. His features contorted and then hardened. He slumped over, the other metal torch sticking through his heart. Celia, eyes blazing, was standing over him. She kicked him away and came to my side.

I looked at Will's lifeless body, my hands shaking. He couldn't be dead. He didn't burst into flames or scatter as dust like all the folklore I knew. His heart didn't beat regularly, and he rarely breathed, making it impossible for me to know if he really was gone.

"What do I do?" I whispered to Celia. My hands shook as I touched the metal handle that still protruded from his chest. I touched his face, moving the hair out of his eyes, when he opened them. Relief flooded through me to see that he was alive, but the emptiness in his eyes and a soft moan reminded me that it could be too late.

"He isn't gone yet, Julia. There might be something we can do. Maybe the blade isn't fully in his heart or maybe it missed it. Whatever the reason, he isn't dead yet so there may still be time." Her commands were short, and she grabbed her cell phone and began searching for a signal. "Stay here," she said. "I think I know what to do. I'm going to go up higher to get help. Just... stay with him."

As if I could ever leave his side.

She took a torch and hurried away. My sobbing was uncontrollable now and swollen tears rolled down my cheeks, my hands unable to brush them away fast enough. Shadows flickered on the walls and the mustiness burned my nose.

"Will," I murmured. "I'm sorry, this is all my fault. All my fault."

Will moved his lips to speak, and I leaned down to him to hear.

"It's not your fault, Julia, I knew what I was getting into." His labored voice was barely audible. "I need to tell you something, before it's too late."

"It's not too late, Will. You will be okay. Celia and I will figure this out and you will get well." I placed my tear-soaked hand next to the gaping wound, near his heart.

"There isn't time. I cannot survive this." He closed his eyes for a moment as his tongue ran over his dry cracked lips. "Julia, I have loved you from the moment I first saw you. You have made me want to be something better than what I am. I'm only sorry that I can't be around to return the favor. I... I love you." His eyes began to fade and his skin became even paler. He couldn't die. I wouldn't let him die right here.

"No, no. This can't be happening. Will, don't go, I need to tell you things, too!" my body fell onto his, and I pulled frantically at the dagger. "Don't you leave me, I love you."

With every last bit of effort I had, the dagger slid out and cold dark blood oozed from the wound and covered my hands. I sobbed loudly letting my tears run down my face. "I... Don't leave me, don't you leave me..." The words kept pouring out of my mouth as my tears mixed with the blood that was all around me. I kept trying to listen for the heartbeat that I knew wouldn't be there, hoping for the impossible.

"Please!" I begged again.

His eyes fluttered and his body tensed. Suddenly, he convulsed sending electric currents though my hands that were still covering the gaping hole in his chest where the dagger had been. And then there was nothing. He was gone. Tears poured down my cheeks and all sound was lost by my uncontrolled scream.

I DON'T KNOW HOW LONG I lay over him crying, before Celia pulled me away. I looked up and wiped my bloodstained cheeks. There were two men dressed neatly in suits standing near me. Their opposite physical build made me think of a comedy routine. They started toward Will, and I instantly became defensive and scrambled back to Will's body.

"It's okay, Julia. These men are okay. They're here to help. They will take him to a special hospital where they will look him over. My father will meet us there."

"It's too late. He's dead," I sobbed. Celia's strong arms pulled me to her and the tears continued. I pulled away and wiped the blood off of my face and hands, her face stoic.

The men crouched over Will checking him over. Suddenly the smaller man stood up with an odd look on his face.

"Excuse me ladies," he said, "He is not dead. We need to get back to the hospital right away to figure out how to save him."

"Not dead? He's not dead? I thought... he stopped moving... and I thought... he took a knife to the chest." I felt hope coursing through my veins at his words. Hope and disbelief.

The man went back to Will's side and grasped his limp hand.

"There seems to be something strange going on within his body. Do you happen to have the dagger still?"

Celia, handed him the small dagger with the ornately decorated handle now covered with blood. The man looked at it intently and then went back to Will.

"He should be dead. I can't comprehend... his hand... his hand is actually... warm."

CHAPTER 21
WILL

WHEN THE DISEASE TAKES HOLD, it doesn't really hurt. At least not at first. After the train accident, we didn't really know what happened. Some were left for dead, some bodies burned in the fire, and the rest of us were taken somewhere. I think now that it was probably the catacombs under the city. The ones that the bootleggers used during Prohibition. The same ones where Chris took us to.

I remember waking up and feeling horrible. I didn't know where I was or how long I had been there. As my eyes adjusted, I tried to make sense of my surroundings. The room was long with beds lining either side. Like an infirmary. Torches dimly lit the walls and it was damp. The air was sour and smelled of blood. It wasn't hard to see why. I could see that I wasn't alone. There were figures in the beds. Some of them looked dead and others looked as if they wanted to be. Bags of dark liquid were hooked up to many. Blood. That was where the smell was coming from.

Suddenly my body shook with a cough and my insides felt like they were going to explode. I drew my hand away and immediately noticed the blood that clotted there. Consumption. I must be somewhere being treated for consumption.

"Will?" a voice tentatively called out. My eyes searched out in the dim light. It was my father in a bed next to me. I don't know why I didn't notice him before. I started to get up but immediately felt dizzy and had to lie back down.

"Where are we? Where's Celia?" I hoarsely cried out.

My father didn't know much more than I did. Celia was in a bed across from us, and I found a small relief that we were alive. If only I knew then what I knew now. I may have regretted surviving, as I have so many times since. Our health only went downhill from there, as the disease wracked through our bodies. The poison slowly freezing the blood in our veins and slowing our heart. Our skin paled and our mortal bodies slowly died. The pain became excruciating as we hardened and during the worst of it, we hallucinated. I would wake up in a cold sweat, with the bedding tangled around my naked body. Sometimes I wished I would get well and other times, I wished I was dead.

I suppose the actual change took only a week, but it felt like an eternity. Even now, as I lay in this place dying from a wound to the heart, I couldn't help but think of the pain that I endured to become this way to begin with. The only difference is that this time, I had more of a reason to live. I had a reason to pull through.

Will. Don't leave me. Her voice continued to whisper

through the shadowy corners of my mind and her presence flowed through me. I thought back on my life... both of them... and willed myself to continue on, not yet ready to leave. Reminding myself that the world is always darkest before the light.

CHAPTER 22
JULIA

I FOLLOWED CELIA AND THE others in a daze, still not sure what had happened to Will. All I knew was that he might be alright if they got to him in time. We traveled in a sleek, black car, with the two men holding an unconscious Will. They seemed oblivious to the blood that was covering us and the seats of the car. Celia, gripping my hand, pressed next to me as we raced to the outskirts of the city, trying to control my shaking.

"Where are we going?" I whispered to Celia, my eyes never leaving Will's face.

"I'm not totally sure, as I have only heard of this place. It's a hospital of sorts, I guess. There are those of our kind who are specialists, who are rumored to be looking for a cure. I hope that they will try to figure out how to help him... if they can." The last sentence came out so low, I wasn't sure that I had actually heard her correctly.

"I don't understand, Celia. I thought that... I mean... it

went right through his chest. His heart..." my voice dropped off, unable to say it out loud. I feared his heart had been pierced. Immortal or not, there would be no recovery from that. I knew there were ways that he could be killed.

"It is. But my father and I have a theory. It has to do with iron and..." She stopped abruptly and looked out the window. "I think we're here."

We had pulled up to a large, gothic mansion. It looked dark and sinister. Rundown. Then again, it didn't look like the kind of place that I would venture up to without being invited, so it made sense. Iron gates swung open and gravel crunched under the tires. They lined up waiting for us on a giant porch.

It took only a matter of moments for them to shuttle Will off behind a set of closed doors and Celia, and I were ushered into a waiting room. But it wasn't the typical sterile waiting room. It was furnished with antiques and carried a slightly musty smell of old things, instead of the typical antiseptic smell of a hospital that burned your nose. In fact, the inside of the building was exactly the opposite of the outside. It looked taken care of, at the very least. Celia and I walked to the couch at one end of the room. The springs groaned loudly when I sat, interrupting the silence between us.

"You really should try to sleep. It could be a long night ahead." Celia murmured.

"I'm okay. I want to be around just in case Will wakes up." In truth, I didn't think I could actually sleep.

"Julia, I have to be realistic with you. There's no guarantee that he actually will wake up. I'll try to find some things out while you sleep. Just lay down right here. I promise I will wake you when I find out anything."

It was useless to argue with her because I knew she was right, so I gave in.

"Well I suppose I could close my eyes for a few moments." The last thing I remember was someone pulling a blanket over me.

CHAPTER 23
WILL

I REMEMBER GETTING STABBED. A brilliant pain threatened to pull my body apart, tearing what little of my soul remained. I remembered Julia and the beauty of her and how she stayed. I told her I loved her and then I was dreaming.

Julia was at the piano, her back to me. A song drew me in, and I stood behind her placing my hands on her shoulders, absorbing the sound illuminating from her. She finished and turned to look at me. She smiled and pulled me down toward her mouth, and I wrapped my arms around her. Before our lips could meet, she turned her head slightly to whisper in my ear.

"I'm afraid," she whispered. Before I could answer, she disappeared from my hold and I was standing in the cemetery alone with the graves of my family at my feet. The leaves of the red maple stirred around me and sadness filled my soul. The wind confided in me and its voice was Julia's.

"I'll never leave you. Don't go," it sang before everything went dark.

I FELT COLD. I DIDN'T even know where I was, but I knew that I registered cold. I tried to open my eyes but couldn't, because a bright light beckoned. So this is what it felt like to die. I almost chuckled in relief at the idea that I was actually feeling. There was a deep pain in my chest that felt as if there was a gaping hole. And then I remembered there *was* a gaping hole. I had been stabbed. I really was dying. I stopped fighting the light and began to relax, trying not to focus on the pain. But the pain would not subside. In fact, it was heightened by a thump. I couldn't put my mind around what this extra pain was. And then it came to me in a flash. I could see her face. Julia. The reason I was here. The reason my heart was trying to beat. The reason I had for living.

Her image came to me. Dark auburn hair, cascading in soft curls past her shoulders and her green eyes. Ah, yes. Her eyes, so deep they penetrated right into mine. And then I remembered her hands softly placed on ivory keys as a beautiful melody erupted. The music that had saved me the first time, began to run through my mind. I held on to that melody and began to fight through the haze that was trying to pull me under. It came to me like a movie. Short scenes, memories, dreams, pictures. It was all there, in my subconscious, fighting to stay. I fought until I could consistently focus on my memories of Julia and her music. I wanted to live. I wanted to wake up to see her face again. She had said it didn't matter what I was. We would figure it out. And for once, I wanted nothing more than that. I loved her, and she loved me and we could take this on together.

"WILLIAM. WILLIAM, WAKE UP." MY mother's voice softly whispered through the haze of sleep. I startled and opened my eyes to see my mother sitting on the edge of my bed back home. I sat up nervously and looked around my bedroom.

"What is it mother?" confusion spread through me. I looked around slowly. The room was exactly as I had remembered, since the time we moved into the house. Although, the thin layer of dust was gone and my hand-carved wooden trucks still lined the shelves. I looked over my mother's shoulder at the snow falling softly outside. Suddenly I knew. It was Christmas morning, and I was 12 years old. It was before everything happened. Before she died. Before I became what I am.

"Merry Christmas, darling," she said, then pulled me into her arms. My head lay on her shoulder, and I inhaled her scent deeply. Roses. I fought the tears from coming, trying to tell myself I was dreaming. I didn't want this dream to end.

THE QUIET SOUNDS OF WHISPERING brought me back at one point. I tried to open my eyes again, but they were heavy and wouldn't obey. My mind was hazy, and I tried to swim through it. I felt as if I was drowning, my chest bursting with pain. I tried hard to concentrate on the sounds around me, so I could figure out what was happening.

"If only I could understand what these readings mean, I would know what to do," a low voice uttered. "I have never seen anything like this."

"Me neither," another voice added. "The only thing I know is that the dagger didn't fully pierce his heart, which is a miracle in itself. That is the only explanation for why he's still alive."

"His wound is definitely healing, but it's not healing in the way I would think. I just can't piece this all together. I actually had to give him a blood transfusion this morning. That is unheard of." The sound of fabric made me think of a shrug. Then a shuffle of papers and the click of the door led me to believe I was again alone.

I am not dead, I thought to myself and fought, again, against the heaviness holding my eyes closed, only to be met by the pain. I could feel myself fading again, and no matter how hard I grasped, I couldn't stop the fall.

A GIGGLE, THEN MUSIC BUT only a few bars before it stopped and the giggling started again.

"Will, please. You have to let me finish practicing."

Julia. Was I dreaming again?

"Try again," I heard myself say. "I promise. I won't mess you up." A scene was clearing before me. Julia and I, sitting side by side on the piano bench while she played. Now I knew I was dreaming because I had always hoped for this.

She struck a chord again, and I let her play longer, but finally couldn't contain myself. I ran my lips along the edge of her jaw line and twisted my hand in the hair at the base of her neck. The smell of lavender. Another giggle, and then everything went black.

A HEARTBEAT. A HEARTBEAT POUNDED through me. It felt strong but not constant and it hurt. I could imagine the atrophied muscles trying to find their rhythm. It was as if it was relearning how to beat. I heard the blood whoosh through my ears and echo in my head. I willed it to continue, wanting so much for it to be there. It was like a metronome counting down for me, and I needed it to continue. I concentrated on that until the sound of voices again. I could only assume at this point that I was in some sort of hospital, and doctors were trying to treat me. The beeping of a machine matched the thump in my chest. I could smell nothing, but I could hear every tiny thing.

"It's getting stronger as he stabilizes. Should we tell his father?" the first voice asked.

"No. It's too soon to tell. We don't want to get their hopes up," the second replied.

"Did you find anything in the medical archives or in any of our research that could help us?" the first voice asked.

"No. It seems as if this has never happened before. I can only hope that what we are doing is working. That human girl loves him so much, I don't know what it would do to her if we lost him." His feet shuffled against the waxed floor as he shifted his weight.

"Perhaps we should let her come in. If they have such a bond, maybe her presence would help wake him."

Yes! Oh yes, just let me hear her voice, my mind screamed. There was no answer. I fought to open my mouth just to let them know I was there. My calls went unanswered, and the doctors left the room.

I LOST TRACK OF TIME. I don't know how long I had been there, or even where I was. Time was standing still and I was trapped in my own mind. Pain came and went. At times, it was excruciating, as if my veins were full of tiny needles set to prick me from the inside out. I wanted to wake up. I needed to wake up. The heartbeat was still there. Stronger now, and full of hope. And Julia was near. She had stayed and I could feel her, which is what kept me fighting to get back to the surface.

CHAPTER 24
CELIA

I PULLED A BLANKET OVER Julia and tried my best to hide my concern for Will. No need to alarm her even more. The truth was, I was terrified. Something wasn't right and for once, I didn't seem to know what the right action would be. Should I stay with Julia and let the doctors take care of it, or should I try to figure out exactly what happened.

After arguing with myself for several minutes, I decided that perhaps cleaning myself up would be best. I was mess. Dried blood that looked like tar splattered all over my clothes and face. It plastered my hair in strange angles and twisted itself in reddish black curls. I didn't know whose blood it was, but it disgusted me. I needed to wash the night off.

The receptionist at the front was nice enough to give me some scrubs and point me to an empty bathroom with a shower. With towel in hand, I glanced once more at the sleeping figure and crept down the hall. Ten minutes later, I emerged clean but not feeling much better. I would have to direct Julia to the shower when she woke.

There was still no news on Will's condition. I glanced at my watch. My father wouldn't be here for another hour. I needed to occupy myself.

The chair groaned when I sat down and began thumbing through a magazine. My leg tapped on the floor in a rhythmic disturbance. This would never work. Unlike, Julia, I could never sleep. She seemed to be able to let the exhaustion take over. Perhaps it was her way of dealing with trauma. She was able to shut down. Lord knows, she had dealt with enough of it.

Eventually, she stirred next to me and then sat up with a jolt, as if remembering where she was.

"Hey," I started. "There's no news. I would have woken you if there was."

"Thanks," she sighed, rubbing her hands on her face, startled when the dried blood began to flake off into her hands. She looked up at me abruptly. "You showered?"

"Oh yeah. I couldn't sit still. The receptionist gave me some scrubs and a towel. You should go too. Get yourself cleaned up." I shuddered, remembering how we got this way.

"Thanks." Julia got up, then hesitated and looked back at me expectedly. "You will come get me if anything changes, won't you?"

"Of course. You will be the first to know." I smiled reassuringly. She nodded and walked toward the front.

A few minutes later, my father rushed through the door. He looked around frantically as I rushed to his side and met him with an embrace.

"What happened? I knew that I should have come with you." Concern etched his face and I could feel his helplessness.

"It wouldn't have helped. Chris ambushed us. He must have been following Will closer than I thought. You wouldn't have been with us anyway." I repeated as quickly as I could, exactly what had happened.

"He has to survive, Father. He just has to. He has come so far." The emotion I had been trying to hide could not be extinguished anymore. It was just too much.

Julia emerged from the bathroom, her damp hair falling around her shoulders. She hesitated briefly before continuing toward us.

"Hello, Mr. Bradley."

"Hello, Julia. I am sorry for getting you involved in this. And please, call me Samuel." His smile was warm and full of concern. Julia took my father's hand briefly but looked at me.

"Don't be," she said. "You didn't get me involved in anything I didn't want to be involved in. Do you think we could see him, Celia? Won't they let me just see how he is?" she pleaded as she turned to me.

"I'll talk to them," my father replied. "You probably won't be able to go in there, but perhaps you can look in on him. I'll see what I can do." He walked in the direction of the front desk and I steered Julia back to the waiting area.

"If anyone can get you in, it will be my father," I reassured.

"I just need to see him," she said, her voice falling off.

My father motioned to us and we hurried over.

"No one can go in yet. They aren't sure he's stable. He's under full surveillance, but I can take you to where his room is. Perhaps you can look at him through the glass.

"Oh, thank you!" Tears sprang to Julia's eyes in gratitude. "I just... I just want to see him."

A doctor came out and ushered us through a swinging door. Despite the ancient decor of the waiting room, the interior of the hospital was surprisingly modern. Each room was separated by thick glass walls. Electronic monitors were scattered all over. This wing of the hospital was empty, except for a room that I suspected was Will's

"It is fortunate that you were already in Chicago when this happened. I don't think we could have saved him if you would have had to travel a great distance," the man leading us commented. I glanced nervously at Julia, but she was white as a ghost and already distracted.

"This is his room. As you can see, we are still trying to stabilize him, so you cannot go in yet. Stand here and look, but I ask that you don't stay too long." He hurried away, his long strides eating away at the black and white tiled floor beneath him.

I pushed Julia forward, figuring that my father and I could wait in the distance. She shuffled ahead, and stood stock still in front of the glass. Slowly, her hand moved up and she spread her fingers on the cold, clear wall in front of her. Her eyes closed and her forehead touched the glass. Her lips began to move, as if she were saying something or perhaps, praying. I joined her in a silent prayer of my own, hoping for the best.

After a few minutes, she turned back toward me.

"Thank you, Samuel," she said to my father. "I'll go back out and give you a few minutes with him." She motioned to the people and the monitors that littered the room.

We watched her go in silence and I walked up to the glass to see Will for myself.

"She really does love him, doesn't she?" my father's voice interjected from behind me.

"Yes, she does. They could be happy together." I smiled at the thought. "He just has to get through this."

My father came and stood next to me, sighing.

"I have always wanted nothing more for you two than to be happy. I should have protected you more. I should have tried harder a long time ago with Will. It's a parent's job to help their child find what makes them happy."

"Father, there is no way that you could have known what would happen. You can't blame yourself for what we are. You couldn't have stopped the attack. I feel like Chris' betrayal had been coming for some time, and I think Will feared it, too."

The doctors continued to work around Will's bedside. I left my father standing there and walked back down the hall. When I reached the waiting room, I could see that Julia was curled up on the sofa asleep, and again, I couldn't help but wish I could shut myself down as easily as she did. And perhaps when I awoke, this would all just be a horrible dream.

CHAPTER 25
WILL

I COULD FEEL MYSELF GETTING pulled again. A song, a melody was pulling me back, and I could feel it through my body. Julia was close, I could feel it. I could feel her near me. She was speaking to me. Whispering in my ear. *Will, I love you. I need you. Don't leave me.* Her voice, a song in my heart that I fought to keep hearing. I would not give up. I would not let this get me. I felt determined, strong, until I tried to pry my eyes open again.

It's too soon, just rest. Let your body heal a voice I didn't recognize said. Yet I felt comfort. I felt at ease and a feeling of peace. *Get strong so that you can take care of my sister.* Aaron, Julia's brother. It had to be. I tried to say something to him, but the pain pulled me under again.

CHAPTER 26
JULIA

W HILE THE SHOWER WASHED THE blood and grime off of me, it didn't necessarily make me feel much better. Seeing Will lying like that was agonizing, and when they allowed me in, I couldn't make myself stay long. I kept on wondering if this would be it. If this would be the last time I saw him, and I didn't want to remember him that way. Instead, I left and went back to the sofa to curl up and retreat into myself, to remember him in my own way, confident that Celia would come for me at the slightest change.

I must have dozed off, because the sky was beginning to lighten up with the colors of dawn. I squinted my eyes, letting them adjust to the dim light of the room and the silhouettes of Celia and her father whispering. I watched the two of them and tried to hear what they were saying. Suddenly, Samuel turned and our eyes met.

"Oh, you're awake, Julia. How are you feeling?" he called

out. I jumped up at the sound of his voice, still clutching the blanket in my hands, embarrassed to be caught eavesdropping.

"I'm doing okay. Is there any change in Will's condition?" I felt a cold sweat break out on the back of my neck as my nerves got to me.

"No, not yet. Actually, I would like to talk to you about something. Regarding Will's condition."

"Okay."

"The idea that he is still alive is such a mystery. In addition to trying to keep him alive, the doctors have been trying to figure out how he even survived the stab wound to begin with. I mean, it appears that Chris was gone instantly from a similar wound." He stopped abruptly keying in to the confused expression on my face.

"I'm getting ahead of myself," he continued, "first I must explain how to kill an immortal and, then I will share a theory with you." He walked to the nearest chair and sat down, with Celia trailing not too far behind.

"We don't actually live forever. We can be killed. We just don't react to sickness like others, because our bodies are in a sort of hibernation. There are, however, certain things that could end our life. It isn't the stab wound that will kill an immortal, it's the chemical reaction that takes place. The virus that is already raging through our bodies, leaving us in a permanent frozen state, reacts to the metal... specifically, iron."

"A chemical reaction? What do you mean by a chemical reaction?"

"It's simple, really. Most knives or swords are steel, and steel contains iron. Since we have very little blood in our systems, there is also very little iron in us. Stabbing an immortal with any weapon with iron in it will take our bodies from being iron deficient, to being poisoned." He paused and let me take in this new piece of information.

"So how come a wood stake or a shard of glass won't kill you? I mean, I know what I'd seen, and it was a blow that should have been enough to kill anyone. And if that knife did have iron in it..." My voice trailed off, the words stuck in my throat. Celia moved to sit by me and placed her hand lightly on my arm. She looked at me and smiled, and I smiled back weakly. I was so wrapped up in my own grief, it was hard to remember that I wasn't the only one who could lose someone.

"I have to be honest, Will should be dead now. He took a hit to the heart with a steel blade, although it wasn't directly in the center. The reaction should be taking over. It's the iron that poisons. In fact, if we are stabbed by anything else, the disease fights back and heals what was damaged." He hesitated briefly, running his hand through his silver hair, reminding me so much of Will. "Will is not dead and he isn't dying. In fact, the doctor's seem to think that he is actually *healing.*"

"Healing?" I asked incredulously. "But you just said that he was stabbed with a steel blade. He should be suffering from iron poisoning, right?" The Will I had seen looked dead. Lying in that bed, hooked up to machines, it was hard to believe that he was healing.

"Well, they are confused as well, because they have never seen anything like this before. I have a theory and this is where you come in." Samuel got up excitedly and came to kneel in front of me. "As you know, most immortals lose their grip on humanity after some time. They become detached, soulless. Obviously, not all doomed to immortality lose themselves. I have been of the belief for decades that we can hold on to some semblance of what we used to be. Celia and I have managed to hold on, because we believe there are certain things that can cause someone to cling to their humanity. Love is one of those. Celia and I have both seen what love has done for Will. He has changed. The light has come back. He's beginning to find a reason to be, and that reason is you. I think that your love has saved him."

"Saved him? My love saved him? But I turned him away. I'm the reason we are even in this mess. If I had only let him talk. If I had let him explain and had some time to think, I would have... I wouldn't have run."

Samuel smiled warmly and placed his hand over mine.

"You can't change the past, and you can't change how you reacted. It is what it is, and it's done. Stop blaming yourself and focus on the future." His words were kind and understanding, and in some strange way, were just what I needed to hear.

"But you do love him, don't you?" Celia offered. "You never stopped loving him. Just because you... needed space, you never stopped loving."

I could feel the tears begin to streak down my face as this all sank in.

"I do love him, but I didn't save him, he saved me. I was broken, I was the one who couldn't cope with my life, and he fixed me..." I could hear my voice slowly fade.

The swing of a door and the sound of shoes on the linoleum floor, caused all of us to turn with a start.

"If you would like, you may go in with him now," the doctor came in with a somber look on his face. "He isn't awake, but we seem to have him stabilized. I think it would be alright for you to do more than just see him through the glass. Perhaps the sounds of your voices will help him."

Celia pushed me forward.

"You go. I think he would want to see you first," she said. Suddenly I was nervous. We had only just found each other again. Maybe he blamed me. What if all of this had made him change his mind?

"But you are his family. Don't you want to see him first?"

"You are family, too. Just go," Celia smiled. "We will give you some time before we come in."

As always, her kindness was too much. I gave her a quick hug and then followed the doctor down the hall to Will's room. He pushed the door open slightly for me and continued in the other direction, leaving me alone outside the room. With a deep breath, I pushed the door open the rest of the way. The room was dimly lit. A series of monitors with flashing lights and numbers stood sentry over the bed, which seemed to be placed in the center of the room. Will was lying there with his eyes closed, hooked up to countless machines. I noticed a stool beside the bed which seemed to be there just for me. He did look peaceful lying there. It was almost as if he were sleeping. His face was emotionless, any trace of feeling erased by sleep. There was a large white bandage over his chest. Purple bruises covered his face and there was a large gash on his forehead. I gripped the side of the stool beneath me, as I watched his face scowl leaving lines in his forehead. Ever so lightly, I brushed my hand on his forehead to try to smooth it out. His face seemed to relax at my touch, so I left my hand on his face.

"Will, I am so sorry. Please don't leave me. Please don't go," I pleaded with my voice, as my hand continued to caress his face. "I'm still here. I'm not going to leave you ever again. You are everything to me."

My forehead pressed against the hospital bed, and I closed my eyes tightly, trying to shut out this pain. I thought of our short time together. I thought about everything I had never told him but wanted to. I willed him to live for selfish reasons. Selfish because I needed him to live. I didn't think that I could survive losing him.

I grabbed his hand and squeezed. His hand was strangely warm. The man in the tunnels had been right. I picked my head up from the bed and looked at him for a moment, puzzled. He was never warm. The monitors began to blink again, and then I noticed the rhythmic beeping. Immediately, I became concerned and turned my attention over to the monitors to try to figure out what was happening. I saw it... the heart monitor. It was beating in slow, regular beats. This wasn't possible. Not from what Celia had told me about their kind.

Turning back to look at Will, I saw his eyes begin to flutter, and I grasped his hand again to squeeze it.

"Will, can you hear me? Are you okay?" I stood next to him and pleaded with him fervently.

His eyes fluttered once more and then began to open.

CHAPTER 27
WILL

T HE LIGHT WAS BLINDING AS I opened my eyes. My lids began to reflexively snap shut, but I fought to keep them open, happy that I finally could. She was here. Julia. Her presence completing my soul. I had been fighting for what felt like weeks, or even months, and I finally felt as if I had made it back to the surface.

"Will!" her voice was frantic. "Oh my god, you're okay! You're here, alive!" I could feel her hand covering mine. Not just the presence of it, I could *feel* it. And I felt warm.

"You stayed," my voice was barely a whisper through parched lips. My mouth and throat were dry. There was a thirst and an ache in my chest, but it was different.

"Your heart. It's beating," Julia gasped.

"It beats once and a while." The effort to speak was excruciating.

"No, it's beating regularly. Like a human." A look of

disbelief shot across her face.

Suddenly the doctors, Celia, and my father rushed in.

"He's awake! We saw it on the monitor!" Celia exclaimed.

The doctor immediately began looking at the computer readouts, his brow furrowed with concern.

"I don't understand," he said incredulously. "These readouts don't make sense."

"What do you mean, they don't make sense," Celia asked.

"These readouts are unusual for someone with the disease. I have been puzzling over them for days, as they have been so inconsistent. But now, they don't make any sense. They . . . they are reading *human* vitals. It's as if you aren't immortal anymore. Will, I'll have to do some more tests, but I think you are cured."

The four of us stood there in disbelief, listening to the monitors beep for a moment before anyone spoke.

"How do you feel?" my father asked.

It felt like a loaded question after all of these years.

"I feel okay. I mean, I actually *feel*. The dull ache, the pressure in my chest, it's gone." He reached for my hand and smiled.

More doctors rushed in and stared at the monitors. They whispered excitedly while pointing from me to the monitors and then back at me. The doctors didn't seem to know how to respond, and from their reactions, neither did Celia nor my father.

"Well, I'm not really sure how it all happened, but it seems that you are now human," one of the specialists finally said, speaking directly to me.

"It is a miracle," my father whispered.

The thought took a moment to sink in.

"I'm human again." I tested the words out tentatively. "Cured." I whispered. I didn't question how it happened, I could only accept it, and know that everything would work out.

The room suddenly became very loud, as all of the doctors began talking at once, gesticulating at the monitors and each other. My father and sister joined in, but I didn't need to hear an explanation. I had been given a second chance, and it didn't matter to me why I was alive, it only mattered that I was. My eyes sought out Julia, who had been pushed to the corner of the room. I could see glossy tears in her eyes and couldn't help my own tears from falling down my face. She began to walk toward me cautiously, and I reached a hand out to reach for her.

"You stayed," I whispered. "I thought I lost you again."

"Never. I will never leave you again," she said through her tears. "I was a fool to leave the first time. You are who I want to be with, and you must know that you aren't the only one who has changed. You make me feel like a stronger person and I can't imagine a life without you in it. I need to be where you are."

At this moment, there was only one place I wanted to be and that was by Julia's side. I pulled her into my arms, never wanting to let her go. I laid her head on my chest and listened to the echo of our beating hearts.

EPILOGUE
CELIA

I COULDN'T HELP BUT STARE out the open window at them. The air was warm and birds sang in the trees. It had been nearly six months since Will came home, and spring was beginning to show everywhere. The garden was alive with new growth and the color of the lake was a brilliant blue. My brother sat on the bench in the rose garden with Julia's head in his lap, while she attempted to read. Will's hand tangled in her hair and a smile played upon his lips. The happiness that they had found together radiated from them. The scent of the newly blossoming lilacs was all encompassing and mingled with the fresh air coming off the lake.

I smiled to myself as Julia giggled and playfully nudged Will's arm when he tried to pull the book from her hand. He leapt out from under her, grabbing the book and began to run around holding it at arm's length, away from her. She followed, chasing him through the pathways, laughing madly. Finally, she grabbed his arm and pulled him to her. Forgetting about the book, Will pulled her into an embrace, their mouths meeting gently.

I turned away from the intimate scene before me. This is how they always were. They were engaged now, with Julia spending most of her free time at the house, having put her own house up for sale. She said she was ready to put her own demons to rest, and besides, she would be moving in here anyway, once they were married. Will was back in school, getting a degree in art, a newly discovered talent. In the fall, they would get married, completing their happy ending. The play they had worked on together was postponed until spring, but when it was finally performed, it got rave reviews, prompting my principal to hire Will as the assistant director for all of the shows.

My father was now submerged in research. He was more positive now than ever before that there had to be an answer to Will's unexpected cure, and he was determined to find it. It gave him a renewed purpose, and he was as eager as ever. He now split his time between here and Chicago, researching. I was finishing out the school year, as life had slowly gone back to normal.

The happiness around me made me long for what I once had, but lost. I sighed and pulled out a yellow, withered picture that I had been carrying around with me for decades. It was my own engagement picture. Jonathan and I were looking adoringly at each other. The picture was faded where I had held it so many times. I brought the photograph to my lips and closed my eyes to prevent a single tear from escaping.

I looked back out to the garden at the retreating forms of Will and my future sister-in-law. With his arm around her and her head on his shoulder, they slowly walked down the path toward the lake. If Will could find love, surely I could too. *Someday. Someday I would have this again,* I thought, the sounds of the laughter below drowning out any sorrow, as if to prove that in the end, it would all be set right.

Acknowledgements:

This book, as with many first books, is a project that has been a long time coming. Writing is the sort of thing that got away from me and then reintroduced itself again later in life. In school, I loved English class. I loved creative writing and have lots of short stories to prove it! When I finished college, I actually was a travel writer/editor for a small magazine, yet never had any thought that I could do this "for real." Fast forward to about 10 years later and something hit me. That book I have wanted to write isn't going to write itself. One day I sat down and started to write. I have been completely overwhelmed by the love and support I have received from my family and friends which has helped make this happen.

First, I need to thank Georgia and Jennifer. The last year has been difficult and Georgia was the one who said, I know what you need to do. You need to publish your book. Until someone actually verbalized it, publishing my books was a far off dream. Thank you for being my friend and for giving me the kick I needed to do this! Jennifer has become more that just another author to me. She has answered countless questions about the publishing process. Jennifer is one of the people who have kept me sane throughout this whole process. I also need to thank all of my TM/EFG girls for their friendship and support over the last few years. I can't name you all, but you know who you are!

I would also like to give some credit to those who inspire me through their writing or who listened and helped me work out plot problems. You taught me more than you know about the individual creative process that goes into writing. Robin Wasserman, Alex Flinn, Lauren Oliver, and Maggie Stiefvater, THANK YOU!

A huge thank you goes out to Kate for being my beta reader, my editor, my therapist, and one of my best friends! She has read this almost as many times as I have and has seen it change drastically. Through it all, she has been my biggest cheerleader. I could not have done this without you!

Finally, I would like to thank my family for being there for me. My husband survived countless nights falling asleep to the sound of typing when I found myself on a roll and didn't want to stop! And, of course, all those times when he corralled my girls away because "Mommy's writing." Thank you for believing in me and following me throughout this endeavor!

To those of you who I forgot, I'll make sure you get a proper thank you in the next book.

—Happy Reading!
Sara

Keep reading for an excerpt from
The Impossible Art of Falling by Sara Fiorenzo,
the first book in the Impossible Art Series.

Coming November 2015!

In a split second, Jena Grayson's life changed forever. In that split second, there was the sickening crunch of bones breaking and the crash of 1500 pounds skidding into the brightly painted poles and the surrounding dirt. The horse had fallen right into the jump, sending splinters of wood into the air and her father plummeting to the earth, head first. Jena knew he was dead, having just watched him crumple to the ground at an odd, unnatural angle. She ran to his side anyway, hoping that she was wrong. Deep down, she knew surviving a fall like that would be nearly impossible. Others scrambled to catch the horse hobbling around on three legs, nostrils flaring, and eyes full of fear. The saddle was shifted sideways and the reins swung back and forth loosely, just like the broken leg swinging limply until the poor animal was pulled to the ground. People swarmed around the fallen animal, quickly putting curtains up to hide the ungodly task before them.

Jena pushed aside the others who had gotten to her father before her, her hands roughly grabbing shoulders and arms to pull them out of her way. Her father lay before her, his lanky body twisted unnaturally. Her hands shook as she searched for a pulse. She was sure she would be able to hear it as the air was full of silence, the spectators staring at the disaster before them. Ambulance sirens announced the arrival of help, but it was too late. Hands reached down and pulled her away and she felt as if she were suffocating. The stadium was a mess of color and undecipherable sound, yet she heard and saw nothing. Ted Grayson was dead, his neck broken, and as they took his lifeless body away from the still arena, it was accompanied only by Jena's screams as she fell to her knees and spilled her grief onto the sand.

A Year Later

She watched through the small window of the hayloft as the gray truck grew closer, meandering through the narrow mountain road, behind it a small trailer. Nothing fancy, just a plain stock trailer in a matching steel grey. A few minutes later, the sound of tires on gravel announced its arrival and still, she didn't move. The door of the truck slammed and a man who was deceptively familiar, stepped out. He had the same slender physique and frat-boyish grin, blond hair peppered with gray peaked out from underneath the ball cap placed on his head. His eyes, though, were a soft brown, while her father's had been almost gold. Mac, the barn manager, strode forth from one of the green and white buildings to greet the man who had driven all this way. They shook hands briefly and Mac placed his hand on Rob Grayson's shoulder. Both men's eyes looked at the gravel beneath their feet. Mac reached for his eye, his fingers fisted, and began to rub. Perhaps his eyes misted over or he was simply removing a particle of dust. The loss of a brother and friend was too much for both of them.

"How is she handling things, Mac?" the other man asked.

"Not well, I am afraid, Rob. She still doesn't speak much and she wanders around the barns aimlessly. It's like she's a ghost," Mac answered. He gestured to the dark horse alone in a small arena near the barn. "And she stopped riding months ago. The poor guy's bored." As if to prove the point, the horse kicked his heels and ran a few circles before sliding to a stop at the fence and shaking his head. His mane and forelock were shaggy, covering a bright white star. The two men walked over to the horse standing at the fence. Rob scratched the horse's forehead.

"Well, perhaps if her mother hadn't taken off a few months later, things would have been easier to deal with." He sighed and it was full of grief. "I guess I can't blame her for being upset. Karen never really got into this farm life, but I think leaving your only child because you can't handle tragedy is a shitty thing to do," Rob replied and then looked around nervously, hoping that his niece hadn't overheard.

"The farm will be sold before long, and the last of the horses are leaving tomorrow with you." Mac looked around with sadness. He could see parts of the white and green barns where the paint was fading. Fence posts needed to be fixed, and the once rolling pastures were overgrown and full of weeds. It had only been a year and the once vibrant farm was now empty and dead, just like the man who built it up. "I guess this really is the end." The sadness and loss was evident in his voice.

"I'm sorry, I couldn't take over," Rob said. "I don't know anything about show jumpers and eventing, and I have my own business and farm back in Tennessee to worry about. I wouldn't be any good for this place. Still, I am sad to see it go." He paused for a moment, his face twisted in pain as he looked around. White planked fences encircled open fields, and the empty barns enveloping them like giant arms. "My brother worked hard to build this farm and became a giant in the horse world. It's what he always wanted and he did it. I just can't believe it's all gone."

"It's not your fault. The clients all left anyway, in search of new trainers to take them to the next level. No offense, but it wouldn't be the same. I mean, Ted was the heart and soul of this place. Honestly, I'm more concerned for Jena at this point. I know that she isn't just a kid anymore, but it's like she has lost both parents. And now that she's stopped riding, I'm worried she doesn't have anything left. The kid loves horses as much as her dad did." Mac turned again, his squinted eyes searching the horizon. The object of his gaze, never really being revealed. Perhaps he just couldn't look into the eye of the brother who looked so much like his lost friend.

"Well," Rob smiled and kicked at an imaginary stone on the driveway, "she has Meg and me, and I promise that we will help her through all of this. I know it's not the same, but we can give her a life in Townsend. And she will remember that she is not alone." Rob began to gesture around him, sadness settling in again. "I hope taking her away from all of this will help her. Where is my niece anyway?" Rob swallowed his own pain away and looked around anxiously. "Jena?" he called out, using his hand to shield the sun. "Jena, I'm here."

Jena descended the stairs of the hayloft slowly, breathing deeply the smell of alfalfa and horses. Out in the driveway, Rob's back was turned and he was looking far off at the field of mares he was taking with him. She slid out quietly and leaned against the post outside, waiting for him to turn around and acknowledge her. She could speak and tell him she was here, but she preferred the silence instead.

She stared at his silhouette. His graying stubble, straight nose and angled jaw line was so much like her father, it hurt. Other than a strong physical resemblance, though, the brothers couldn't have been more different. Her father was constantly on the move and lived for the competition. Rob preferred to live quietly on his farm. While her father thrived in the limelight, her uncle was content in the shadows. He must have felt her stare because he turned around.

"Oh Jena, there you are!" Within a few strides he was in front of her, pulling her into a bear hug only an uncle could give and she felt six again, instead of eighteen. "I missed you. How are you doing, kiddo?" She shrugged against him and bit her lip, a new habit to stop the constant flow of tears.

"Fine," she whispered meekly, forcing a crooked smile.

"Are you all packed? Do you need help with anything? I figure we can take the rest of the day to get things packed up. We'll load the horses first thing in the morning, so we can get back to Tennessee by late afternoon. That will give you and the horses some time to settle in. I've closed the trail rides for the next few days so that we can get things situated. And maybe you can introduce your boy to life on the trails. . . " Rob trailed off at the blank look in Jena's eyes. Mac had said that she had stopped riding. They were taking her horse with them, but he wondered if she even cared.

"Let's go see what we can scrounge up for some lunch." He put his arm around his niece, and the pair began to slowly walk toward house.

There wasn't much food left, but they managed to find enough to make some sandwiches. Rob, Mac, and Jena sat down at the big dining room table. The house was fairly bare, with only a few large pieces of furniture left. The bank would be auctioning off what was left to pay the lien on the farm, and the staff had all been let go the month before. Mac had stayed to help keep things going until Rob could get there to handle what was left. Mac had known Jena since she was a kid and, although she was now old enough to take care of herself and had been over the last few months, he didn't feel he could abandon her like everyone else had. She had continued with school in order to graduate, and he had made sure that there were groceries in the fridge and that she was fed. Today, he joined her and Rob one last time before heading down to Florida, where he had taken a job as a barn manager for another stable. He figured that staying through to the end was the least that he could do repay the kindness the Grayson's had shown him over the years.

"Have you heard from Karen?" Rob asked, to no one in particular and not sure which one would answer. Jena continued to stare down at her plate, which was all the answer that he needed. He couldn't help but think of what a cold and heartless woman she was. At first, he got it. After his brother died, everyone was lost, himself included. The grooms tried to run things as usual, thinking that Karen Grayson would continue to run the farm or allow Jena to start taking over. But one by one they left as well, once they realized that she stopped paying the bills... and them, and that Jena had no interest or money to run the place. What had happened to the farm's money, one could only guess, although Rob was sure that Karen wasn't exactly collecting any money from the boarders. Finally, she walked out one day, leaving the farm and her daughter. At first, Jena had tried to call her mother, to urge her to come back or at least come and get her, but Karen was too broken. She wanted nothing to do with the horses or her daughter, because they were a constant reminder of what she had lost and the life they used to lead. Every time she looked into her daughter's eyes, she was reminded of the husband she lost. In many ways, Rob thought, it was a blessing that Karen decided to sell the farm or rather, let the bank take it and auction it off little by little, to pay the bills she refused to pay. The immaculately maintained green and white buildings of Grayson Stables would never be the world class stable it had once been. And Jena certainly didn't deserve to be left with the mess of a father who died too soon and a mother who let it all fall apart.

"Not in a few weeks," Mac replied, answering Rob question. "She called once just to see how many horses were still here and if anyone from the bank had been by." He leaned closer to Rob. "She never even asked for Jena."

Jena continued to stare at her plate while taking another bite of her sandwich. She hated how quickly she had become the subject of conversations, instead of a participant. She hated how everyone tiptoed around her and treated her like a child. Or like a priceless vase that would break at the slightest movement. Mac's eyes darted toward her nervously. Rob knew she had heard. She knew her mother's shortcomings, but would never talk about them. In fact, when she did talk, it was only to say a word or two and she never mentioned either one of her parents. Her face was a constant mask of stoicism that sometimes opened up to either sadness or anger. There hadn't been any happiness in many months.

"I think you will like it in Townsend, Jena," Rob said, changing the subject. "The mountains are your backyard. And of course, there are the horses on the ranch. We were sort of hoping that you could help us with the trail rides through the park this summer. If you want to talk about going to college, we can talk about that to. University of Tennessee is only a short drive away. We weren't sure what your plans were." Having finished her sandwich, Jena shrugged in non-commitment and began to bite her lip again while she took her plate to the sink. Apparently, this topic was off limits, too. Rob was beginning to wonder exactly what they *could* talk about. It would be a long drive back to Tennessee.

"I suppose we should start loading the truck up with the

things we're taking with us. Mac, perhaps you could help me? Jena, just put what you want to bring at the foot of the stairs. I'll put it in the truck." She nodded and then slowly walked up the stairs to her room. Rob watched her slowly retreat, her shoulders hunched, her stride slow and sad.

"She'll be okay, Rob," Mac assured. "You really are doing the right thing. This place is full of nothing but the ghosts of the past for her. She needs to find something else to help her get back up, get back on her feet. I know she's old enough to be on her own, but in many ways, I don't think she's ready. And being with family will help her heal."

"Yeah, maybe you are right. I still just keep wondering if taking her away from the life she knows is the right thing. Maybe she would be better on her own. " Rob ran his hands through blond hair that was graying at the temples. "This is the only home she has ever known. Not only that, but I'm taking her to a different world. She's grown up in the spotlight, traveling around and showing since she was old enough to walk. Hell, she's been on the Olympic track for the last several years! I'm afraid my small farm isn't going to be enough for her."

"Maybe the spotlight isn't what she wants anymore." Mac stood to leave, his boots echoing on the hardwood floor. "You are doing the right thing, Rob. You may not know it and she may not realize it, but taking her away will help her." He placed his hand on Rob's shoulder and stood for a moment, both men silent. "I'll go tend to the horses."

Jena listened from the top of the stairs. Her uncle was wrong, of course; this was the right thing. At least for now. She knew she couldn't stay here at this farm, and she had nowhere else to go. She just needed a place to be for a few months. She needed enough time to figure out where to go next, and then she could leave... start over somewhere new. As far as competing? Mac was right on that one. That part of her life was over. There would be no Olympics in her future. In fact, she wasn't sure she would ever ride again.

About Sara:

SARA LIVES ON THE SHORES of Lake Michigan with her husband, two girls, dog, and horse. She has been known to speak only in movie quotes, randomly break out in song, and spend hours on the internet researching abandoned places. Her friends think she is a great date to an amusement park and a decent, but slow, running companion. In addition to being a writer, Sara is also a high school English teacher. Riding horses and music make her happy and she believes that bacon should be included at every meal.

CONTACT SARA:
https://www.goodreads.com/sfiorenzo
https://www.facebook.com/sarafiorenzobooks
https://www.facebook.com/sarafiorenzo.author
http://sarafiorenzobooks.weebly.com/
sarafiorenzobooks@gmail.com